Lake of Sighs

Meli Sarkissian

818-515-9628

ISBN: 1981522255
ISBN 13: 9781981522255
Library of Congress Control Number: 2017919179
CreateSpace Independent Publishing Platform
North Charleston, South Carolina

For Mom, Dad, Asbed, and Lalique

(Following is the translated poem that follows Tamar's experiences)

Akhtamar

Into the moonlit waters of the sea of Van
From the shores of a tiny hamlet
Enters the water as thief in the night,
Each and every night a lad.

He enters the night without a boat,
With arms powerful and virile,
Parting the water he swims on,
Towards the island on the opposite shore.

From the dark island, clear and bright
A beaming light beckons him on
A powerful beacon just for him
To help guide him on his path

The fair Tamar every night,
Prepares a fire on that isle,
And she awaits him impatiently,
In the dark bushes nearby.

The untame water crashes and roars
And the lad's heart crashes along
The water howls in frightful screams
And fight it does menacingly.

Now Tamar, with her heart pounding,
Finally hears the sounds nearby

The splashing of water and with all her being
She's ablaze with love severe.

Silence, along the dark shore,
Stands a lone shadowy figure
Alas! It's he, they find each other,
On this mysterious quiet night.

Only the waves of the sea of Van
Now gently caress its shores
Subsiding as they retreat
Murmuring intelligibly

You may say they're whispering
And the stars arched above,
Glance down and slander away
At impudent, shameless Tamar.

Their gaze disturbs the maiden's heart
It's time to part, and once again,
One enters the turbulent sea
Whilst the other prays on its shore.

Who might that daring young man be?
Intoxicated with his love
His heart void of dread or fear
He crosses the sea by night.

He swims from the opposite shore,
And our Tamar he does kiss,
Snatching a girl from our hands
What does he take us for?

Thus they spoke in bitter pain,
The young men of this island,
And Tamar's hand-lit light
They extinguished this one night.

Bewildered in the darkened sea
The swimmer lad, her beloved
And the wind lifts, and it carries,
His merciful sighs, "Ah! Tamar!"

His voice is near in the deafening darkness, wedged be-
tween the jagged rocks,
Where the untamed water roars,
At times muffled and at times lost
And at times feebly heard, "Ah! Tamar!"

At dawn the calm water floats in, upon the shore it leaves a corpse,
On his stiffened and frozen lips
Perhaps you'd say at time of death
Frozen were two words, "Ah! Tamar…"

—Hovhannes Toumanyan (Armenian poet: 1869-1923)

Prologue

MY EYES WERE closed. All I felt was his touch. His fingers traced the contours of my face, as though he were planning a long and winding journey through the mystery that was me. He was slow and deliberate, stretching out the strands of time with his measured movements. I felt him linger at times, as though a certain spot needed more attention than the rest: the arch of my eyebrow, my lower lip, the line of my jaw. He tugged at the skin there, and I felt his breath catch. Through the darkness of my eyelids, I could almost envision the look on his face. Just as he traced my face with his fingers, I traced his with my memory. My thoughts smoothed over his skin, over the hardness of his jaw, his set pursed lips that always seemed ready to say something but rarely did, his soft eyes that always gave his turbulent thoughts away. He traced the skin on my neck, and I lifted my chin, my lips parted in preparation for a kiss that I needed, a kiss that breathed life into me. But it did not come, and the anticipation hung suspended beyond my eyelids.

"Have you found it yet?" I breathed.

"Found what?" came his voice almost immediately.

"Whatever you are looking for."

There was silence, and he lifted his finger from my skin. The sudden absence of his warmth was startling. Worried I had said something wrong, I blinked open my eyes. He was only a few inches away from my face. The starry sky was reflected in his dark eyes, and I gazed into them, mesmerized, certain he could see the same reflection in my eyes.

Without breaking his gaze, he put both hands on my cheeks and murmured, "I have already found the greatest treasure in all the world."

He kissed me then, his lips soft against mine.

It was anguish when it was time to part. He held onto my hand and kissed the veins at my wrist. With his other hand, he lifted my chin and caught my eyes. "I will see you soon."

"Must you leave already?"

He looked out at the sun that was beginning to peek over the horizon. "Yes, there is much to do. I must leave. But, Tamar," he said, his voice faltering.

"Yes?"

He looked down at me, a small smile on his face. "I can't let you go without making you mine first."

He pressed something into the palm of my hand and closed my fingers around it. With a firm kiss to my forehead, he said with resolve, "Soon." Then, he jogged toward the water. I watched him wade into the waves, which sparkled like jewels in the reflection of the rising sun. I watched him until he was but a speck and I could not see him anymore, like a faded promise that echoed with the word, *Soon...*

I beheld the item in my hand—though my heart already knew what it was. Tears came to my eyes as I saw the ring. It was fashioned from two thin pieces of metal, intertwined and twisted into each other. I knew that he had made it with his own hands, and the simple ring I looked at was more precious to me than anything I had ever known.

I kissed it firmly and uttered the same prayer I had sighed at the lake for months.

Please bring him back to me, Lake Van.

When I was little, my father would sit on the ground with me in his lap and surround us with piles and piles of paper. We would giggle as the wind made them flutter around us like waves on water. But then, I would become serious, as the important task fell upon my shoulders. I would shuffle them around—careful not to smudge the charcoal lines upon them—and inspect the sketches on each sheet. Each one told a different story, and it fell upon my shoulders to pick which sketch would be the lucky painting my father would devote his time to for the next several months.

My memories were like these sketches, fleeting and faint. Many were forgotten, left at the bottom of the pile, but some were so well drawn and so vivid that I could already see the missing colors bringing them to life in my mind.

This was one such memory. When I closed my eyes, I could see the sketch of his face, as he traced the features on my face. The shadows were placed perfectly against his cheekbones and his nose, changing his expression with every direction that he turned his chin.

I would have chosen him for a painting. A million times, I would have chosen him.

But then, the sheet drops, and another memory is picked up.

A figure of a girl, fallen to the floor with her head in her hands. The water around her swirls violently, desperate and frantic. Hundreds of colors make up the mystery that is the lake, and swallowed by those very same swirls, a boy breaks through for a brief moment and reaches out with the last drop of strength that he possesses, desperate to reach the girl who weeps for her beloved.

I drop the sheet of paper and pick up the last one.

A girl in a crudely made rowboat, rowing with all her might against the waves that threaten to send her back home. But she is determined, her eyes shining with the stars that dot the vast skies. She has finally found her own light—her own path—to guide her out of the life she was never meant to have.

Chapter I

FOUR PAIRS OF bright eyes watched the pastel blue sky above. One pair, dark brown, belonged to me, the younger of the two. I was a little girl of four who giggled at nonsense, such as the clouds shifting before me and the lone worm that poked its head at my toe. My brown hair splayed out around my head and tangled with the grass, tickling my head and making me squeal with every movement. I was known to have a sprightly countenance, eager to show all my emotions at once with exaggerated tears and laughter. The second pair of eyes shone crystal blue and belonged to the elder, a girl of seven, named Aleena. She had a porcelain face, with charcoal-black hair that twisted around her head like Medusa's curls. She had a quieter way about her, lurking the hallways of the home, mischievous and solemn, looking for all the world like she hailed from some ethereal world that we would never know of. Though we were drastically different, our greatest similarity was the love that we held for each other.

We were lying on our backs on the lush green grass, watching the clouds above shift restlessly. Eventually, my sister sat up, and I followed her lead, as I usually did. But she sat quietly while I played with the fragile strands of the grass, splitting them daintily as if they were petals in the hands of a lover. They tickled my legs and etched light scratches onto my skin that did not hurt, which used to surprise me immensely. The sky stretched high above us, a dome of blue with smudges of softest white. The colors around us were vibrant, reminding me of my father's paintings, which lined the walls of our home and traveled far and wide in fame.

I remember he had painted my sister once, having her sit quietly on a stool while I reclined in my mother's arms. His hands fluttered over the canvas like the flight of a hummingbird, but his eyes never left my sister's form. He caught the way the light shone on her black curls, the way her eyes sparkled but were indifferent at the same time. She sat without a single fidget, her eyes watching my father, her lips pressed together in calm solemnity.

Her expressions could change so drastically that she often determined the mood of the house. If she was happy, we were all happy. If she was upset, we were all upset.

While I played with the grass, she smiled sweetly at my unnecessary caution in splitting the strands of grass evenly down the middle. She rarely missed a detail, for her eyes shone with a keen curiosity. Our shoes—uncomfortable laced boots that pinched—were beside us. We wiggled our toes and felt the cool air caress our skin. Not too far away, our parents sat on an ornate tapestry we usually brought out for picnics. My father sat with his two greatest friends, Baron Avedis and the priest, and they laughed heartily, their voices reaching us with the wind. My mother sat quietly with her two sisters and sisters-in-law. They talked in low voices, smiling politely and sweetly. But my mother was anything but subtle. She was strong-willed and proud—the perfect queen.

Eventually, the priest's daughter, Lilit, approached us and sat next to me. We were of the same age and looked quite similar with our dark hair and dark eyes, but her skin was the same porcelain tone as my sister. We had become used to each other's presence in our lives, since the priest came to our island quite often. Aleena seemed to like her as well, so all was well within our little group. As we played quietly in the fantasies of our own minds, Baron Avedis's youngest son decided he would join us, although we gave him no inclination of an invite. We were strictly a trio of girls, and any boy was an intrusion on our fun. He had been sitting a few feet away, watching us with a frown on his face. But now, he sat too near me, tearing at the grass fiercely and disturbing my simple pleasure.

"Bedros," said my sister, her voice tinged with hardness, "go play with your brother."

The five-year-old glanced up with his dark eyes, gave her that certain defiant look only children can manage, and then looked back down at the grass. Seeing my neat grass strands being demolished by his clumsy hands, I began to cry, the tears running down my cheeks and my chest heaving. Lilit absentmindedly tried to arrange the torn-up grass into a neat little pile, attempting to bring peace. Through my tears, I noticed my mother glance over from the corner of her eyes and then look away again, no doubt exasperated with our never-ending drama with the boy. I raised my voice slightly, hoping she would look back and come to our aid. Aleena rose to her feet, her fists balled at her sides and her eyes two hard glints of ice shards. "Bedros, go away."

"No."

"I will tell your father."

"No!"

"I'll thrash you!"

She would not have dared, of course, for the adults would have intervened immediately, and Aleena would have been promptly punished. But her tone was enough to instill the necessary amount of fear in him. Bedros opened his mouth to scream but choked on it when a shadow fell over us. A voice boomed, "What are our children doing?" We looked up at the great hulk of a man that was Baron Avedis. He towered over us with his great body and silenced our raging emotions, from my incessant crying to Aleena's threats. He was our father's dearest friend from childhood and so was appointed as our godfather. He was known for his great size, especially in comparison to our small forms, but his giant smile and jolly laugh always erased our fears. We loved him dearly as if he was our own uncle but despised his sons.

Vartan, Bedros's older brother at nine years old, stood at his father's side, his mouth prim and proper and his pale blue eyes bored. He watched us as if we were pieces of dirt strewn about the floor. He thought himself quite mature, although every word uttered from his lips was in want of something. He often lurked around the adults, wanting a place to sit among them, but they ignored him, for a child was not their equal.

Aleena, for a reason I would not understand for a long time, had a special aversion for him that was the true reason Vartan avoided sitting with us. She made him feel very unwelcome with a mere piercing glance.

Bedros, meanwhile, was filled with the usual mischief that most children harbor. He had dark features as well, although he possessed the same blue eyes that his brother did. But Bedros's eyes had a brighter glint in them, which made him a little more pleasant to look at.

"Nothing, godfather," muttered Aleena with a frown on her face.

I admired Baron Avedis's warm countenance. I never understood why his sons never inherited that trait of his. They seemed to take after their mother more—a prim woman who enjoyed discipline. Baron Avedis gave my sister a look from underneath his bushy eyebrows, but she kept her face devoid of anger and watched him coolly with her crystal eyes.

"Well," he broke the silence, smacking his lips. That smile that we all loved so dearly grew over his face. "We must remedy that. Run along and have some dolma your chef has so kindly prepared for us," he suggested, grinning at the thought of the rolls of rice wrapped tightly in blankets of grape leaves. He leaned down and picked up Lilit, pinching her cheeks and making her giggle. "Come along, girls," he called to us, as he turned to walk away with my friend in his arms.

"Yes, we will," chimed Aleena, reaching down and tugging me to my feet. I let the strands of grass fall from my fingers, watching as the soft breeze caught some of them and lifted them lightly. I wanted to see where they would land, but Aleena was pulling me in a different direction, and I quickly forgot about them as soon as I turned my back.

Bedros was watching us with a pout on his face, and I wanted to laugh at him. We had won this round. I managed a small, unsuccessful kick in his direction before Aleena took off running much faster than my legs could carry me. She half-dragged, half-pulled me along with her, disregarding the capabilities of my body. We ran, not toward the picnic where the adults looked so comfortable on the tapestry and surrounded by delicacies, but toward the dense thicket of trees surrounding the clearing. We ran and ran, dodging trees and ducking under branches, my hand firmly in Aleena's strong fingers. Her grip never loosened, and I managed to stay up the entire time, my trust in her unfailing. She was only seven, but she was my constant companion and the wisest person I knew. The ground beneath us sloped up into a steep climb, and we ran past rough-looking trees, but I was unafraid, even though my body moved awkwardly and I had to drag my legs at times.

"Almost there," she muttered breathlessly. *Almost where?*

She was gripping my hand so tightly it hurt. The ground was still steadily climbing, and we found ourselves grabbing at broken tree bark or roots and low branches for support. Right when I thought I would collapse backward down the small mountain, she stopped abruptly in front of me. I continued running, too tired to stop immediately, but my sister reached over and grabbed me around the waist right before I would have plunged straight off the edge of the rocky cliff that lay an inch away from my bare, raw feet.

There was silence for a few moments as we struggled to register the height of where we stood and how death had come so close to claiming me. We breathed heavily, trying to catch our breaths from the wild run, as the realization of my carelessness dawned on me. It was still an abstract concept to me—that one could cease to exist—so the idea of it frightened me, that I was so close to something I could never understand. I tried to step back, but my sister was there, so I could not move.

The lake crashed vengefully against the bottom of the cliff, so far beneath us. If I had fallen, it would have shown me no mercy. It roared at us, angry that we were so far out of its reach, leaping at us desperately and stretching its terrible arms in our direction with every crash against the wall. But the longer we stood there, the more I realized how protected I was, so far above on that sturdy rock. I knew I was safe as long as my sister kept her arm around my shoulders. We stood like this for some time—my eyes on the cliff while her steady breathing calmed my fast-beating heart.

Finally, my sister leaned her head down and whispered, "Tamar," into my hair, stirring the strands and tickling my scalp. "Look up."

I looked up at once, and my eyes widened.

The lake stretched out for miles in front of my eyes, as if it were a glittering blanket sewn with millions of diamonds. Looming mountains rose in the distance, topped with white snow at the top, and though I could see no sign of civilization, I knew there were people there. A smooth bluish glow rested over the horizon, calm and gentle. I knew we lived on an island, but it had never occurred to me that there was land beyond our great lake, and seeing it for the first time was astounding. Suddenly, I felt smaller—a tiny speck lost on a tiny island.

Where we stood, the wind was harsh, battering at our hair, threatening to rip it from the tight braids that hung over our shoulders.

"I want to be over there," whispered my sister.

I understood her desire. I wanted to fly over the lake and stand on the horizon. My heart ached with the longing. The wind was unnervingly persistent, pulling at my body and coaxing me to leap into the sky.

I remember waiting for my sister to say something—to break the silence—but she made no move to do so, and together, we gazed out at the beautiful scene stretched out before us. I was going to finally make a sound when she squeezed my shoulder slightly, and that was when I heard it: faint music from the land in the distance.

It was low and whisper-thin, like smoke, traveling over the vast stretch of water and caressing us smoothly. We were mesmerized and stood still, as if any slight movement would make the music vanish, like a dream. Somehow, the more I listened, the louder it grew, overtaking the roaring of the waves and the wind, and dancing with my thoughts. My sister had closed her eyes, while a small smile spread over her serene face. But my eyes were wide with wonder and trained on the land. I imagined the people there, the villagers, dancing in time to this music, and wondered who they were and what they were celebrating.

Why was I not there with them?

It was that thought that opened our hearts to the idea. That maybe one day we could join them. That maybe one day, this lake would not be a barrier to the other side and we could cross it just as easily as we had climbed this cliff.

Underneath the music reverberating in my mind, I was able to hear the faint rustling behind us as someone approached us fast, and I craned my neck up to look at my sister, but she was still smiling with closed eyes, seeming oblivious, as her thoughts were filled with the music.

"Aleena," I muttered. I reached up and tugged at her dress.

She looked down at me, opening her clear eyes, and nodded, smiling. "I know, Tamar." I remember noticing for the first time how blue her eyes really were and how much they differed from my own dark eyes. Looking up at her, I saw the glittering lake reflected in her eyes—a reflection of such hypnotic beauty. I was looking at a doll, come to life with a flush just by listening to the music. This was not the same Aleena who sat quietly in my father's painting, docile eyes gazing out, her head slightly cocked to one side as if she were the one studying the viewer in a painting, instead of the other way around.

No, this Aleena was *real*. Everything about her was real. And she was beautiful.

I wanted to somehow express this to her through my limited childhood vocabulary, but I was hardly able to squeak out a sound before several of our father's guards burst into the small clearing where we stood right at the cliff's edge. With only a moment's hesitation coupled with much panic, they reached forward, and one grabbed Aleena, while a second grabbed me by the waist. Aleena was smiling still, amused at their haste.

They perhaps believed we would have jumped foolishly straight into the lake's snarling mouth. They lifted us easily into their strong arms and carried us down the side of the mountain back to the picnic, neither saying a word while they breathed sighs of relief, even as Aleena and I lay limply over their shoulders, eyes fixed on the horizon.

⤙⟞◦ ◦⟝⤚

My father took us out often to explore the island. He had a great black horse named Vrej, which I knew meant "revenge." And true to his name, Vrej's eyes raged and his nostrils flared, as if there was a never-ending war occurring beneath the stretch of his hide. Father would place me in the front of the leather saddle with Aleena behind me, and he would sit behind us both, arms pulled around us to cage us in between his arms and the reins. Being in the front, I would pretend I was the only one riding Vrej, and I would squeal with unrestrained joy. Mother always fussed terribly when he took us riding, for he would ride fast, not wanting to slow down the tempered Vrej.

Besides the exhilaration, I learned much from going outside, for I was able to see and experience what everyone at home would recount to me. I learned more about our tiny island that floated on the moody Lake Van. The lake stretched far and wide, though we were not in the middle but rather pulled to the side. Thus Aleena and I were able to see the land and hear the music clearly on one side.

When we passed through the village, I noticed how differently we were all treated. The people lived in desolate brown huts wearing brown outfits, and they all seemed to have brown faces. But every time we passed through, dressed in our crimsons and golds, they put down their buckets and tools and came outside to greet us with brightly lit faces. They seemed absurdly excited and eager to see us, though I could not imagine why.

I finally asked my father why they did that.

Before he could reply, Aleena, instead, grinned at my innocence as she replied, "He is the king, silly. They have to."

King?

I did not understand the term, for I had not yet started reading books and novels to fully comprehend the magnitude of that title.

Father, one night, took us to a church on our island. It was on a thinner stretch of the land, so it was easy to see the water on three sides. I saw it in the distance as we trotted down a narrow, winding path from the top of a hill. It seemed so small and insignificant from that distance: a small pebble of obscurity, blinking in the fog that descended with the coming dusk. When we neared it, father slowed his horse and helped us dismount, freeing Vrej to graze on the surrounding grass.

I tottered toward the church, my neck craning back to take in all of it. I had not noticed that Aleena had stayed behind and was watching Vrej with a troubled expression. Vrej gazed back at her calmly.

"What is it, darling?" asked my father.

"Why does he not run away?" she asked.

"Why would he run away?" he questioned her, smiling patiently.

"Because he is a horse. And he is the wildest horse you have. Does he not want to be free?"

"He *is* free, my love. He does not run because he knows the island is surrounded by water. There is nowhere for him to go. He is smart enough to steer clear from it."

"How does that make him free?"

There was a pause. Father's smile faltered for a moment. Aleena's gaze was unwavering. Then he sighed and answered, "He does not look beyond the water. All that exists to him is on this island. And that makes him free."

I would never know what Aleena's answer would have been to that, for I chose this very moment to trip over a crack in the ground. The lush grassland had ended, and the ground was now a hard rock, crisscrossed with cracks and coated with a fine layer of sand. Father came to me and helped me up, explaining, "I brought you two here to show you why I am king."

"Because of God?" asked Aleena.

Just like death, the idea of God was something that had never been fully explained to me. I stayed quiet, hoping I would understand what our father would tell us.

"Look at the church. What do you notice about it?" he asked.

"It's brown," I piped up immediately, excited that I could answer a question.

He chuckled. "It is actually pink tufa, dear—volcanic rock. It has become browner over time from the sand and dirt. But I was asking for more of the details."

"The people on them," chimed Aleena.

"Yes," he replied. He picked me up into his arms and walked toward the church, closer to the raised markings on the walls. They were the faces of different men, circled by a ring, as they hovered over figures of people and horses. There were many; they surrounded the entire length of the wall, each set in different scenarios. Aleena touched one of the horses, and a bit of the tufa crumbled with her light touch.

"They are images of saints, biblical figures, as well as people from different places and stories around the world. Very important people are portrayed on these very walls." He pointed to a figure of a large man holding a sword and shield, standing across from a smaller man who held a stone in his hand. "This is David and Goliath. David defeated Goliath with just that one rock, even though Goliath was much bigger and stronger than him. This is an important story, showing that it does not matter what you look like or who you are; if you are smart, you will succeed."

He led us inside, where the walls seemed to grow higher and narrower. It felt as though they had closed in on us, and the darkness grew more intense. There was a dome directly over us as well as a narrow and thin window across the doorway, where the moonlight shone through and illuminated the cave-like interior.

The walls were completely covered with paintings! Aleena and I were wide-eyed and hushed at the pale beauty of the etchings. Saints, in their full forms, were holding the folds of their robes or gesturing toward *us* as if they had something to say. They were painted with blue and red and black, but it seemed faded, and a lot of the pieces were chipped and weathered.

"God speaks to us in different ways. He guides us and rules over us, without making himself known. This is why I am king. He has chosen me to be king, as he chooses all the rulers. Someone must keep control of God's people." His voice was soft, but it echoed loudly against the walls and surrounded us, as though ten of him were speaking all at once. I was confused, puzzled at this powerful God, who seemed to rule over my father, the man everyone else bowed under.

We walked back outside, embracing the cool air once again. My father pointed to one of the faces in the rings. He said, "That was the king who oversaw the building of this church: King Gagik the First. He was a strong man—first a prince regent, then a beloved king. All knew of him. I will rule over my land just as he ruled over his as well, until the day that I must pass it on, which will be when Aleena marries." He smiled at her.

She wrinkled her nose in response.

I had a memory here of my mother, who would sit in the parlor with Aleena on a stool in front of her. She would glide her gilded silver brush through Aleena's curls slowly, as that would keep the hair fresh and clean. I would be sitting in the arms of a nursemaid who pampered over me and kept me still as I tried to get a glimpse of Aleena's brushing. Mother would talk to Aleena about everything, almost as if she were talking to herself. She told Aleena that she was beautiful and that, because of this, she would marry someone who would take over the kingdom. She told Aleena how important she was and how talks of her beauty would range far and wide and touch the hearts of many dukes and princes. "We live on a small island, Aleena, but with a face such as yours, we will capture the attention of many. Our island will finally be known for its beauty, and not for its tragedy."

"What tragedy?" Aleena had asked immediately, the only part she was interested in.

"It is not important. What *is* important is *you*."

And Aleena glanced at me from the corner of her eyes and folded up her lips to bare her teeth and furrow her eyebrows, so she looked quite the monster. I would explode in a flurry of giggles, and my mother harshly would command the nursemaid to keep me quiet. That was always the way with her. I was raised with the orders to always remain quiet, while Aleena was raised as a true princess.

I was not the face of beauty. I would not glorify the name of the island.

That was what my mother believed.

I sometimes wondered why I was not important. As Aleena wrinkled her nose at my father, I wondered why I could not marry like her and rule the island. It was as much my home as it was hers. But I could not conjure up enough words to explain my unsettled feelings, so I turned my attention back to the church, such a beautiful and sad building, which had been forsaken over the years and was beginning to harbor cracks.

Aleena walked over to me and put a hand on my shoulder. When I looked at her, she smiled at me—a beautiful and sad smile.

I would slowly begin to understand that we were all similar to that church: fragile enough to crumble at the slightest touch, but strong enough to remain standing for years to come.

Chapter 2

ALEENA, AT THAT young and fragile age, was given a tutor, a plump woman that we called Digin Galia. I was passed along to my mother and several of our aunts when Aleena could not be with me, and life suddenly became very dull and bothersome. I learned that adults have no ability to act normally in the presence of children under the age of six. I was coddled and petted until my cheeks were raw from constant pinching, and I began to cry as soon as I saw an adult walk toward me. I missed Aleena terribly and would call out her name when we sat in the parlor during a tedious hour of sipping tea and sewing. But she always somehow sought me out at the end of the day and smuggled me little sweets and delights and read me stories from books Digin Galia had given her. All my misgivings were forgotten and joy entered my life when she would read to me.

I especially loved the stories of tragedy and romance, for the heroine would always remind me of Aleena, and she would prance around on her horse in my imaginations. I did not know any men at the time, and when I confessed to Aleena that I always thought of her with Vartan, she would get angry. So her lover became a dark shadow of a man, always hidden, but always there in a hazy silhouette, ready to defend her honor against villains and fiends. It seemed better that way, anyway. Vartan was not the sort of man to be dashing and romantic and dangerous.

Like every story of heroes and heroines, there had to be a villain, and we had conjured the most perfect one. My sister would tell me wicked stories of Digin Galia, the witch of a woman, who had whips made from dragon's tails and had claws that dripped with poison. I began to fear this tutor I had never met and would fuss when Aleena had to go to her lessons. What if she was hurt? But my sister would always pat my hair and whisper that our tutor would never harm us as long as Aleena was there to protect us. Brandishing an imaginary sword, she would yelp and scamper off, ambushing unsuspecting servants and frolicsome squirrels or mice, until our mother saw and scolded her endlessly.

I remember once sitting in the library by myself when an old woman walked by, her skin a weathered relic against time. Eyes sunken behind layers and layers of sagging skin peered out rather curiously at the little girl who sat in a chair much too big for her, staring intently at a book she surely could not read.

I knew it was *her*: Digin Galia.

And when this ancient woman stopped and looked as if she were about to approach me, I shut the book with a *thud*, leaped down from the chair, and darted away as fast as my little legs could carry me toward the safety of my chambers, where Aleena had put a magic spell of protection.

⇥⟫ ⟪⇤

When I turned six, I was finally formally introduced to Digin Galia, who cast her shrewd eyes over my rumpled dress and tangled hair. With several biting words to my mother about my well-being, it was agreed that she would also tutor me, although Mother decided it would be most beneficial to stick to basic reading, writing, and history, as I would not become queen and did not need the extra lessons.

I was old enough at this point to have dismissed the wild tales Aleena would tell me about the woman, but I was still young enough to fear her. Throughout my time with her, I learned that maybe some of the tales behind Aleena's stories were true. Her whip was certainly not a dragon's tail, but it brought just as much horror in me when it was taken out. I decided immediately that I would dislike her.

I still bear the mark of my first whip on my knuckles, brought on by her discipline on the second day of my being with her. Aleena and I both feared her infamous whip. It was made of a soft, thin wood, torn from a pomegranate tree, so when she struck us, it made an awful *whip* sound and drew a thin line of blood, which stung for days on end. The reason for my first whipping was because I forgot to address her with the respectful title of *Digin* and just called her by her first name. I never forgot to use titles again. Women are *Digin* and men are *Baron*.

Through all this, she did manage to teach us reading and writing, claiming that although we were only girls, all royalty must be more educated than the common peasants. I was horrified that the villagers were denied education. They did not know how to read? How could they live in a world with no thoughts of fairies and dragons and true love?

"What do they do all day?" I once asked Digin Galia.

"They work, child. They survive."

"Do they have fun?"

"Yes, sometimes they do."

"Can we have fun with them?" I asked, in all my innocence.

Digin Galia looked as if she was going to scold me, but a thought came to her. Her face softened for a moment and then turned into one of determination. She stood resolutely and said, "Get your sister and Lilit."

"Why?" I asked, but she was already striding purposefully out of the room, barking commands at the maids nearest to her.

Excited and anxious, I ran down the hall, and, upon reaching Lilit's room, I pounded on her door. Her wide-eyed maid opened the door, and I said, "Digin Galia says Lilit is to come with me!" Without waiting to hear the maid's response, Lilit bounded out from behind her, and, hand in hand, we ran down the hall, giggling.

"You've saved me!" she laughed, breathlessly.

"Let's get my sister," I said, turning down another hall toward Aleena's room. We saw her walking out through the doorway, and she looked at me, surprised. "Digin Galia says we are to go with her."

Always up for a change to the daily routine, she nodded and grinned excitedly, following me as we ran back to my chamber.

We saw Digin Galia standing in front of my door, with a stern look on her face. "What have I told you about running?" she hissed, grabbing my hand roughly.

"Only horses do it," I recited obediently.

"You are a princess, not a horse," she nodded. She gave us three shawls—one for each of us to put over our shoulders—and taking Lilit's and my hand with Aleena marching ahead boldly, we left the castle.

I noticed some of my father's guards walking some distance behind us, keeping an eye on us but making sure to stay out of our way. They were always around in some way, making sure we were protected. We never minded them, never really noticed them anyhow. Our little group entered the village, and I couldn't help but to give a little skip of excitement.

There was a sort of festival happening in the village, and I gathered quickly that we were there to watch it. Aleena gave a shout of delight and almost made ready to run off, before Digin Galia held her arm tightly. "None of you leave my side, or I'll have the guards drag you back to the castle," she threatened. We nodded, though I could see that Aleena had pursed her lips in quiet defiance.

We made our way through the crowds purposefully. Many people turned to look at us and parted immediately when they saw our attire. They smiled and grinned, some reaching out to touch Aleena, who they knew was the eldest from her striking appearance. Aleena shrank back timidly and took my hand. I was a bit surprised at her reaction. I never knew Aleena to shy away from anything or anyone. Digin Galia said to us, "Look at them, girls, the way they are, the way they act. They are different than you three. They have common blood in them. But they are your people. They are your family. We are not here to have fun; we are here to learn from them and to show them who you are."

I cast my eyes around us, looking at the free and easy way that the villagers moved. We walked toward the center of the village when the music suddenly began. I craned my neck to see where it was coming from, and I saw three men sitting on the side, playing the traditional *zurna* and *dhol* instruments. Aleena whispered in my ear, "This is like the music we hear from the mainland."

"Look at the dancers!" cried Lilit excitedly.

With silly smiles on their faces, some of the men grabbed each other's hands so they made a loose half-circle and began to dance together, rowing their hands back and forth and stamping their feet on the dusty ground. Every few steps, they would let go of each other and dance in place in a little circle, before rejoining hands and continuing.

Digin Galia leaned down to our level and said, "This is called the Fisherman's Dance. It is a dance specific to our region, because of our precious Lake Van and the food that it provides us. Look at their movements, and you will see how it resembles fishermen and the work that they do to provide us with food."

As the men danced, the women joined them, giggling and linking hands. They all rowed their clasped hands back and forth, as if rowing a boat. The men fell to their knees and pretended to catch a fish and then reel it in. It was a fascinating and beautiful retelling of a rather mundane task that the villagers did on the daily.

I looked at Aleena's face, and she was wide-eyed, with a smile on her face. She suddenly turned to Digin Galia and pleaded, "Please teach us!"

"This is not a dance for the royal, Aleena. This is a village dance," she replied. There was a distant look in her eyes as she watched them, as if she were miles away. Aleena pursed her lips and made ready to argue, but a woman recognized our tutor and captured her attention.

The two women clasped each other in a warm embrace, and in that split moment, Aleena took Lilit's and my hands and pushed us deeper into the crowd. In the rush, I was suddenly separated from the girls and found myself alone in the middle of the crowd.

Weaving in and out among the villagers and trying not to panic, I suddenly bumped into someone and sprawled onto the floor, coughing as the dust fluttered up around me. My shawl flew off my shoulders and gathered next to me.

"It's an angel!" I heard from near me, hushed with awe.

"It's the princess, idiot," responded another.

A pair of hands reached down and helped me up, and I quickly began dusting off my white dress. Digin Galia would kill me. My shawl was thrust abruptly in my direction, and I grabbed it quickly, throwing it over my shoulders. I finally looked up and found myself looking into warm brown eyes. The boy looked to be Aleena's age, and he stared at me with wide eyes. There was an older boy standing next to him, and he pulled the younger boy away from me. "She's a princess; don't stand so close," he said quietly. My face flushed in embarrassment. They both had tanned dark skin, with brown and beige village clothes on. The younger one's clothes were more tattered, and they both had scrapes on their knees and dust streaks on their cheeks.

"I'm lost," I managed to say. I heard a different song start up, and I perked up in excitement. Another dance!

"What is your name?" asked the eldest.

"Tamar." I pulled my attention back to the boys.

"I am Kevork, and this is my little brother Aleek. Where is your mother? Where is the...queen?" The eldest said it awkwardly, as though the word was foreign on his tongue.

"I came with my tutor," I said. Kevork looked at Aleek, who shrugged.

"Tamar!" I heard. I looked around as a hand snaked out of the crowd and grabbed my elbow. Aleena appeared, with a worried Lilit behind her. "What have you done to your dress? Digin Galia is going to kill us. Who are these boys?"

"Kevork and Aleek—they are brothers. This is my sister, Aleena, and my friend Lilit."

Kevork's face was flushed, unused to being in such company, but Aleek was looking between Aleena and me with fascination on his face.

"Real princesses!" He gawked at us. Kevork nudged him angrily.

Aleena nodded at them and then turned to me. "I found Janna in the crowd," she said, naming my mother's maid's daughter and playmate, who was my age. "And we have to find Digin Galia. Come."

She took my hand and led me back into the crowd, but I managed to glance quickly back at the incredulous boys and call out, "Bye!"

Then we were back in the crowd. Aleena led us to another part of the circle, where I saw Janna in the center with the dancers, dancing with her mother. She danced wonderfully, and my eyes grew wide with awe.

But before I could do or say anything, I felt a sharp slap on my wrist, and I glanced up in horror into Digin Galia's burning eyes.

Aleena stepped forward to shield me and said, "It was my fault; I'm sorry!"

"I said do *not* leave my side, you foolish girls! Tamar—your dress! You ungrateful girl!"

She grabbed us and led us back to the castle, muttering and threatening us the entire time, warning of what would face us when we returned home.

But I was not upset. In fact, my heart was racing with excitement, and I could see the same in Aleena's and Lilit's eyes.

Later that day, I sat with my sister and Lilit during playtime, wondering what I could do. I tried to ignore the rumbling in my stomach, as we were all punished with no dinner. "I'm going to teach Janna how to read," I announced suddenly and determinedly.

Aleena glanced at me languidly and pursed her lips. She looked down at the red slap mark on her arm, pressed a finger onto it, and watched in fascination as the color changed with her touch. "Don't be ridiculous, Tamar."

"If I teach her how to read, she will teach me how to dance."

"I will help you," smiled Lilit.

"You will only get yourselves in trouble," warned Aleena.

I ignored her and turned toward the door. "Janna!" I called loudly. After a moment, I heard the patter of steps down the hall as Janna ran toward the room. When she entered, I sat her down across from Lilit and me and put a piece of paper in front of her. "I'm going to teach you how to read, and you will teach us how to dance." Janna's eyes grew wide.

"I'll keep watch," said Aleena with a frown on her face, as she moved toward the door. For the next twenty minutes, Lilit and I taught Janna how to write letters and how to pronounce them. A flush came to Janna's face as her excitement grew during the lesson.

Then suddenly, we heard a commotion at the door. Looking up and leaping to our feet, we saw Vartan push his way past a furious Aleena and into the room. "What are you doing? It's not nice to keep me out," he said. His eyes traveled over the scene: three girls standing in front of an arrangement of papers and pencils. Bedros followed closely behind him, looking at me with wide eyes. I was reminded of the two boys I'd met earlier that day. How I wished they had run in instead—instead of these two.

As much as we begged Vartan to keep our secret, it was all in vain. He scurried to my mother and told her everything.

We waited sullenly in the playroom, with Aleena and I on the bed, Lilit perched on the couch, and Janna sitting on a chair across from Lilit. I was nervous, my skin stretched tight at the imminent punishment. I fidgeted with the tassels of my bedcover, while Aleena watched me closely. Suddenly rising to my feet in a huff, I began to pace around the room. "She's going to kill me!" I announced.

"She will not kill you, Tamar," piped up Lilit immediately.

"Yes she will." I turned to Janna and said, "When I die, I would like for you to have all of my books. Lilit, you may have my clothes and jewelry. Aleena..." I began, turning to her, but Aleena was laughing. "This is not funny."

She stood up, crossed the room to where I stood and took my hand to lead me back to the bed. She sat me down among the bed sheets with my back to her, and she began unbraiding my hair, pulling her soft fingers through it soothingly. Then she began to speak.

"There was once a man and his wife, and they had three daughters. The father was working in the field, when he got thirsty because it was a hot day, so he told his eldest daughter to go to the spring and get him some water. She went to the spring and saw a beautiful large tree next to the gushing water. Looking up at the tree, she said, 'One day when I get married, I will have a son named Kikos. Kikos will grow up and he will climb this tree, but he will fall from the tree and hit his head on a stone, and he will die! Akh, my poor little Kikos!' and she began to cry relentlessly."

Lilit and Janna were both smiling as Aleena acted out the scene, raising her voice as though she were crying.

"At their home, the father sent the second daughter to find out where her sister was. When the eldest daughter saw her sister approaching, she shouted, 'Come quick and look what happened to your poor nephew, Kikos!' Her sister asked, 'who is Kikos?' and the eldest told her what happened to Kikos, and soon both girls were wailing about poor little Kikos!"

Lilit began to giggle and Janna and I exchanged an amused look. After combing out my hair with her fingers, Aleena was now braiding my hair again.

"Soon, the youngest daughter appeared at the spring, and the same thing happened, so now all three girls are crying and wailing about poor Kikos. And then the mother finally went to them and they told her how her grandson Kikos fell and died and the mother began weeping as well. Finally, the father appeared, and they told him the story of what happened, and after he cried for a bit as well, he decided they should go and have a feast in honor of Kikos's memory. So they went back to their home, killed the last ox they owned, invited their neighbors, and had a feast in his honor. Only after all that was the family able to move on with their lives."

She patted my head comfortingly, indicating that she had finished.

"They got carried away with something that had not even happened yet," said Janna.

Lilit glanced at me. "You are crying about your poor Kikos."

"I know," I muttered.

Aleena grinned at me. "You will be fine. Mother's punishments are never terrible. They are harsh, but not terrible."

At that moment, the door opened and my mother and Digin Galia entered, followed by my father and Baron Avedis. My mother's eyes shone with disappointment and anger, but I was not so upset, as Aleena's story had calmed me down significantly.

"Tamar, you have overstepped your boundaries today. That is twice today you have broken the rules! It is unseemly for the royalty to engage in such behaviors. You are forbidden, and I wish to never see you disobeying me again," she scolded. Vartan, with an insolent smirk twisting his lips, stood behind his father with his pig nose in the air. I could imagine him years into the future, kicking a beggar child in punishment for asking him for help.

My punishment was not terrible, as Aleena had proclaimed. I received some slaps to my wrists, and they took away some of my novels. But I was in a foul mood at the unfairness of it all. Before Aleena left my room, she came to me and muttered, "Meet me an hour after midnight in front of my chambers."

I was excited and could not sit still in my room that night. I was alone, for Janna and Lilit had left and Aleena was in her room. I tried to read a novel, but it could not hold my interest, for my mind was with Aleena, trying to figure out what she would do tonight. As I waited, there was suddenly a knock at my door. I stood up as my father entered my chambers, glancing at me with an apologetic look. I sat back down and watched him as he walked through my room and sat at the edge of my bed, fiddling with the tassels on his coat. He lifted a hand to the red mark on my wrist from Digin Galia's earlier slap and sighed. "Does that hurt?"

"No," I said.

He smiled softly. "You are different from your sister. You are strong."

Had I heard that correctly? "But…Aleena is the strongest person I know."

"No, Tamar, her heart is not as strong as yours. You will do anything for kindness and justice, and unfortunately, there will be many people who try to stop you."

I frowned. "Why can I not teach Janna?"

"You are too young to understand. But never forget: though we are ruling over them, we are not necessarily above them. Your mother forgets that sometimes."

"It is not fair."

He put his broad hand over my hair. "You are a young girl, Tamar. Nothing will be fair to you."

He left then, giving me a small kiss on my forehead before closing my door.

I waited the necessary amount of time and then managed to scurry through the dark hallway until I found my sister standing in the shadows. She was wearing her white nightgown, as was I, and we stood together, two conniving ghosts ready to haunt our victim. I noticed a small bowl in her hands. "What is that?"

She held it up to my face, a mischievous glint in her eyes. I sniffed and recoiled, my nose wrinkling. "Piss?" I hissed.

"Vartan behaved more of a child than you today."

"What will you do with that?" I asked distastefully.

"We shall make sure he learns his lesson," she said, her lips pursed. She took my hand and led me through the maze of our palace to his chambers. Baron Avedis's entire family had extra rooms in our castle, for when they visited and stayed for long periods. We knew exactly where Vartan's room was.

"Shall I wake up Lilit?" I asked, as we passed her room.

"No, she shares her room with her mother."

I nodded and followed her. "What if he awakes?" I whispered, unable to keep quiet.

"I can bang on a dhol in his ears, and he would not wake up."

I put a hand over my mouth to smother the snickering, imagining Aleena banging over his head with the giant barrel drums. I was already feeling better when we reached his chambers, excitement taking the place of my earlier anxiety. We opened the door slowly and saw his still form under the covers in the shadows. Tiptoeing to the bed, we made sure we made no noise and avoided the toys and books that lay sprawled on the floor. For such a supposedly proper child, he was a bit of a mess. I made a mental note to use this fact against him one day, if need be.

Holding my breath, I reached out and pulled back his covers, my muscles taut in case he would wake and we needed to dash for cover. When it seemed safe, Aleena slowly poured the piss on his bed sheets, careful so that it did not touch him and wake him. When we finished, we shuffled out and shut the door, our hands clamped over our mouths to stifle the laughter aching to burst from our throats.

The next morning, Vartan did not appear at breakfast. The adults were unusually quiet, and Baron Avedis and his wife were not at the table. The clink of utensils against the plates was unbearably loud, and Aleena and I ached to learn what had happened. I caught Aleena's eyes and gestured to Bedros, but she shook her head. I leaned in to whisper into her ear, "He must know what happened to Vartan."

"It will be too obvious if we ask. He will tell us himself."

"But how do you know?"

"He is a boy. He will tell us."

As with most things, Aleena was right. After breakfast, during our tea hour, Bedros pulled us aside. His face was red, and I thought he had been crying, but when we were alone, I realized he had been laughing. "Vartan pissed in his pants last night."

Aleena feigned shock, but she pinched my arm discreetly. "What happened?"

"He should not be pissing in his pants at this age. The servant found him and told mother. She scolded him, and he is not allowed to leave his chamber. They are bringing in the doctor soon to explain why he did it. He might be ill."

"Oh dear!" she said, giving me a look. "Poor boy."

And later, hand in hand, we snuck out of our palace and found ourselves on our beloved cliff's edge where we could do what we want, and we laughed and laughed hysterically at her brilliant scheme.

"I wish I could have seen his face!" she chortled. I smiled, looking at my sister, who always knew exactly how to make me feel better.

We often went to that cliff, loving the walk and the feel of the nature around us, devoid of people and noise. We made sure to cover our mouths and hair with a headscarf, wrapped tightly around our necks and held scrunched in our hands. We did not want to chance being seen and recognized, and it was not strange to see women and girls with the scarves, though it was not common among the people.

At the cliff, we would sit for hours, feeling the strong relentless wind but not cowed by it at all. We knew we were safe as long as we did not fall from the cliff, and we were careful not to sit too close. There, we were not afraid to let loose and do things that our household would find incredibly unseemly. We made fun of the people we knew and belched with no restraint. We screamed at the top of our lungs and laughed with the most idiotic and silly faces. We told each other our greatest fears and our greatest desires. And for children in those years, everything was a dream, and so we believed our wildest dreams would come true eventually, especially if we wished with all our hearts.

Sometimes when Bedros and Vartan were visiting, they would press us to tell them where we always ran off to. I could not understand why they cared so much. It was not as if we were friends in the least. Especially Aleena—she could not abide them at all. I realized though that I sometimes enjoyed Bedros's presence. I only told Lilit of our adventures, but she did not seem interested in joining us.

"I'll tell your father if you don't tell me," Vartan would always say, lifting his chin.

"Oh hush," snapped Aleena once. "You'll do no such thing. We are only playing."

"I want to play," said Bedros.

"Play with your toys and leave us alone," I said haughtily, taking on Aleena's tone. She looked at me proudly.

"Don't tell me what to do, baby," he retorted.

"I am not a baby!" I set to wailing, losing my momentary bravery, and Aleena would rush to my rescue, as she always did.

"You'll show them one day," she would say and wink at me.

Chapter 3

WHEN ALEENA TURNED twelve, she was given a different tutor. Mother insisted that it was not right for sisters to share the same tutor. I never met this other tutor, but I began to dislike her even more than I disliked Digin Galia. She kept Aleena away from me until I rarely saw my sister; we were kept apart, though I could not imagine why. Oftentimes I waited for her to find me as she used to when we were younger, but she was finding less time to do so. Sometimes I would wait in her chambers, but she would arrive, tired, and tell me that she wanted to rest.

Left with not much to do and frustration from my boredom, I took to reading and drawing, although my sketches never appeared as well as they did in my mind. The colors were so dull in real life; no matter how many colors I mixed, they never seemed to match. Father tried to help me a few times, but he seemed to realize from the start that I was doomed in the field of artwork. I never finished a sketch or a painting, but I managed to read countless books. The joy I found in words was unmatched. On other days, Lilit stayed with me. I grew very close to her, and we played often together. I took her to the garden or to the library, and we would always have such a good time, but her father often wanted her with him. I tried to learn how to dance with her during our free times. We would hold hands and make up moves, trying to remember how the Fisherman's Dance that we had seen in the village so long ago. But it was half-hearted and mostly for fun, for we did not know the moves, and we did not have the music. We tried to bribe Janna to teach us, but she was frightened of the consequences if we were caught. So Lilit and I managed as best as we could on our own.

On one particular day cooped up inside with my tutor, I had angrily crumpled another sheet of paper, ruined by my poor drawing. Dismayed by my poor treatment of something as valuable as paper, Digin Galia kicked me out of the room with a sharp slap on my knuckles, announcing that I was a spoiled brat and I deserved nothing as fine as paper. Sulking and rubbing my reddened knuckles, I roamed from room to room, looking for something to do, until my father found me.

"How about an adventure with Vrej?"

"Yes!" I exclaimed.

Not long after found us galloping through the country—my father's arms protectively pulled around me. We rode around the village, so as not to attract attention, and I found myself yelping for joy as the wind pulled back my hair. It seemed much too soon when we arrived at the church, and my father dismounted before helping me dismount. He had packed a lunch, so we sat on the grass a little ways off from the church and ate the quaint assortment of food, reveling in the moment.

"Do you ever go into the village?" I asked of him.

"Yes, of course."

"What do you do?"

"I speak to them, visit the workers, see if there is any work I can help with, and I make sure they are all healthy and safe."

"In my novels, the king is always in his palace."

He nodded absentmindedly. "Would you like to hear a story, Tamar?"

"Yes!" I said, laying down on the grass and sipping at cool tea that he had packed for us. I loved stories.

"There was a king living inside his palace, and he was looking out of the highest window with his advisor. He was eating a pastry that was covered in honey and admiring his magnificent city, when suddenly a drop of honey fell from the pastry onto the windowsill. The advisor was about to clean it, when the king said, 'It's only a little drop of honey; it's not our problem.' The honey trickled out the window and fell into the street, when a fly landed on it. A lizard came and ate the fly. Then a cat jumped onto the lizard. Then a dog jumped onto the cat! The two animals begin to fight, and the advisor said, 'Shall I go break them up?' The king said, 'no, no, leave them be. It is not our problem.' Soon after, the cat's owner came out and saw the fight, so she began to beat the dog. The dog's owner came out and began to beat the cat. They began to fight each other, and then their friends appeared and a large fight began in the streets. The king again said, 'It is not our problem.' The police were called in to break up the fight, but the people began to fight the police and it turned into a riot. The army finally appeared and the riot turned into a civil war, with looting and destruction occurring all over the city. Finally, that magnificent city was reduced to a pile of ashes. And only then did the king say, 'maybe that little drop of honey was our problem...'"

I smiled at him. "That is a good story."

"What do you think it means, my dear?"

I thought for a moment, furrowing my brows intently and sipping at my tea. "A king can't ignore his problems?"

"Sure; but also that a king must always be a responsible leader. It was his duty to clean the honey, but he left it alone. We make mistakes, Tamar, and that is normal and healthy, but to address those mistakes and acknowledge them...well, that is honorable."

I nodded, understanding. There was much in this world I did not understand, but when my father spoke about the island and the people inhabiting it, I felt the passion reverberating off of him, filling me to my core with the pride and honor of being a part of this family.

Later that day, with lighter spirit, I went out into our garden, strolling down the winding path that was surrounded with trees that leaned curiously over to peer down at me. It would be a shame not to describe the garden's beauty. Mother and Father had commanded the island's most brilliant artists and gardeners to make this stunning garden, filled with the most dazzling flowers. Splashes of vibrant colors adorned the lush green bushes and trees, and an assortment of sweet smells mixed so that the perfume lingered on our clothes until they were next washed. Flowers of every kind resided here, blooming and glowing under the soft light of the sun. Cannas, bright and yellow, swished their soft petal skirts, as if they were dancers in the sun. Pink cherry blossoms, imported from the east, flirted sweetly with blue bells, which covered much of the garden grounds. And roses of all kinds filled the garden with their dewy petals and promises of love. It was my favorite place on our land, second on the whole island after the cliff's edge, and I often came here to read or gather my thoughts.

As I walked along the many paths in the garden, I found Aleena sitting near the pomegranate tree, the prettiest plant in our garden. My sister was wearing a lovely pale pink dress, which fit her sweetly, so that she looked similar to the flowers that surrounded us. It was slightly longer than mine, as she was not a child anymore, and a short dress would have been unseemly for her age. My own dull green dress reached my knees. I tugged at it anxiously. How fitting that I should be wearing green, I thought dryly. I was a stubborn weed in comparison to the flower that was she.

She was sitting on a small boulder at the foot of the beautiful tree, which had spread its red flowers up in a great stretch, as if it had just wakened from sleep. Hanging from the branches were the red spherical fruits, dull and thick on the outside, though they held such treasures inside.

Aleena looked up and I noticed that a pomegranate was cupped in her hands. She had split it open and had been looking inside at the deep ruby seeds. A serious expression adorned her face, and I stared at her in much the same way. My head was cocked slightly as our many cats around the palace would do occasionally when they were puzzled.

"It is such a beautiful fruit," she muttered in a soft, musing voice.

I nodded slowly and sat across from her on the warm ground, not caring if the grass stained my dress. The weather was wonderful, and the birds were twittering and I'd just returned from a wonderful ride in the countryside with Vrej and my father. I did not want to stand. Aleena was acting slightly strange, however.

"All beautiful fruits are forbidden," she continued.

"They are not!"

"They were once. You can eat an apple now, but you couldn't before. God did not allow it. The apple is the devil's fruit. The pomegranate is Hades's fruit."

"Digin Galia says it is not right to tell tales."

"Stop it, Tamar," she scolded, suddenly, making me jump. I was taken aback. I had never seen her like this before.

"Stop what?"

"Stop being like *them*."

"Like *who*?" I asserted. When she said nothing, I whined, "You're not making any sense."

Aleena sighed and looked back at the fruit, shaking her head as if to rid herself of her thoughts. It seemed to work, for she did not look angry anymore. She avoided my question, however, and I could not find the courage to repeat it.

"Nothing will happen if we eat it now, right?" I asked instead.

"We believe in God, dear, not Hades," she said distractedly.

"Then we can't eat the apple?"

She looked at me as if seeing me for the first time, her eyes clear and blue, like the lake that surrounded our beautiful island. She shook her head slowly, a small smile spreading over her face, almost sadly. "You may eat an apple if you so wish. And you may eat all the pomegranate seeds you want." I nodded with a small sigh of relief. I liked apples, and I liked pomegranate seeds. I spread my legs out in front of me and watched with an amused expression as a snail edged towards my feet.

Aleena reached into the split pomegranate with a finger and pulled out a single seed. It was as if she held a tiny gem in her hands, juicy and sweet and rich. "They say there are three hundred sixty-five seeds in a pomegranate: one for every day of the year. And each one shall bring you luck." I cocked my head again. She was looking straight at me, her eyes slightly narrowed. "Do you suppose if I count the seeds, there would be three hundred sixty-five of them?"

"If they say so, then yes I suppose." I shrugged.

She nodded slowly, observing me quietly. I had a vague feeling I had failed some sort of test and was on the verge of asking her what I had said wrong, when she held the seed out and slipped it between my lips, stopping the words. As I felt the seed burst in my mouth with a splash of sweet flavor, she took out another one and put it in her own mouth. After a second, she took out yet another one and put it to my lips again. "For extra luck." She winked as I ate it. And just like that, her musings disappeared, and her old self came back. She leaned forward and said in a low, hushed voice, "I have a brilliant idea! If you wish to meet, send me a letter by pomegranate!"

"What do you mean?"

"Put it in the pomegranate. So no one sees! It'll be like a romance straight out of a novel! I must go now; my tutor is waiting." She stood to leave abruptly but turned back for a moment, as if I had pulled her back brusquely with a string. "Baron Avedis is visiting for the week."

"Is he bringing the boys?" I asked immediately.

She made an exasperated face, and I knew they were coming. "I shall see you soon, sweet sister," she said instead. She leaned forward quickly and kissed me on the forehead, her sticky lips leaving the residue of the pomegranate seed on my skin. Then she ran off down the path without a backward glance. I sat still, frowning at her sudden mood change, until I realized she had left the split pomegranate on the boulder in front of me. I took it in my hands, barely able to wrap my little fingers around it, and gazed into it. I saw the clusters of seeds, shining radiantly within the darkness of the fruit.

There were three hundred sixty-two now. After a moment's hesitation, I took out another seed and popped it into my mouth. I took the fruit in my hands and stood up, feeling all the better for having eaten my third lucky seed.

"What are you doing here?" asked a voice suddenly from behind me. I turned and saw Lilit walking toward me.

"I was about to go back to my chambers," I said, smiling at her. She sat where Aleena was sitting before and made herself comfortable.

"What's this?" She picked up a book that was placed gingerly against the boulder.

"Aleena's book?" I leaned in to get a closer look. "She must have forgotten it."

"A book of the world," she said, sifting through the pages. I saw maps and descriptions of different regions. "Why does she have this?"

I shrugged. "I suppose to learn about them. I should give it back to her." When I reached out to take it from her, she jerked it away from me with a giggle and bounded up to her feet.

"Not if you can't catch me first!" she challenged, running off between the trees. Her dark hair flew out behind her as she nimbly jumped around flowers to avoid stepping on them. A smile on my face, I shouted, "I'm faster than you!" Leaping to my feet, I pelted after her, dropping the pomegranate and forgetting about my encounter with Aleena, focused only on catching my friend.

⋯⋙ ⋘⋯

That night, after cleaning up and dressing in more appropriate attire, we children sat in the parlor with the adults as they drank tea and had small, colorful desserts. The table was lined with puff pastries filled with sweet cherry or apricot jam, baklava brought by Baron Avedis's family, small bowls holding pomegranate seeds, bread, and all sorts of dips. Aleena and I were seated at a table off to the side with the two boys, all of us eyeing each other distastefully. We were hungry for the desserts but dared not approach unless we were invited. Vartan seemed especially sore that he was unable to sit with the adults, once again. "I should be sitting with them. I am an adult now."

"You are fourteen. You are still a child," sighed Aleena, playing with the ornate tablecloth. It was sewn intricately with gold and dark green thread that glittered every time the cloth moved. I watched it quietly as she played with its folds, making the colors catch the light. My eyes fell toward the beautiful Persian carpets that lined the floor of the parlor. I had never really noticed them. It was amazing how simple hands could work to make this masterpiece of interwoven colors, all put together to make one beautiful image of swirling designs.

"Don't get him started," sighed Bedros, matching Aleena's tone.

Vartan's brows furrowed. "You must stop teasing me, Aleena."

"I don't see why I must," she responded smoothly, not even gracing him with a look. Her eyes roamed around the room, as if looking for something that was hidden in the walls.

"You are a princess. You can't act like a child. You'll be marrying soon."

"Nonsense," she laughed, sending me a disbelieving look.

"No, really," said Bedros, his dark eyes glittering. "I heard my father talking about it. You two must marry at some point."

"Not anytime soon," I told him, coming to Aleena's rescue.

"Not for *you*, anyhow. Aleena's time is coming. She knows it too," Vartan said with a shrug. He stood and walked toward the adults, making another attempt to sit with them. They paid him no heed, but he lingered around them as if he were a thought sitting in the back of someone's mind, ready to come out but hesitant and waiting for the right moment.

Aleena had meanwhile gone quiet, but only I could see her mouth working quietly to spit out words she knew she could not release.

"He's stupid," announced Bedros, trying to make her feel better in his own way. She glared at him and stood, walking toward the garden. I looked after her, knowing that she needed to be alone. Bedros looked at me and shrugged. "Well, I don't want to get married either. Girls are such a bother."

"Boys are too," I countered.

"Girls are more."

"We wouldn't be if it weren't for boys."

He laughed and stuffed a piece of baklava into his mouth. I watched distastefully as the crumbs stuck to his lips and fell to the floor. He glanced at me from the corner of his eyes. "Well, you're all right, I guess. You're not a baby like most I've met."

"You haven't met any girls except for me and Aleena and Lilit," I retorted. "But I guess you're all right too, for a boy," I said and shrugged.

My father suddenly stood with Baron Avedis and clasped his hand warmly. "The priest is here, my friend."

Baron Avedis glanced over at us. "Where is Aleena?"

I shrugged, unable to keep from noticing how pale Vartan was, as he sat primly next to his mother. A small nudge from behind me interrupted my misgivings. I turned and saw Digin Galia, eyeing me angrily. "Do not shrug; you are not a peasant."

"My apologies," I murmured distractedly, for the priest was being accompanied in. Mother handed him a small cloth pouch tied with a pink ribbon. I felt a movement at my side and looked to see that Lilit had joined us quietly. The wild girl in her had disappeared as her hair had been braided properly, and her dress had nary a wrinkle in it. I smiled at her in greeting, but before I could say anything, Bedros tapped my elbow, and I glanced at him.

"What do you suppose is in that?"

"I don't know. He's doing something to it."

"It looks like he's blessing it."

"What's in it?" I asked Lilit.

"I don't know," she said. "My father did not tell me. He only said that today is a big occasion."

Why would he be blessing the bag? What was in it?

We watched silently as the priest murmured traditional words and waved a golden cross over the bag and its mysterious contents. My mother shuffled out of the room toward the garden, and I knew she was going to find Aleena and bring her back. I felt a grave dread spreading over my skin, like thick syrup that one could never really wash off, as I wondered what he had been called for and what the occasion was.

But somehow I knew it would be a while until I found out.

Chapter 4

THE POMEGRANATE LETTERS became a regular practice and we communicated often with them. I would cut open the pomegranate with careful precision, scoop out some of the seeds, and place the folded letter into its depths, telling Aleena to meet me at the cliff at a certain time, and she would do the same when she wanted to meet me. That way we would not be scolded for straying from our duties.

When I was thirteen and she was sixteen, we knew the route to the cliff by heart. Instead of walking the entire way, we rode there by horse. Aleena had a sweet chestnut horse named Noor—"pomegranate"—which Mother had pronounced a ridiculous name for a horse, but Aleena had insisted upon it. My horse was black with a fire temper, but he was his sweetest self with me. I called him Asdgh—"star"—named for the white star on his forehead. Father and Mother would have been horrified if they found out where we always disappeared to with the horses, but we bribed the maids and servants with little delicacies so they would not tattle on us.

Sometimes I took the road to the village, riding straight through boldly but with a shawl over my face, so no one would know who I was and tell my parents. I told myself I was just looking at the different people and learning about the village, but I was always looking for *them*—the brothers I had met all those years ago. They had fascinated me, and I knew they could teach me many things about village life. I felt a connection with them, especially with the younger one who had not flinched from me. The more I dwelled on it, the more I was desperate to meet him. My face would flush as soon as the thought of him would cross my mind. To my everlasting disappointment, I never saw them as I rode through the village. They had disappeared since that day, and I began to wonder if I had imagined meeting them at all. I wished I could remember their names, and I was often very restless to go riding through the village in pursuit of them.

On one rather dull day, while I was aching to go galloping with Asdgh through the village, I was sitting in the library with Digin Galia, reading a difficult passage of history through a raging headache when a maid walked in with a tray. "Pomegranate?" she asked in a small voice. She placed the tray in front of me, and I took the fruit quickly into my hands, abandoning the book that only droned of kings and war strategies.

"Tamar!" admonished Digin Galia. "I gave you no permission to take that fruit!" She waved away the maid dismissively, who left without a backward glance, but I knew there was a note inside. I had the fruit in my hands and noticed the crack that ran down the center of the fruit. Placing it on my lap so the old witch could not see, I quickly spread the lips of the orb with a crackle and was greeted by the sweet smell of the seeds.

"Tamar," repeated Digin Galia, emphasizing every word, "do… not…eat…the…pomegranate."

I glanced up at her, my eyebrows furrowed in anger and my lips pulled down into a bitter frown. "I am hungry."

"Put it back in the tray," she said tersely, holding out the small iron tray.

I glanced down at the pomegranate, then at the tray, then at Digin Galia's pursed lips. With a move hidden under the table so that Digin Galia would not notice, I slipped out the note and slid it into my pocket. But I was not going to let my pomegranate go.

It was now a battle of wills between a child and an adult. "I want a seed."

"I forbid it."

"Why?"

Her eyes widened. "You *shall* obey me."

For a moment, I hesitated, my eyes flickering to the pomegranate whip she kept at her side, but I was much too angered to pay any heed to my fear. Why choose this moment to teach me a lesson? I was hungry and I wanted a seed. I was not a baby any longer; I could make decisions on my own. Without looking away from her piercing eyes, I pulled out a single seed and popped it into my mouth.

In a sudden move, her hand snaked out and slapped the pomegranate from my hands, so the fruit skittered across the floor, its seeds spilling out onto the smooth marble and staining it with its red sticky juice. A part of her hand had hit my mouth, and the pain shot through my head. And just like that, all my defiance and anger dissipated with my shock, and I became a child again. Tears pooled in my eyes as I watched the fruit roll away and the seeds become soiled by the ground. My hand cupped the side of my mouth, as if I could protect it from any more pain. The seeds were untouchable now. Their beauty faded the moment they touched the floor. When she saw the tears, she leaned back in her chair and sighed, her anger gone as quickly as mine had disappeared.

"You *must* learn to obey your elders," she began with emphasis. I said nothing, only looked at the fruit. "You love to read, do you not?" I nodded slightly, avoiding her eyes, and she continued, speaking with desperation to will me to understand her. "In your stories, when the hero or heroine disobeys an order, there is always a tragedy. If you want to avoid tragedies, you *must* follow the rules!"

As she said this, I thought of what Aleena would say to this. I was certain she would sigh romantically and say that tragedies made life worth living. She would say that without tragedies, life was too easy. It would just be a straight path with no obstacles, no adventures along the way. It is much more romantic to die for love than it is to wither away in loneliness.

I was going to open my mouth and tell Digin Galia this, but to my surprise, she slipped straight into a song, humming the tune first and then singing the words. I could not understand, as her voice did no justice to the song, and her voice scratched through the words. But I somehow knew it was a sad song. It swayed and danced, then grew melancholy, as if it was mourning for someone. I tried to listen, but I could not understand, and I grew frustrated as deep sorrow filled me to the core. I was not sure, but I could swear I saw a tear roll down Digin Galia's face, and I wanted more than anything to understand its words.

I numbly sat in my chair, hand cupping my mouth—though the pain was long gone—as I listened to the song. My eyes were trained on the seeds that were scattered across the marble floor, but my vision was blurred from the tears that filled my eyes. The red juice swam before my eyes until it looked like splatters of blood, oozing out from the heart of the dying pomegranate.

When I left the castle an hour later, her cracked voice still scratched throughout me, and I longed for the beautiful soft music we always heard at the cliff's edge. I rode hard toward the village, veering onto another path, so no one would know that I was arriving from the castle. I passed through—unnoticed—and reached the grass clearing we'd had the picnic on so long ago. I saw Noor tied to a tree, and I knew Aleena was already here. I tied Asdgh next to her and climbed to the cliff.

Upon reaching the top, I stopped immediately, as I always did, and gazed solemnly at Aleena's back. She was sitting calmly at the edge of the cliff, her feet dangling in the air and a soft song humming from her throat, as if she did not notice the deadly drop beneath her. I hesitated, still afraid of the terrible height, but she turned and smiled at me reassuringly, patting the space next to her.

I came over slowly and sat next to her, joining my feet with hers. I looked away from the angry waves beneath me and tried to ignore the idea of dangling meat in front of a wild beast.

"You have been crying," my sister said at once, to my surprise.

"No, I have not," I replied.

She reached out and touched my cheek gently. Then she brought her finger in front of me so I saw the splash of my tear on her skin. "Then, I don't know why," I said and shrugged. I wiped at my wet cheeks with my hands. I looked up at her and realized she knew I was lying. She was waiting for an answer. I hesitated for a moment, but my curiosity was too strong. "Digin Galia told me a story today.

A song, actually—she sang it. I think it was a romance…or a tragedy. It sounded quite sad."

"What was the story?"

"I don't know, but I heard my name in it."

Aleena turned away, taking a deep breath. It almost sounded like a sigh. "It *is* sad," she said, her voice trailing off. She looked off toward the mountains, her face serious. "It is the most important story of this island."

I had a vague memory of my mother mentioning the tragedy that we were remembered for. Was this it?

"Do you know it? Will you tell me about it? I could not understand her."

She was quiet for a bit, pondering, her brows furrowing. When she began, her voice was low, as if it was the voice of the very wind itself. I leaned in to her, eager to hear what she had to say. A story from Aleena was far more precious than any lesson I could ever learn from Digin Galia.

"Do you think, perhaps, you may love whom you wish to love?" she mused.

"I suppose."

She glanced at me, but her eyes were not seeing me. "*Akh,* Tamar," she breathed, and the words seemed to echo through my heart. "If only you never feel what she felt. If only you could be free to love whom you wish. That was Tamar's greatest fault. She did not know the rules, or if she did, she chose to ignore them. You would think that, as princesses, all we have to do is wish for something and we shall have it. Mother and Father would see to it immediately. We would never want, but we would wish and it would be ours. The illusion—damned illusion—is that we cannot have the one thing that has the power to give us the most happiness." She paused, her brows furrowing again in concentration. "See that land over there?" She pointed off to the mountains, the source of our mysterious music, which danced faintly in the distance. I nodded. "A young man lived there. He was in love with a beautiful young woman who lived here on this island."

"Tamar," I said.

She nodded. "Tamar and the nameless boy."

"Nameless?"

Her eyes grew hazy with feeling, as if she was remembering the story from her own personal memories instead of telling it as just a story. Shivers ran down my spine at this new feeling that had spread over her, like an ominous cloud approaching over the horizon. "He was *nothing*. She was a princess, like us, but he was a commoner, dirt in this great world, kicked underneath all our feet. The story does not even honor him with a name." She looked out at the land angrily, the wind whipping at her hair fiercely. "They were not allowed to see each other. A princess falling in love with a commoner? One who did not even live on the island? It was absolutely unacceptable. But Tamar—she would not have it. She had found love, and *nobody* would take it from her!"

Aleena suddenly snaked out her hand and clutched at my wrist, tugging me up from my spot and to my feet. For a disturbing moment, I thought she was going to push me off the cliff. I lost my footing from fear and tipped toward the edge, horrifyingly looking down at the mouth that opened wide to swallow me whole, but she tugged at my arm hard and pushed me the other way, so we both ran and stumbled down the path. I did not ask where we were going, even when we veered off onto another path that was unfamiliar to me.

I knew she saw the story before her eyes and was wholly consumed by it. I stayed silent, as I always did. She looked back during the run and, eyes shining, shouted, "They were not allowed to see each other. Ever! Him on the mainland, her on the island. But their true love had consumed them entirely. They had become obsessed with each other." We were running downhill, crossing past the cliff, which we so often sat on. Branches whipped at my face and tugged at my hair, but Aleena's speed tore me past them. I kept my eyes closed, blindly following my sister.

"What would *you* do for love? For true love?" she asked, suddenly pulling us to an abrupt stop. Her voice had grown soft.

I blinked open my eyes and took in my surroundings. We were standing at the edge of where the dense trees ended. In front of us stretched a small pebbly beach, hidden from view by our own dear cliff. I saw the water slamming into the rocks at the base of the cliff a few miles away from where we stood. But the water at this shore was calmer and sweet, almost inviting us into its embrace. And in the distance, we saw the lake stretch for miles until it touched the mountains. I had never been here before, and I did not know how Aleena had found it.

Together, hand in hand, we walked out onto the pebbles. The wind was calmer here; a soft breeze instead ruffled our hair. I walked to where the tranquil water of Lake Van barely touched my feet. It lapped at my toes, tickling my skin and washing it clean of the traces of dirt it had collected from the run. I could hear the music so much stronger here than from the cliff, for it echoed against the rock wall behind us.

"She sat here and lit a single candle. With only the candlelight for guidance, he would swim all the way from there to here in the dark of the night. She would wait for him impatiently, worried for his safety and wanting to see him so desperately," Aleena said softly, coming up next to me. We sat together on the ground, comfortable despite the smooth pebbles rattling underneath us.

"But as every secret in the world, hers was revealed. Some of the young men of the village decided that what she was doing was not seemly and must be stopped immediately. They approached on a particularly dark and stormy night and snuffed out the candle. They dragged Tamar back to the castle."

My eyes were wide as I looked across at the mountains. I could almost hear her wails, her screams, echoing against the walls of the cliff.

"He was trapped in the middle of the lake, where, for a split second, the land on both sides completely disappears. With no way to find land, as his only guiding light was gone, he drowned, and his body was found on this island. His last words had been in anguish, and they were the simple words, 'Akh, Tamar.'"

Ah, Tamar.

"And this is what our island is named after…Akhtamar." Her voice trailed away with the wind, and we sat silently, hearing the waves break on the shore.

"What would you do if you were her?" asked Aleena softly.

"I do not think I will love as much as she did."

"But *if* you did, *if* you loved that man and it was forbidden."

"I don't know," I whispered, closing my eyes. She stayed quiet as well, but I knew she wanted to say something, so I looked at her expectantly.

"You know, don't you, what Father and Mother have planned?" she asked. There was a hesitant quiver that shook her voice and frightened me.

"No."

"I shall marry in autumn of my seventeenth year."

I turned to look at her, shocked. "Marry? In a year? To whom?"

She looked up at the sky, her eyes wide and a sad smile on her lips. "Who else?"

"Vartan?" I cried. She nodded. My mouth had dropped open.

"The very same."

"But why?"

"There has been an arrangement. That day when we decided to send pomegranate letters was when they brought in the rings. It is called *khosk-kab*, the engagement, when the families decide on the arrangement and bless the rings. They told me about it a day before." She shrugged. She suddenly looked younger than sixteen. I remembered that day and finally understood her odd behavior, as she had sat solemnly underneath the pomegranate tree. She turned to me, and I was surprised to see that her eyes were shining with unshed tears. "Tamar, I do not wish to marry Vartan. He is arrogant and heartless, and I hate him." I opened my mouth to try and console her, but she interrupted me suddenly. "But marry him I must. *You* have more freedom; you will not rule the kingdom, as I shall. You *must* fall in love and escape the constraints of your status, Tamar! Do not shake your head at me; you must do as I say. I want you to feel that happiness that Tamar felt every time she saw her love swimming toward her."

"And the same heartbreak when he drowned?" I snapped angrily.

"Heartbreak is something you do to yourself," she said, simply. We drifted into silence here, gazing off at the water that ebbed back and forth across from us. It was so peaceful here, and I closed my eyes absentmindedly, allowing the moment to relax my body. "Have you ever thought of the possibility that perhaps we were put on this island for the purpose of leaving?"

I opened my eyes and looked across at Aleena. She had a pensive look on her face. "What do you mean?"

She sighed. "Just think about it. People are born into their families and traditions and they stay there for years. Especially on this island. But what if our point in this world—as princesses—is to lead people to realize they can be free?"

"I suppose that could be true; but then if we leave, who would rule the people of this island?"

"Does this tiny island really need a ruler?"

"I'm not sure. I believe we all have our roles that we are placed into and we should be content with that. Father is a magnificent King and has done so much for the island. Imagine if he just decided he didn't want to be king anymore. That would be dreadful!"

"But that is Father's joy—his fate is to be this leader."

"So how are we supposed to know which is the right or wrong path?" I was frustrated.

Her eyes were searching mine. Then she stood up and took me by my hand, pulling me to my feet as well. She led me closer to where the lake touched the shore with longing waves, as if they were the soft caresses of a forbidden lover.

"Do you know what happened to Tamar after her lover died?" she asked. I shook my head. "I don't either. It does not say. It is assumed that she lived her life dutifully, put back on the *right* course of her life." She bade me hold out my right hand. I did, palm facing the skies. She held it softly in her palm. "But to Tamar, that was not the right path. To the rest of the world, it was. Don't ever be *obedient*, Tamar. If you feel that your path is headed somewhere else, then take it."

"But *you* will be *obedient* if you marry Vartan! Don't marry him, Aleena!"

She smiled sadly. "*I* have no choice, sweet sister."

"Why not?"

"One day, you will understand."

She looked down at our hands that were facing the sky and said loudly, "Before your fifteenth birthday, you shall fall as much in love with a boy as Tamar did in our legends. And you will change that story. We will have a new Tamar. I will not be the reason we forget our tragedy, as Mother always likes to say. *You* will. You are meant to."

"How can you say that?" I winced. "You are beautiful and spirited and strong."

She raised an eyebrow. "They may call me those words, but your heart beats stronger than mine. Though Mother named you after the story of this island, you are stronger than that. Your story will be different. I promise."

I saw a sudden flash of quick light, and before I could yelp, she brought the tip of a sharp sea glass down to my palm, slicing my skin cleanly. I cried out as a lightning jolt of pain shot up my arm and beads of blood bubbled out of the thin gash. It was only about an inch long and very thin, but my eyes were bulging, and my mouth opened in horror. "Aleena!" I cried. "Why did you do that?"

"I want you to remember this day. No matter what happens to me, no matter what happens to everyone around us, I want you to remember this day. And that"—she gestured to my hand, which was now dripping with blood—"will help you remember."

She then brought the glass down on her own palm and sliced the skin there. Her face hardly changed, and I was not certain that she even felt the pain. There was a hard glint shining in her eyes, and I almost couldn't see their color. The blood glimmered as though we were both holding precious rubies that contrasted darkly against our skin. She tilted her hand over the water at the shore and let several drops of her blood fall in. A moment later, she leaned down and washed her hand in the water. I watched the blood spread and, after a moment, leaned down next to her and washed my hand as well. My hand stung, but I stayed silent as Lake Van lapped at my wound, wondering if it would continue hungering for my blood after the taste I was allowing it to take.

→══◎ ◎══←

I never forgot that glint in Aleena's eyes when she spoke that wish. Forever it stayed with me, and if I wished for the memory to disappear with the gash, it did not. It spread its sticky tendrils in my mind even as the mark became a pearl-white scar on my palm. I always caught myself staring at it, wondering if love would ever come for me. And if it did, would it hurt? Would I cry as Tamar had cried? Would I scream as the dying, nameless boy had screamed?

From then on, I made a vow that when I did fall in love—for Aleena's wish would come true—I would not be pained by it. It would only be ruled by happiness and bliss, as all my fairy tales were, bound within the safety of my books. It would free me.

With this thought firmly in mind, I regarded the scar with a lighter heart, and Aleena seemed to believe I was ready for my rebellious love story.

So I forgave her for her cutting my palm.

I always forgave her.

Chapter 5

THE NEXT YEAR passed in a blur of quick preparations. The arranged marriage was made public and announced happily to the people of our island—happily to all except, of course, to the bride and her little sister.

In a year, Aleena had become a beautiful young woman at the age of seventeen, with her long dark curls and crystal blue eyes. Meanwhile, I had recently changed my wardrobe for the longer dresses I was so eager for. I was now fourteen and felt as much an adult as Vartan had when he was that age. Vartan, now eighteen, was the luckiest man alive for getting to marry her, though the same could not be said for Aleena. I vaguely wondered what the boys looked like now. It had been several years since we had last seen them; in fact, the khosk-kab had been the last time. I found it odd that I had never really thought about them growing up. In my mind, they were both the same children who would torment my sister and me.

Although the occasion was not something Aleena and I could celebrate with smiles on our faces, the ceremonies for weddings were our favorite. Preparations and traditions were the highlight of any wedding, and even Aleena managed to find a bit of excitement in realizing that she would be part of it all. Lessons began for Aleena, such as what to do, what to say, and which dances she would partake in. After every lesson, she would come to me and teach me what she could remember. They were slower dances and a bit flirtatious, though I could not image Aleena dancing these across from the pig Vartan. Did he even know how to dance? I doubted it.

A month before his arrival, all of our closer female cousins and aunts gathered in our guest rooms for *shordzevk*, one of the family traditions. The maids had prepared several dozen needles and rolls and rolls of thread. We sat and organized who was to sew which part of the bride's dress. Mother was in charge of distributing the duties to each cousin and aunt, and she was terribly excited to finally be at the head of the tradition. I wanted the belt—for truly I could not make anything else—and it was agreed that Aleena and I, along with Janna and one of our cousins, would design the belt. The rest of the party would create the dress from scratch. One of my aunts, married happily for several years, was to make the headdress and eventually put it on Aleena's head, as this would bring good luck to Aleena's marriage.

Tradition dictated that the bride's dress would be made of a crimson color, with gold embroidered into the bodice and sleeves. The crimson was made from a bug that was found at the base of our beloved Mount Ararat. The deep red color was unique to our land, and we took great pride in this. Lace, also one of our culture's prides, was to adorn the headpiece, as well as some of the creases throughout the dress. All the lace was to be sewn by Aleena, for this was part of our younger education. A young girl needed to learn how to sew lace, for she would be expected to sew it for her own dress. I was definitely lacking in this skill and kept my head down for fear that I would be reprimanded harshly.

Mother, thankfully, was incredibly distracted. She was in charge of the gold, and she found great pride in this. I had never seen her as happy as she was on this day. The dress itself was to be loosely fitted, with the ornate belt tied around the waist to give it extra volume at the hip. The headpiece, my favorite part and also the hardest part, was made of cotton and silk, wrapped into a tube with ornate designs around it and a long train of soft silk material, brought in from China.

We sewed with much enthusiasm, eagerly passing around the colorful strings and ribbons to share, and calling out directions and ideas. I caught Aleena's eyes over the rolls of cloth. "It's going to be beautiful," she murmured as we sewed, a glittering awe in her eyes.

"I am excited to see you wear this," I said and smiled brightly.

"Yes." She nodded, looking down at the lace that was becoming a gorgeous design in her delicate fingers. She was truly an artist when it came to sewing. I worried about how I would manage my own wedding dress. When I tried to make lace, I created a twisted tangle that Digin Galia would disappointedly turn away from. "I only wish it wasn't for my wedding," Aleena added. I had nothing to say to that, so I managed a small hopeful smile and continued sewing.

The room was a clamor of excitement as all the women in our family piled in. The couches, which were given as a gift from the Far East, were soft and oriental, and some of my favorite pieces of furniture in the room. They were comically overtaken by mostly heavyweight fluttering women and rolls and rolls of cloth. They all bonded between sewing, sips of tea, and numerous dips with lavash and pastries. It was one of my favorite traditions, for it truly brought the family together. There were the few small arguments when they could not agree on a section, but it was always resolved with a compromise and a laugh. I had never seen my mother in such good spirits before; her cheeks were flushed, and a small smile rested on her face. Every once in a while, her eyes would flit across to Aleena, and she would smile, content.

She did not realize that Aleena's spirit was fading. Or if she did see it, she did not care. Her eldest and most beautiful daughter was to marry a nobleman's son. What more could a mother ask for?

The dress had to be flawless. Occasionally we would stand Aleena on a small pedestal and try the pieces against her body to make sure that the dress was made for her—and only her. The colors had to be perfect, the sewing and material professional, and the dress unable to fit anyone else. We sewed until our eyes crossed and our fingers were aching, but the dress was getting along absolutely exquisitely. I caught Aleena's gaze and gave her a big smile, and she smiled back a little sadly, but it was a grin nevertheless, and I was content.

The dress was finished in three weeks. At the end of the last day, Mother brought forth a small box the size of the palm of her hand. She presented it to Aleena with a proud smile. Inside the box, nestled among the softest silk, was a ruby, held delicately by a silver chain, shining brilliantly and lined with the smallest diamonds. "It was from my wedding, and now it will be for yours. It is made for the queens of Akhtamar."

The Queens.

I watched as Aleena and my mother bent their heads together, dark curls falling over their shoulders as they gazed upon the glittering ruby. Aleena lifted up her hair, and my mother clasped the necklace around my sister's neck, letting the ruby rest against her porcelain skin. It shone brilliantly, the blood red contrasting against her skin tone.

And as I saw my mother look up at Aleena with shining eyes, I knew she did not care about the ruby. Her most precious gem was—and would always be—her eldest daughter.

Knowing that Aleena was overwhelmed from the past several weeks, I peeked my head into her room one night, where I found her curled against her window, reading a book. "Aleena," I whispered. She looked up and quickly grabbed the pomegranate I tossed at her. "Let's go."

Of course she was willing, putting down her book and the pomegranate immediately and grabbing her coat. We snuck into the stables and found Noor and Asdgh, who both became skittish in eager anticipation for the coming ride. Mounting them, we galloped off into the night, heading toward the little abandoned church. The night was incredible, the dark sky above clear and dotted with millions of stars. I felt as though if I stared too long into the sky, I would get lost. It was a mesmerizing feeling and I smiled into the wind. When we arrived, we let Noor and Asdgh free to graze, while we roamed around the church.

"It's so different here than from anywhere else on the island," mused Aleena. "It almost makes you forget."

I walked around the corner, my fingers trailing the wall of the church at my side. "Forget what?"

"That we're surrounded by water. That we're just a tiny little island in a huge world."

I came to stand next to her as she looked up at the proud structure across from us. "What are you looking at?"

She pointed up at a raised carving of a bird. "Is it not ironic, sister, to carve a bird into the side of a wall? Birds are meant to fly, but this one is forever fixed in stone."

Remembering a previous conversation we'd had, I grinned mischievously and said, "Ah, but that bird's destiny is to remain locked inside that stone."

She raised her eyebrows at me, amused. "One day, I shall fly away from this island, and you shall follow me, and we shall be free," she proclaimed, throwing her arms out and twirling melodramatically.

"But what will Vartan do without his lovely wife?" I asked.

"He shan't even notice my absence. In fact, no one will notice us missing, for we will dress two women like us and they will not even realize it is not us. We shall be free forevermore!" Aleena skipped to me, grabbed my hands, and began twirling me in a circle, spinning faster and faster until we both threw our heads back and laughed breathlessly.

"We will be free!" I cried out, managing a look at my sister while we spun dizzyingly fast. The world was a blur around us, but she was clear, her eyes shining and her hair lifted above her head, as her laugh rang out for all to hear. It was a moment I committed to my memory forever, as such joyous bliss was a rare occasion to witness. In that moment, all was perfect. It was as it should be.

→═◉ ◉═←

For the next several days, all our cousins and aunts were on alert for the next tradition, which would happen through the groom's family. A single person from that family would be designated to be the *aghves*, the "fox." He would arrive here earlier than Vartan and the rest of the guests and try to get into our palace. We had to prevent him as best we could and find him out quickly, for letting a fox into our home was unacceptable. The idea was that the fox would steal our bride and take her away from us forever.

We did our chores, prepared Aleena, helped with the food, cleaned the castle, danced new dances to wonderful music played by our cousins, and bonded with our family, while keeping our eyes peeled for the fox. It was during this time that the priest arrived, much to my father's joy—to mine as well, for this meant that Lilit would be staying with us. The priest would marry Aleena with Vartan, so he was beaming with pride and honor as he beheld my parents. Meanwhile, Lilit bounded into my arms, and we hugged tightly, not having seen each other in such a long time.

"You're so much taller now!" I cried, slightly envious for I was slight of body.

"You're beautiful," she said and smiled, holding the length of my hair softly in her hand. She had truly become beautiful herself, with wild dark hair and shining, glimmering eyes. She had a mischievous smile on her lips, and I saw how much she had become a woman, though she was only fourteen, just like I was.

We had a wonderful time for the next few days. We practiced dances together and managed to even persuade Digin Galia to teach us some steps. They were slow and honey-dense dances, bouncing slowly and tensely to the beat of the song. We practiced them for hours and hours, improvising the dances in ridiculous ways and dissolving into laughter. It was refreshing to be careless and silly.

Some nights Lilit stayed with me inside my chamber, and we stayed up talking in low voices so no one would hear us. I found myself opening up to her, as my worries had been aching to release from my chest since I had first seen Lilit. I finally told her about my concern for Aleena, unable to hide it from her any longer. I had not told anyone else. "Do you think she'll be truly happy?" asked Lilit.

I sighed. "Not as long as she is with Vartan."

"I never liked him," she sniffed.

I laughed. "I do not think anyone ever liked Vartan."

"We shall have to find a way to make this bearable for her."

I frowned. "With every day that brings us closer to the wedding, it becomes more impossible."

Lilit gave me a hopeful smile. "You care a lot for her, and she sees that. Knowing that you are at her side is most definitely a consolation to her, I promise."

I nodded in agreement, but a sliver of doubt had wormed itself into my mind, making me believe that Aleena would never really be happy again.

A week after shordzevk, we women were drinking tea in our parlor, while the boys and men were in the library, perhaps guzzling down their spirits and discussing what men normally discussed. We were never allowed in there, so we contented ourselves in the parlor, sipping the delicious tea instead. The adults were in a half-hearted conversation about an acquaintance of my family who had recently received a large sum of wealth from an uncle who had passed away.

The conversation went on, and their words droned around my head like buzzing flies.

My aunt, the ever-constant gossiper, was saying with a resolute sniff, "To be honest, it seems very odd to me. Who was this uncle of hers? Why did he give her this sum?"

My other aunt responded, "I heard when he was ill once, she took great care of him. Maybe he feels he owes her for this."

"She's not telling us something."

"She never *told* us anything; we have just been hearing rumors."

"You know what I mean. She's keeping something hidden."

"Well, I've never cared for her."

I exchanged a look with Lilit, who rolled her eyes. She never cared for gossip either. Janna, who was sitting next to Aleena, stifled a giggle, and I turned to Aleena to see her reaction, but she was looking down and stirring her tea distractedly.

My mother sipped her tea delicately, dabbed at her mouth elegantly with an embroidered handkerchief—ever the proper queen—and said, "Why waste time in idle gossip? I have the right mind to invite her to call on me one day. Then the story will be cleared."

"Hear, hear," said my elder cousin, smiling as she stood up.

"Talin, where are you going?" asked her mother.

"I want to take this piece of cake to my brother. He dearly loves them."

"Would you like me to accompany you?" asked my other cousin.

"No, I'll be back soon," said Talin, smiling.

"Do hurry and leave the men to their affairs," said her mother, with a sniff and a rather large bite of a pastry.

Mother glanced distastefully at the crumbs that fell from the woman's mouth and disappeared into the colorful carpet. I knew she was making a mental note to set a maid on the carpet as soon as the guests left. And when she gave me a piercing glare as I scratched a scab on my leg, I knew she wished she could also set a maid to fix me.

Talin, meanwhile, made her way out the parlor with a small glass plate holding a modest slice of cake. The moment she was out of hearing, my aunt said, "Talin is coming to the age of marriage, as well."

Her mother fluttered her hands. "Oh dear, I know. She is such a bother about it."

"Have you found her a young man to marry?"

"Not yet. Do you know of any?"

"There is Bedros, our Vartan's brother."

"He is a very suitable man, but Talin cannot abide him."

"And why is that?"

"I shall tell you. The simple reason is that he is a rascal."

Some of the women feigned shock, as if they did not know this. Lilit nudged my side. My mother noticed the movement and cast her eyes across to me. I made my face a stone, so she would not think anything.

Of course Bedros was a rascal. He had been a mischievous fool all his life.

"Have he and Talin had…relations?" ventured an aunt.

Talin's mother bristled. "I will not have that sort of talk about my daughter."

"Dear, she meant nothing of the sort," soothed my mother, giving my aunt a piercing look. My aunt only looked off carelessly and sipped at her tea. "Talin and Bedros are not suited for each other. We shall find her another man and Bedros another woman." My mother gestured for her maid to fill her teacup as she said this. Janna's mother quickly did her duty, while my mother's eyes flickered to me again. I looked away quickly. I had a bad feeling for whatever was on her mind.

"I do know someone else who is coming of age," said another aunt, who winked in my direction. I accidentally sipped too much tea and burned my tongue, but I made a show of not caring, as that would be humiliating to my mother. Janna glanced at me and made ready to help, but I shook my head at her. The rest of the women preened at me, as if I were still an infant. "You shall be fifteen soon, dear—such a young woman!"

I felt Aleena finally looking at me, but I dared not lock eyes with her. Lilit nudged me again with a stifled giggle.

"Do you have your sights set on anyone yet?"

"Not yet," I responded, my tongue raw from the burn. My face was bright red, as all the attention in the room turned toward me.

"She will soon. It will be a good match, I promise," said my mother, sighing as if she was tired from just the thought of finding a match for me. "She will be just like her sister. They do adore each other so."

The women continued on with their gossiping and chatting, leaving us be. I finally glanced at Aleena and the worry in her eyes made me uncomfortable. She slightly shook her head and I nodded in agreement. We both sensed Mother's determination at pairing me with Bedros. I could feel the thought sifting off of Aleena.

The scar on my palm tingled, a constant reminder of the bloody pact.

"Have you seen him?" whispered Lilit into my ear, as soon as the room's attention drifted toward a topic that thankfully excluded my future.

"Who?"

"Bedros."

"No, I have not. I saw him last when I was only nine." I glanced at her and saw in surprise that her face was flushed. "Have you?"

"Yes, and I do believe you would approve." She winked at me.

"Oh dear," muttered Aleena.

"Lilit!" I nudged her. "Please do not let my mother hear you."

"You could do worse." She shrugged.

"Hush," said Aleena, leaning in towards her. "That will not happen for Tamar."

Lilit was going to respond, but Talin came back at that moment, followed closely by her brother and a young woman who was a stranger to us. The cake was still in Talin's hands, though I could see her little brother eyeing it longingly. He looked desperately guilty, and we perked up, with the worst fears in our minds. Mother cried, "Talin, what has happened?"

Talin put a hand on her hip and raised her eyebrow, saying with a smirk, "We have found our fox."

"They sent a girl!" Lilit dissolved delightedly into giggles, after a moment of shocked silence.

"I thought she was a maid who wanted water," said Talin's brother, as his mother scolded him soundly for letting the fox into the castle.

"Is *that* what she wanted?" I whispered naughtily to Lilit. Aleena scoffed.

The scolding was all half-hearted, and my aunts laughed and made a joke out of it. "May I have my cake, please?" he asked, reaching out for the plate.

"No," said Talin, moving away from him.

"Mother!" he cried.

"Talin!"

"Why did they send a girl?" asked Talin.

I involuntarily looked across at Aleena, who I expected to snap with, "Why *not* send a girl?" but she stayed quiet. She suddenly seemed incredibly fascinated with the small paintings on her teacup: pomegranates, little pomegranates, with the seeds spilling out of them. When Aleena was not interested in her surroundings, nothing could pull her back.

Instead, Lilit piped up with, "A girl is smarter!" Talin's brother shot her a glare.

The fox shrugged and responded, "They figured I'd have the best luck."

"Targeting the vulnerable young boys, I see," chuckled my aunt. Talin's brother blushed.

I patted the empty space across from us for the girl, who grinned and made her way forward to sit there, no doubt eager to sit by the younger girls. Janna stood quickly and prepared a cup of tea for our guest. "I am Vartan's younger cousin. He will arrive in a week," she announced, taking the tea and ignoring Janna. I nodded with gratitude at my maid, frowning that the girl had not done so herself. "Congratulations on your betrothal, Princess Aleena!"

Aleena smiled politely, glanced at me with a heavy look, and then glanced back down into her tea, as if wishing she could drown in its depths. I dearly wished for the marriage to be called off, as Aleena's spirit was gradually being locked down into a cage, and it was unbearable watching it happen without being able to save her.

Chapter 6

AFTER THIS, ALL that was left to do was to wait for Vartan's great arrival. Aleena seemed to be in a constant state of agitation, and I did my best to keep her calm and keep her mind on the excitement that was going to accompany his procession. She tried to smile, but it never seemed to reach her eyes anymore.

Our doctor came by a few times to see her, though no one would tell me why. I assumed it was her nerves and emotions. Mother was constantly worried. I was worried too, of course, but there was no need for every person in the household to break down, so I let it go eventually. As much as I could, I went to her rooms and sat with her, often reading a book, while she leaned her head against my shoulder, listening to me drone on and on.

Father, meanwhile, seemed to distance himself from us during this time. He was incredibly excited with the arrival of all his friends and cousins and brothers. They went out hunting for small birds, using the time to talk politics and gossip in their own ways. Mother was hosting, bustling about in order to make sure everyone was comfortable and had no needs.

A week after the fox's arrival, Lilit, Aleena, and I were in my chamber, speaking of the dances we had learned and the dances we wished to learn. I sat on the cushioned bench underneath my window and looking out at the view, which never ceased to amaze me. Janna was sitting in a chair near my dresser, organizing clothes quietly, and I knew she was overhearing our conversation. I spoke a bit louder and glanced at her a few times, so she would know that she was included. I knew about her knowledge of dances and longed for her to contribute. She seemed unusually quiet, and I hoped she would say something. To my great joy, when I paused my rambling for a moment, she timidly added, "Sometimes there are celebration dances and flirtatious dances, and then there are war dances."

"War dances?" I asked, turning my full attention to her. Since my punishment so many years ago, she usually never volunteered to tell me about dances.

Aleena leaned over Janna and picked out a pink silk piece from the pile of clothing across her. She placed it gingerly against the dark of her hair and said, "Tell us about these war dances."

She nodded timidly. "Both sides pretend they are in a war. It's not a circle dance, like the others. You just stand across from each other and dance as if you are competing, and it appears as though there is a battle."

Lilit leaped up to her feet and extended an imaginary sword in my direction. "Stand and dance, you villager."

"I'll show you who's the villager!" I shouted, leaping up to my own feet and pretending to parry her blows. We twisted around and pretend-fought, while matching the moves with dance steps that we knew. Aleena laughed while Janna began humming a tune to match our steps, but it was all incredibly disorderly, and Lilit and I fell into a heap on the floor, laughing and trying to catch our breath. Aleena clapped theatrically for us, as though we were at a play.

"One day, we shall learn the real dance," I said, standing up and fixing my dress.

"Women are not allowed to learn the war dances. These are men's dances."

"Dash it," blurted Lilit angrily. Janna gasped, with wide eyes, at the curse.

"Lilit," warned Aleena.

"What? Women can be as strong as men. I could do the war dances if I wish."

"Yes, you may," I nodded, as the fire in me sparked all of a sudden.

"But—"

"But, nothing!" I interrupted Janna. "I am a princess of Akhtamar, and if I wish for us to learn the war dances, then they must obey me. And I shall teach you too, dear Janna," I said and smiled at her.

Aleena raised an eyebrow challengingly at me. "And who will teach you, little sister?"

"I will find someone to teach me." Before she could say anything else, we heard the rattle of a carriage rolling over the cobblestones outside. Lilit and I rushed to the window and leaned out to see who it was. Janna quickly stood up as footsteps sounded in the hall outside our door.

There was a knock, and I heard Janna's mother call, "Lord Avedis is arriving. He sent a letter to say he would be riding several hours ahead of the main procession."

Lilit and I glanced at each other excitedly and ran out the door and into the hall, much to Janna's warnings that my mother would be angry. Of course she was right, but I was eager to see my godfather.

It was as if our palace had awoken from a long nap. Everyone had sprung into action, preparing for the arrival of the actual guests. I realized that Aleena was not with us, and I turned back to my room to see her standing at my window, looking as if she was going to be sick. I walked over to her and stood next to her to look outside at the four-horse carriage that had pulled up. As soon as I saw the jolly man wave at us from his seat, excitement took over, and with a "come on, Aleena!" I ran down the great marble steps of our palace with Lilit beside me. We pelted straight for the door, which several servants had opened to welcome him in.

He stepped forward in a flurry of excitement and enveloped us in a tight hug, sweeping us both off our feet and making us squeal with joy. "Look at you two! I hardly even recognize you! How old are you now?" he cried.

"We're both fourteen," giggled Lilit.

"You have grown into a beautiful young woman." He smiled warmly at her. Then his gaze fell upon me, and he said, "Ah, and look at this; I have a true princess in my arms." I beamed, laughing as his scruffy beard tickled me as he kissed my cheek and put us back on the ground. I would never understand how this man could possibly be Vartan and Bedros's father. Before I could say anything else, however, his eyes slid over my shoulder to where Aleena was standing with a solemn expression, her hands clasped properly in front of her. She had floated gingerly down the stairs while Lilit and I had behaved like puppies seeing their master for the first time. My face turned red.

He reached out a free hand in Aleena's direction, and, after a moment, she smiled wanly and joined our hug. "Princess Aleena, the beauty of Akhtamar, but to me, you are all the same little girls, and that means we can still escape to the kitchen, yes?"

Since the kitchen meant stealing warm bread and cookies from the cooks and hearing his elaborate stories, we nodded enthusiastically. We were led into the kitchen, which was bustling with cooks preparing for the many feasts headed their way.

I always loved the kitchen. It was the one place no one seemed to mind my rank in the land. Although we were always quickly found out and shooed from the room, without so much as a "please." We never minded, though. It was the warmest part of the house, lined with clay ovens that resembled large mouths, opened wide for the hot bread. When I was younger, Bedros told me stories about how the *tonir* would eat me if I neared it, and I grew deathly afraid of the kitchen until Aleena found out and throttled him for frightening me.

I learned soon that they were essential to our living. They were holes dug into the ground—tonirs—which were used to make bread like our beloved lavash. I would sit and watch the women, busily slapping the bread onto the sides of the walls of the tonir and then glancing at it constantly to make sure it was baking right and not burning or tearing. The result would be an incredibly thin and soft bread, round and smooth, and tasting absolutely delicious, especially when still warm from the tonir.

In the midst of the incessant chaos in the kitchen, we dutifully found a corner out of the way and sat comfortably in a circle, munching on newly made cookies. In the background, we heard a woman steadily pounding dough and then twisting it round and round on her hands until it was flatter than a sheet of parchment paper. As soon as it was flat enough, she threw it in the direction of an older woman, crying, "*Kptsroo!*" And the woman slapped it against the wall of the tonir. It was a show in itself, and I was always mesmerized by the dance to make bread, wishing that I would be able to learn one day.

As if Lilit read my mind, she asked aloud, "Will we learn this one day?"

"You won't have to, if you marry well," said Baron Avedis with a wink. Aleena pursed her lips, and he noticed that slight motion. "I have a surprise for both of you," he began with a twinkle in his eye, trying to make us smile. I turned my attention back to him and saw that he had crumbs in his beard. Aleena chuckled as I tried peeking around him to see what he was hiding, but he shook his head. "They will be here the day of your wedding, Aleena."

Aleena's smile quickly faded on her pale face, and she looked away. "You shouldn't have, godfather."

The cookie turned bitter in my mouth, and I brought it down from my lips, realizing these were her wedding cookies. It was so soon.

She seemed to realize this as well and put down the cookie, rubbing her fingers slowly together to lose the residue that had lingered on them.

Baron Avedis's smile also faded, but it was quickly replaced by a sympathetic, kind expression. He put his palm on her clenched knuckles and said, "I know Vartan can be unbearable on occasion, but sometimes, Aleena, sacrifices must be made for true happiness. Isn't that what you want? He shall provide for you; he will make sure you are happy. And *I* shall be your father-in-law and will make sure to give him a slap on the wrist anytime he mistreats you. You shall never want for anything."

She kept her eyes glued to the floor, and he leaned back, sighing. "Shall I tell you what the surprise is, then, so at least you have something to look forward to?"

She said nothing, so Lilit nodded instead and said, "Please do."

He smiled and said, "I have invited dancers from the mainland."

Aleena's head shot up as Lilit and I gasped, wide smiles spreading over our faces.

"They shall dance for us?" asked Aleena hesitantly.

He nodded, smiling, and then stood, for a maid had called him to appear by our father. "Until later, ladies," he said as he bowed extravagantly before striding out of the kitchen.

"Dancers!" cried Lilit. "I'm going to tell my father; he will be overjoyed!" She bounded up, grabbed some more cookies, much to the dismay of the angry cook, and left the kitchen.

I was alone with my sister. In the background, there was the steady pounding as the women made bread. The sweet and musty smell filled the air. But all I could see was how Aleena gazed distrustfully at the cookies as if they had been poisoned.

"They are delicious, are they not?" I asked. She only glanced at me. I frowned, unable to keep the silly smile on my face any longer. "Please talk to me."

"What do you want me to say?" she asked. Her eyes were filled with such sorrow.

"What is on your mind?"

"My freedom is slipping away; it is as though I'm trying to hold water in my hands, but it is just dripping away and I can't do anything about it."

"I know," I said, frowning.

"No," she said, almost fiercely. "You don't. And you will never know; I will not allow it."

"I understand, but I still feel what you are feeling. As your sister, I know you better than anyone else, so I know what you are going through."

"But I don't want that!" she snapped. Her eyes were feverish. "This entire marriage is ruining everything, and I am sinking down into it, and I'll be damned before I allow you to sink down with me."

"You said yourself that heartbreak is what you do to yourself! You don't have to suffer!"

"But I am suffering, Tamar. I am so envious of you. It is easy for you to smile when you are sad. It is easy for you to do something when you don't like it. But not me, Tamar. I cannot pretend to be happy when sadness surrounds me. I cannot pretend to be joyful when I see only pain in my future. I cannot pretend to love when I am only hating with all my heart. I cannot ignore so easily as you do."

She was envious of me, but I only heard insults in her tone. "I am not as obedient as you think I am, Aleena." Much like a child, I threw my cookie to the ground and ran out of the kitchen, leaving her sitting behind me. I ran straight to the stables, where Asdgh was watching me with his large brown eyes. I hugged him and began to cry, upset that Aleena had said what she had. After a brief moment's thought, I threw the saddle onto Asdgh and mounted him. A stable boy cried, "But, Your Highness, you can't leave. The procession is arriving soon."

"Open the gates, please," I said coolly.

"But the queen—"

"The gates!"

He obeyed reluctantly, and we shot out, thundering down the path.

Asdgh knew exactly where we were headed, and I closed my eyes partway and reveled in the wind blowing against my face. I felt the tears stream across my face as I cried, clutching Asdgh's soft mane, which billowed wildly behind him. After a moment, I leaned over and buried my face in his neck, wanting to disappear and live among the tiny hairs on his skin. I knew she did not mean it maliciously, but I could not help but take it that way. I did not have Aleena's same spirit, though I wished desperately that I was more like her. I felt so small and insignificant all of a sudden, and I cried for both myself and her, wishing I could change our lives with a snap of my fingers.

Several miles away from the castle, Asdgh's pace suddenly changed beneath me, the strong and smooth stride becoming jerky and wrong. There was something in the path.

I opened my eyes and lifted my head to see a long line of decorated carriages, rumbling slowly toward the castle. Vartan's procession!

I ducked my head the other way, and we passed them in a flurry of excitement, but from one of the carriages, I heard a man's voice call, "Asdgh?"

Damn!

I thundered on faster, pressing my heels into his side. We rode on, and I glanced back occasionally, but I did not see anyone behind us. Good. I did not want to see anyone from the wedding at this moment. I was sick of the entire event. When we finally burst into the grass clearing, I was already breathing easier. I slowed Asdgh into a trot so that he could relax as well. We trotted into a large circle around the clearing, then I slowed him to a walk, and finally to a stop. I dismounted smoothly and let him walk freely in the clearing to graze to his heart's content.

I made ready to sit under a shady tree, when I suddenly heard a lilting voice say, "You're going to sit on the grass and ruin your pretty skirts?"

I whipped around, my hand shooting to my side where I always kept a hidden knife, unbeknownst to my mother and tutor. But instead of seeing a village miscreant, I saw a handsome young man on a dark brown stallion. He wore the crimson and gold colors of nobility, and his chin was raised haughtily. He dismounted smoothly and walked toward me, slowly so as to give me time to recognize him.

It was plenty of time.

My mouth dropped open. "Bedros?"

He bowed extravagantly. "Hello, Princess."

"Did you follow me?"

"Oh yes, of course—I recognized your horse and could not let you leave without saying hello, especially as it's so long since we saw each other last."

I said nothing, unsure of what to make of him. Had I changed as much as he had in these years? What did he think of me now? Anxious for the answers to those questions, I slowly made ready to sit again.

"Wait." He held out a hand. I waited. He jogged to his horse, who stood obediently on his own, and grabbed a small blanket; he then spread it out extravagantly on the grass. "You may sit on this. I also took the privilege of bringing some fruit."

"A picnic?" I wrinkled my nose.

"We do not have to call it a picnic. We can call it a reunion." He grinned. I smiled, shaking my head with disbelief, and joined him on the blanket.

"Now," he said, as he settled across from me, "I would like to know what you reached for at your side when I startled you?"

I gave him a look and said, "You did not startle me."

"Of course I did not," he said, raising his eyebrows. I hesitated for a moment, and then I slid out my knife. He immediately set to laughing. "A kitchen knife?"

"I read it in a novel once. Somehow I do not think my mother would approve of my carrying around a dagger," I responded, a flush rising to my cheeks. I was unsure of how to act around him. I suddenly understood Lilit's face flushing when Bedros was mentioned. She was right. I did approve. I felt uneasy, as though he were a different person entirely.

"I do not believe she would approve of you carrying any sort of knife. Regardless, a kitchen knife will hardly do anything against a man who wishes to do you harm. But luckily, I am not a man who wishes to do you harm."

"We shall see," I muttered suspiciously, casting a shrewd eye over him as he looked about at the clearing I had grown so fond of over the years.

"Is this where you and your sister disappear to all the time?"

"Yes," I said immediately.

"It is not polite to lie."

"It is not polite to ask for what is none of your business."

He nodded. "Is it any of my business to ask why you've been crying?"

"No," I said, frowning.

"Will you tell me anyway?"

I sighed and wondered if I should tell him. He would not tell Aleena, and he was not close enough to Vartan. "It is nothing. I only argued with Aleena."

"The two inseparable sisters…arguing?" He feigned surprise.

I made a face at him. "We grew up I suppose."

"I seem to remember how headstrong she was."

"She still is, but then so am I."

"You are different than her. Just as Vartan is different than I."

I looked at him, observing his rigid jawline, smooth brows, and dancing eyes. "I wish she were marrying you."

"I am two years younger than her. It would not be the ideal marriage."

I took a piece of apricot and put it between my lips, observing him even as he observed me. He took a large bite of an apple, and while the juice ran down his chin, he said with a sparkle in his eyes, "In fact, *we* would be the ideal marriage."

I watched him distastefully as he wiped his chin with the sleeve of his shirt. I knew he did it on purpose to repulse me. I was my mother's daughter after all. I averted my eyes, deciding to ignore his comment, and asked, "When did you grow so tall?"

"When did you become so beautiful?" he replied immediately.

"Oh hush." I rolled my eyes. "Your tongue is as smooth as silk."

"And yours as sharp as a snake's." I stuck my tongue out at him, and he grinned, taking another bite of his apple. Nonchalantly he asked, "Do you like how I look as a man?"

Cheeky. "You are fifteen. You are still a boy."

"And you are fourteen, but you look quite the woman."

I gave a small scoff and looked down at the fruit. He was handsome, but he was still incessantly infuriating. He glanced down at the grass, taking a piece between his fingers and dropping it lightly to the ground. He was looking at it with the same memory that resided in my thoughts. "As I recall, I was once scolded by you and Aleena for touching your grass."

"I shall do so again if you lay a hand on it."

He put a hovering hand over the grass.

"You *shall* regret it."

"Will you scratch me with your kitchen knife?"

I raised my eyebrows challengingly as he grinned mischievously and then laid his hand flat on the grass. Immediately I grabbed his clean, embroidered handkerchief and ran from him before he could retrieve it. "Hey!" he cried, running after me. I was laughing as I ran toward Asdgh, but on the way, I tossed the cloth into a small dirt pile and mounted my horse. While he rescued his cloth and gathered up the picnic quickly, I galloped away, but I heard him shout, "My horse is faster than yours!"

I galloped hard, but in no time I heard him behind me, approaching fast. I looked back, my hair whipping around my shoulders, but his horse *was* indeed faster than mine. I tried as best as I could, urging Asdgh with shouts of encouragement, but they caught up to us, and Bedros leaned over and grabbed my reins.

"Let go!" I shouted.

"I've won! Surrender!"

"Can't make me!"

"I can make *him*!" he said, pulling hard on the reins. We both skidded to a flustered stop and dissolved into laughter.

"You might be taller and handsome now, but you are still a monster. I shall have to warn all the girls who fall in step beside you," I said as we calmly walked our horses toward the castle.

"You might be exactly the same height as before and prettier, but you are still the same bossy little princess."

I shook my head, trying to contain my smile. I wasn't *short*.

He nudged my side. "Did I make you feel better at least?"

"I shan't admit to it." I raised my chin, but I smiled at him.

"Stubborn," he muttered, but we were both in a better state of mind, and I was secretly glad he had followed me to the clearing, although I would never admit to it.

Chapter 7

THE MARRIAGE WAS to be in three days. Preparations were at full speed now, and the maids and servants were near to collapsing from exhaustion, as caring for the guests and preparing for the ceremony all at once was difficult.

I was hoping to see Aleena and talk to her—to make right the argument that we had had. But she was nowhere to be found, and I found out from a maid that my father was painting her wedding portrait. The maid reported that my sister was dressed in her wedding dress and seated on a chair in my father's study, while he watched her closely, attempting to capture my sister's beauty. No one was allowed into the study during this time, and I grew frustrated at the distance.

Why did he have to choose these few days to paint this portrait?

He would certainly have to leave the project at some point. The night before the wedding was to be the *azbanstum*, the lads' party, where all the men gathered and celebrated without the females. My father would be obligated to attend, and I would have some time with my sister.

I never quite understood the party, for they stood around and discussed what they always normally discussed during teatime. Some of the traditions I never really cared for, partly because I had never seen or been to them. I had always wanted to attend the lads' party, but I was a female and, therefore, could not. It would be incredibly unseemly. I might have been able to go in disguise had I been younger, but my woman's chest was already protruding far enough that I would be found out immediately.

The day of the azbanstum, I was walking around aimlessly, my mind anxious that I still had not spoken to or seen Aleena at all. Tomorrow was to be the big day, and I had always dreamed of Aleena and I giggling together as she was married, but it did not seem as though that would be happening. I walked slowly to my chambers, though I really did not want to go back to my room at all. Thoughts of Vartan slipping on a fruit peel and cracking his head ran through my mind, and it gave me an odd satisfaction to be thinking of him injured and unable to make it to his own wedding. I shook the thought from my mind. It would be useless to think of such things.

Not far from my door, I suddenly heard a patter of footsteps getting louder down the quiet hall. Before I could turn and see who was running full blast toward me, I felt someone grab me from the back and thrust me toward my room. The heavy door swung open with our weight, throwing us both in. "Close the door quick!"

"What in heaven's name!" I cried in fear. I turned and saw Bedros, shutting the door with his back to it, his face red from laughing so hard. "What are you doing?" Then I noticed the silver plate of desserts in his hand. He held them out in front of me with an elaborate bow.

"I stole some lovely desserts for you."

"They are for my sister's wedding! Take them back!" I cried.

"Shh!" he hissed, his hand shooting out to be placed over my mouth, while his other arm held me to him. I was stunned into silence, more from shock at his nearness than the fear of what we were being kept silent for. We heard the patter of footsteps outside my door. I couldn't breathe. His hands smelled of sweet pastries, and some crumbs were left on his fingers from the sweets he had stolen. I was able to taste the sugar on my lips, and my face flushed such a bright red at this intimacy.

"Bedros!" called a woman from outside—his mother. "Bedros, where are you? Oh, that boy!"

She knocked on my door, and we both tensed in anticipation. He held me closer to him, though I was sure he did it just to frustrate me at this point. "Tamar?" she called. "Tamar, are you in there?" She was met with silence, and I heard her sigh, exasperated. A heartbeat later, we heard her footsteps fading as she walked back down the hall. When she was gone, I left his arms quickly, without facing any resistance from him, and he laughed while I crossed the room to get as far from him as possible.

The nerve of that boy to hold me so close to him! Did he not understand manners at all? I turned away and wiped my lips to rid them of the crumbs that had stuck to them from his fingers.

He sat on one of the chairs as if it were his and looked around curiously. "Ah," he sighed, "so this is what a princess's room looks like." After a moment of observing, he commented, "I must say, I am a bit disappointed."

"Disappointed?"

"Yes, you have a rather dull room."

"I am not sure what you were expecting. Gold and diamonds to be hanging from every corner of the room?"

"Now *that* would be an interesting room. I wonder that you don't have portraits or mirrors or girl things."

"Girl things."

"Scents and fluff," he said, twirling his hand loosely as if that indicated fluff.

"You have an odd view of girls," I muttered. "I suppose I don't like...fluff."

He shrugged. "I can't see Aleena liking fluff either. Both of you are odd. Here, have one," he said, offering a pastry. "The best tasting food is the one that has been stolen," he said when he saw the look I gave him. But after a moment of hesitation, I decided that there were more for the guests anyway, and I took a small one and ate it while he grabbed one as well.

"That is a terrific motto and one that is very safe for your reputation, of course."

"Of course," he said and grinned.

His reputation...I was suddenly aware of us being alone in my chambers. Where was Janna when I needed her? I remembered the gossip about him being a rascal, and my face reddened. It seemed to be doing that often around him.

"Whatever is the matter? Your face is red! Are you shy in front of me?" he exclaimed. He might have been amused too, that scoundrel.

I rolled my eyes. "Should you not be preparing for azbanstum?" I asked, turning away so he wouldn't see what I was thinking.

"That is tonight, isn't it?"

"Bedros," I admonished, "it is your brother's party."

"Yes," he sighed, "and I shall, no doubt, be named my brother's bodyguard for the wedding, and all shall be well and happy."

"Of course you will be his bodyguard. Tradition says the groom's closest companion. That is *you*!"

"I am not his closest companion, but he does not really have any other companions, so it makes me the only option. It shall be the dullest event of the marriage. I hope someone tries to attack him, so I can do something at least," he said.

"You're horrid," I remarked, sitting across from him on the floor.

He cocked his head at me. "You have an odd habit of sitting on the floor."

"I am most comfortable on the floor."

"Do you still have your weapon?"

"Yes, and I am not afraid to use it."

"Wouldn't want to bruise me with that stick you call a knife. Your parents might think you a savage beast."

I gave him a look. "Maybe I am. I turn into a werewolf when the full moon is up in the sky."

"That is wrong." I cocked my head at him. "That is a wrong legend. Werewolves can transform at any time they want."

"No, it is always with the full moon."

"A werewolf, Tamar, is a woman who is punished for being bad. The punishment lasts seven years, and when she transforms, she has to wear the pelt that is given her. When she wears it, she has beast instincts. She haunts the villages at night, craving and eating little children as food. The only way to kill her is to burn her pelt, which she hides when she is human."

I wrinkled my nose. "That is a story that your nurse would tell you as a baby to frighten you."

He shrugged. "It is told, nonetheless."

"What happens to the men?"

My question surprised him, and he thought for a moment; then he leaned back with a knowing grin. "The men sit around a table, smoke their cigars, guzzle their wine, and write the stories that condemn women for every wrong that they do."

My smile slipped from my lips. He almost sounded like Aleena when he said that.

"So who punishes men?"

He shrugged. "Other, more powerful men. And then those men are punished by God."

I fidgeted with my skirt. I did not like having this conversation with him. It seemed wrong. "I wish I could see a werewolf."

He smiled, giving me an appraising look. "It would eat you up in less than a heartbeat."

"No, it wouldn't. You said it eats little children."

"You are a child."

"No, I am not."

He grinned. "I suppose you and your sister grew rather quickly."

"You did as well," I said. "I can't say the same about Vartan unfortunately."

His laugh was a bark. "No, of course not, Vartan is something else."

"Why does he have to marry Aleena," I sighed wistfully. I lay down on my back, turning my eyes to the ceiling.

"They'll make some beautiful blue-eyed babies."

"Bedros!" I admonished.

His laughter rang through my room. "I wish you were a man," came his abrupt response.

"Pardon?"

"So you can come tonight as well. We'd have a hell of a lot better time."

"We would destroy the place," I giggled.

"Exactly!"

I looked him up and down and wrinkled my nose at his crumpled outfit. "Might I offer a suggestion?"

"Yes, Princess."

"You need to change."

"Ah, Princess, and here I thought you liked me."

"Your clothes, silly!" I laughed. "Come with me; I shall help you."

He let me take him to his chambers. I hadn't seen his room before, for Bedros had only arrived a few days earlier and was arranging his room to be comfortable for him. I looked around, expecting to see a mess, but I was surprised at the order I found. Everything was in its place. Even the bedcovers were smoothed to perfection. "You have the audacity to comment on my room when you have a similar one?"

"I was hoping for a change of scenery when I came to yours," he said and shrugged. "Also, I don't actually *live* here."

He led me to his wardrobe, where we sorted through his clothing and picked out more formal traditional clothes that would suit the style of our island. He came from a different region, so they had a different requirement for outfits. For every piece of clothing that I placed on his chair, his frown deepened, and he looked at them as if I were asking him to wear peels of an onion for the rest of the night. "I feel like one of those Russian dolls. How many layers do I need to put on?"

"Not too many, so stop complaining. You just have the trousers, a blouse, a vest, and a sash for a belt. It's quite fetching really."

"I'd like to see you wear these," he grumbled, as I turned my back to him for modesty's sake.

"You should count yourself lucky that you are not wearing a dress. And I doubt your vest and trousers would do me justice." I giggled. I heard him pull off his clothing, and my face flushed again. I was in his room while he was changing. Oh, if only my mother found out.

"How is female clothing worse than this? You're wearing a dress."

"We have more layers than you've ever seen underneath these dresses."

He finished buttoning his vest and stood awkwardly. "You see?" he cried stiffly in the outfit. I turned and glanced over him.

"Believe me when I say our dresses are worse."

"I don't understand how one can breathe in these belts."

"You don't need to breathe; just smile," I advised. Remembering Aleena's accusation of my conformity, I sighed.

"Have you spoken to your sister yet?"

"No," I said, not bothering to be surprised that he knew I was thinking of her. Bedros knew me well enough to see the changes in my expressions. "I'm afraid. I don't want to spend every moment fearing my encounter with her. Her *wedding* is tomorrow. I never thought this would be the way we parted."

"Aleena has changed. I have seen it in her since I arrived here a few days ago. But I'll wager that she will come to you."

"You think so?"

He stood across from me and nodded. "Sisters will always have a bond. I've always envied that of you."

He envied me? But then, I supposed, there could not be much of a bond with Vartan.

"Thank you," I murmured, looking over him. He looked handsome in his layers of crimson and sapphire and gold. I smiled at him. "You look great."

"You do too. Now, give me a hug, and run along to your chambers. I have a feeling that your sister will visit you before the wedding."

⚬

When I walked out of Bedros's room, I made my way directly to my own chambers, but I was surprised to see someone standing in front of my door.

"Lilit?" I asked.

She turned to me and lifted her eyebrows. "I have asked everyone where you were, and no one knew! Now you shall tell me where you ran off to, or else I shall die of curiosity."

I looked around down the hall, and finding no one, I pulled her in my room and closed the door behind us. "I was helping Bedros pick out his outfit for tonight."

Her eyes grew wide. "In his chambers? Did he change in front of you?" A giggle bubbled up out of her throat, and she began laughing at the scandal.

"Lilit! I did not watch him change!" I admonished.

She began to sing a teasing song about a lovesick woman yearning for her lover's touch. I threw a pillow at her, and she ducked.

"Now don't be violent, Tamar. Be a princess," she teased.

We heard a scuffling noise to the side suddenly, and we both whipped our heads over to see Janna sitting on a chair. When she realized we had seen her, her eyes grew wide.

"How long have you been here?" I asked.

"Long enough to know you were in a boy's room, unescorted," she murmured, a flash of anger in her eyes.

"If you tattle...," warned Lilit in a level voice, but I shushed her.

"Janna," I said, desperation making my voice stronger, "you mustn't tell mother about this." When she did not say a word, I repeated it, emphasizing every word.

She nodded finally and looked up at me with wide eyes. "Please do not do it again. I do hate to disobey my mother and *your* mother. I cannot lie to the queen."

"But you *will* stay quiet about this?" asked Lilit, pursing her lips.

"Yes," said Janna, standing up. "I will go to my rooms now. Good night, Princess Tamar. Good night, Lady Lilit."

As we watched her leave my room and disappear into the shadow of the hallway, I could not help but realize how much we had all grown up—and how all of our actions were watched and judged in some way.

Chapter 8

LATE THAT NIGHT, as I was preparing for bed, the doors to my chamber opened slowly.

I half expected that I would see Bedros traipsing in, but instead, I saw Aleena in the dim glow of the candle that she held up in front of her. Her pale face glistened like porcelain, and the circles under her eyes were unusually dark and filled with shadows. She looked as though she were ill in her long white nightgown and unusually lanky hair. Her brows were furrowed, and a small frown pulled her lips down. For a moment, I believed her to be a ghost, and my heart stood still as I waited.

I said nothing, and I held my own candle up, so I could see her more clearly. The flame hardly flickered, and the shadows crawled slowly over the walls, in an agonizing dance with the writhing smoke.

This was not how I had expected her to visit me. I realized I was afraid of her and her thoughts as she turned her eyes around the room, looking at everything except for me. I half wondered if she knew I was in here.

She walked slowly on light, bare feet to my window. She placed her own candle down and opened the latch with her free hand, swinging open the glass. Cold air rushed in desperately, filling the room as fast as possible and almost extinguishing the candle. It did not succeed, for Aleena moved it slightly to the side out of the wind's way. She was silent, as she slid something out from her pocket. I looked closer and realized it was a pomegranate, shining almost black in the dim light. She held it in both her hands, feeling the leathery surface with the tips of her fingers, as she pressed it against her chest. Half to herself, she murmured, "Baron Avedis was wrong." Her cold voice scratched against the darkness, as if beetles were crawling over the walls. I shivered. "You must never have to sacrifice for true happiness, for you have already lost something that was a part of you." She turned to face me, her eyes gouging deep holes into my face. "How could one be happy without being whole? If I lose my desires, my dreams, then I am nothing. And I am losing them, Tamar; I am losing them."

Then, with a lingering glance at the pomegranate, which she had left on my windowsill, she left my room, the light fading with her as she closed the door. I waited a bit, knowing that I could only go when it was dark. My heart was pounding with anxious beats, fear gripping it tight in its clenched hands. The pomegranate seemed to wink at me menacingly in the darkness from its perch. The lake glistened in the distance, haloing the fruit with its shine. There was no note inside the pomegranate. There was not even a seam where it had been cracked open. It was a whole pomegranate, untouched except by Aleena's hands.

But somehow, I knew she wanted me to go to the cliff. This was the first time she had dared for us to go at night.

I wasted no time dressing warmly, for a cold wind was steadily blowing in from the lake. Winter was approaching fast, and I could feel the chill in the air. I could not leave from the door, for someone would surely hear me. Rooms lined the halls, with servants and visiting nobles and guests behind them. We were never alone in our great castle. With heart pounding, I crossed my room to the open window and looked out into the dark night. The lake glittered brilliantly in the distance, and far away, the faint smudge of mountains rose high up into the sky.

I surveyed the way down from my window. It was high up, but many roofs lay under my feet. If I jumped smartly, I would make it safely to the bottom.

I turned and found a thin length of thread. I placed my candle slowly in the frame of an empty lantern and tied the end of the string to the rings of the lantern. Slowly, I let it out the window, watching the dim glow of the light venture into the darkness below. When it touched the next roof, I judged it to be about ten feet below. Not too bad. For the moment, I tied my length of the line around the curtains loosely.

I took off my shoes and decided I would go without them today. Mother would notice the ruined shoes and assign Janna to supervise me at all times. As much as I liked Janna, she was difficult to sway onto my side when my mother was involved. I was already lucky to not have her sleep in the same room as me. Other girls are not as lucky. When I felt the frigid air envelop my feet, I took two pairs of stockings and put both on, warming them slightly. I would make less noise with the soft padding.

I neared the window and let go of the line, so it fell to the lamp on the lower roof as I sat on my windowsill, feet dangling and skirts and hair flailing in the wind. It felt as if I were sitting on the cliff's edge.

Without intending on it, I let that feeling take over. It was odd, as if I was weightless, gravity pulling me down to the waters below. I lifted my chin and felt the air and wind in my face. I almost tasted the salty lake and almost felt the spray settle around me.

I was suspended, held by a string.

My heart was telling me to jump, but my mind was telling me to shut the window and crawl under my covers, safe from the cold; but I knew Aleena was out there, and both my heart and mind forbade me to abandon her.

With my eyes closed, I pushed myself forward, falling straight into the darkness, as if it was swallowing me whole. I half expected the water of the lake to take me into its embrace, but it didn't. Instead, I landed on the roof safely, though a little flustered.

The rest of the journey went smoothly. I wished I could have taken Asdgh with me, but I would have awakened the stable boy, who would have surely told my mother. She was frightening, but she commanded respect, and tattling on disobedient children was respectful to her. But all went well tonight. I slipped away unseen. The only trouble I had by the time I reached the cliff was my fear of the shadows in the darkness, but they were merely shadows and threatened only in my mind.

I climbed the mountain to the cliff, wondering what my sister would tell me there. But if I expected our usual frolicking that night, I was gravely mistaken.

Aleena was curled near a rock, several feet away from the cliff, with tears running down her face in great torrents. She was half in hysterics, her face twisted with pain and fear. When she heard me, she looked up, her eyes swollen from the tears and her arms stretching out tentatively in my direction, as if I was an angel come to save her. I had never seen her in a state such as this. Without a moment's hesitation, I ran to her and held her close, feeling her trembling body in my arms. My eyes were trained on the rough waters beneath us that were violently reaching their arms out to grab hold of us. I was trembling just as much as Aleena, fear coursing through my veins at the thought of what possibly had made my big sister cry. She held me tight as the wind raged around us and cried loudly, her voice becoming one with the wailing gale.

Then she told me what had happened.

I held her tighter as if I could change anything, but we both knew I could not. Her words resounded and vibrated through my entire body.

"I almost jumped."

⇥ ⇤

We stayed on that cliff for a while, listening to the festivities slowly end on the mainland along with Aleena's tears. I had been holding on to her, refusing to let go, even when she stopped crying. We were silent for some time, but eventually I began aching to say something, so I mumbled, "I am glad you did not."

She sighed, so low it was barely audible. It was nothing compared to the wind that gusted in our faces, but I knew that Lake Van gathered sighs like lovers collected flowers. I wondered how many times Aleena had sighed over these beautiful and treacherous waters, and wished I had been there to collect them instead of the lake. She smiled wistfully. "It would have been instant glory for Vartan. He would be king."

"But he is not married to you yet!"

"Father has no choice but to make him king; we do not have cousins who are old enough. He'd inherit the kingdom immediately."

"There's still me," I mumbled, almost offended.

Aleena looked across at me, her eyes clear and shining with the lingering memory of her tears. "You would refuse it I hope. You will not marry a prince or duke or any such person who will only take pleasure in controlling you. You will fall in love before you marry— in a year's time—and I hope to be there to see it."

I gave her a warning look. "You *will* be there to see it." She looked out over the waters, and I watched her expression. It seemed as though she always had a constant battle inside her mind. I smiled wanly into the darkness. "What if I fall in love with a prince or a duke?"

"A prince shall take one look at you with your wild flowing hair and thick feet, and he will turn away!"

I snorted. "I do not have thick feet; I am wearing an extra pair of stockings! And I shall give you one of them, for you are freezing." I reached down and peeled off the top pair, gesturing for her to hold out her bare feet. They were terribly cold, and I wasted no time in pulling the stockings over them. After doing so, I rubbed them vigorously, bringing warmth into my sister as much as I could. For a moment, we were silent, both lost in thought.

"I am sorry I said those things to you," she muttered at last.

"I am sorry I could not understand you."

She put her head on my shoulder and closed her eyes.

She was so strong and yet so fragile. My father's words came back to me, about how I was stronger than her, but I did not want to believe it. Perhaps I would break down just as easily when forced to marry someone against my will. *If* I was forced. I grimaced into the darkness. Aleena was my better in every way.

When I spoke again in a low voice, I knew she heard me more clearly than if I would have shouted the words. "If I do fall in love, I shall make certain you know every little detail of it."

Aleena managed her first real smile of the night and sighed once more. "That is all I ask. Then I shall better be able to endure Vartan."

There was a calming breeze now ruffling our hair, and we both reveled in this pleasure.

"Aleena."

"Hmm?"

"What stopped you?"

She was silent for a little while, and I wondered if I had asked the wrong question. I heard her breathing steadily near my ear. "I knew you were coming here."

"That stopped you?"

"If I was not here when you arrived, you would never know exactly what happened to me. You would be lost, forever, just as I would be lost forever. The only difference would be that I would be in the lake, drifting off into its depths, while you stayed here, searching endlessly for me. You would never be at peace, Tamar. What kind of sister would that make me? I love you too much to have you go through that."

I kissed the top of her head. "I love you too."

We watched the water beat against the cliffs and listened to the mesmerizing music in the distance. How I wished I could take Aleena and whisk her away to that beautiful place. "I have been learning some dances," I told her.

She smiled and looked down. "Yes, my tutor has been teaching me as well. There are many wedding dances I had to learn."

"One day, you can teach me. I cannot imagine it going well if Digin Galia had to teach my wedding dances," I scoffed, thinking of the bitter woman teaching me the graceful moves.

"I wonder if she ever married. Or if she's married now," said Aleena, cocking her head slightly.

"Perhaps not," I said quietly. I had never thought of that. I hardly knew anything about Digin Galia, though I spent so much time with her.

"You never know, sweet sister. Perhaps Digin Galia would teach you better than I would."

I frowned. "Yes, well, I would much rather you teach me."

She nodded, not saying anything more. I knew she wanted some silence for a bit, but I was never good at that.

"We shall be all right, won't we, sister?" I asked.

She glanced sideways at me and smiled faintly. "We shall always be all right. Even if the sky falls on our heads, we shall be all right."

I smiled. "Good. I am glad you are not going far at least." Baron Avedis and his estate were across the lake, farther than the village we heard music from but closer than the next city over. It was beautiful, from what I had heard Bedros recount to me in great detail.

And she would remain with us on the island until their rooms were ready at the estate.

"Yes, we did manage that bit of luck, didn't we?" There was more silence, and then staring across at the lake that glittered in the moonlight, she said, "We won't see each other much, but remember we can still meet whenever we want."

I nodded. "Pomegranate letters were your best idea."

"They were, weren't they?" she smiled. "I am excited for the dancers tomorrow night," she said before I could say anything else.

"I wonder how long they shall stay."

"I believe Baron Avedis said one night. They shall leave the morning after," she sighed.

"You do not want them to leave?"

"I would like to learn how to dance."

"But we know how to dance," I said, puzzled.

"No," she countered, "we know formal dances that only the royalty perform. Can you not imagine how different and beautiful village dances are? We climb a mountain and sit on the edge of a cliff only to hear their music."

A slow smile spread across my face as I realized what she was saying. "Oh! After all these years! We shall finally be part of it to-morrow!" I cried with an excited gasp.

"Exactly!" She grinned, giggling at my dawning realization. We suddenly realized how strange it was to laugh again, and our giggles slowly rose in pitch until we were laughing as if we had never laughed before, our voices carried high by the wind.

She stood suddenly and pulled me up to my feet, shouting, "Dance with me!" We began to dance to the distant music that we would finally hear loudly tomorrow, and we stomped our feet to the rhythm of the dhol. The adrenaline of the night coursed through our veins and made us wild. We cried and shouted and yelped as if we were five again and had just realized the strength of our voices. They competed in power with the angry roar of the waves, violent beneath us. We were finally going to hear our music and see our dancers, and Lake Van was not happy for us.

I flung a rock off the cliff, where it disappeared into the roiling waves. "Take *that*, Lake Van!" I shouted loudly. Aleena stood next to me, laughing, and joined me in flinging rocks. Her eyes shone, and this time, it was not just with her tears, but also with excitement as well, a shine that had disappeared for some time. "You thought you could separate us!" I threw another rock, to the everlasting rage of the waves. We dissolved into laughter, unrestrained and free.

We watched the rocks disappear and stood in silence for a while. When we knew they had been swallowed by the lake, we glanced up and smiled at each other. Tomorrow we would meet the dancers and learn something we had ached to learn all our lives.

Tomorrow Aleena would be wed to a man who despised her just as much as she despised him. But we would find a way through it. And she would show Akhtamar just how strong she was. Side by side, we would make it.

Chapter 9

THE POND WAS a smooth crème layer of calmness. I watched how still it was, how it seemed as though one could walk over it with no trouble. Why was our lake not this way? Why was it, instead, so violent, so threatening? There was so much anger and rage in it, one would fear ever nearing it. One wrong thought and the lake would pull you under, silencing your cries for help, reducing you to a mere memory that would eventually fade away in time. I wished it could be like this pond instead, inviting and beautiful, with promises of comfort. If I had the choice, I would swim in the pond at this instant. I could imagine the honey-sweet liquid washing over my body, caressing my skin with low murmurs of relief and care. But, of course, under every body of water, secrets lay hidden. What was under the pond?

I reached in slowly and stirred the serene layer as gently as I could, and after a moment, a faint gasp escaped my lips. A bright red layer oozed up, mixing immediately with the crème color of the pond. It was dense and thick and kept rising, overtaking the beautiful calm of the pond. It spread its red tendrils all over the surface of the pond, like an intricate web, until the crème was gone and only the bright red appeared. And if I looked closer, I could see blotches of something in the red...What were they? I looked closer and saw—

"Tamar, stop playing with your food!"

My head shot up at my mother's sudden hiss. My eyes blurred from the sudden change of focus, and I blinked several times to clear them. She shot a piercing glance at me, and I looked down immediately at my bowl. "My apologies," I muttered. I stuck my spoon into the soup.

Beans—those were the blotches.

I could feel Aleena across the table looking at me timidly. I looked up at her and saw the dark circles under her eyes. I knew I had them too, as we had hardly slept. We were going to need all the strength possible today. It was going to be a busy day.

I felt a nudge at my side and looked over to see Lilit looking between us worriedly. "Is everything all right?" she asked.

"Yes," I said, smiling what I hoped was a convincing smile.

She nodded, but she did not seem to believe me. She looked at Aleena, and both girls stared silently at each other. Lilit studied her intently, while Aleena maintained her gaze defiantly. I touched Lilit's arm, and she looked at me again, breaking their gaze.

"We are fine," I said firmly. She nodded. "It will be time soon to get ready! We will have fun." And with that, I pulled a tentative smile out of my friend.

The morning sun was greeting the world early, and everyone was already up, bustling for the preparations. Breakfast was our only calm moment of the day, and even this was rushed. As soon as we were finished, everyone was whisked away into a different corner of the castle, and the table was made spotless, even while I struggled to swallow my last bite.

It seemed as though I turned around for a split second, and when I turned back, Aleena was taken away to a separate room with bustling maids, in order to prepare her there. Janna appeared at my side with some other maids and said, "We are instructed to prepare a bath for you."

"A bath?" I wrinkled my nose. "I do not want one."

"Would you like to attend your sister's wedding smelling like a horse?" she asked, raising her eyebrows.

I raised my eyebrows back at her. Lilit giggled at my side. I smiled finally and said, "Fine, I shall take the bath. But only if you pull up a bath for Lady Lilit too. She looks a bit dusty, don't you think?" Lilit's smile disappeared as the maids began to bring in pails of heated water from the kitchen.

"Good luck!" I giggled at Lilit's wide eyes, as Janna pulled me toward my bathroom.

As much as I disliked baths, I had to admit that the steaming water against my bare skin was soothing and much needed. A few minutes in, Janna entered the room and added scents of rose into the water, and I wanted to sink back into it and fall asleep for days and days. My body was weightless and felt so light and free.

But after Janna cleared her throat, I was snapped back into the present. There was much work to be done. Still, I grumbled at her to make a point before dipping my head forward into the water and scrubbing my scalp, working in the rose-scented water. I scrubbed the important parts of my body as well, and when I was finished,

Janna wasted no time in bundling me up into a towel and removing me from the warm bath.

An hour later, I had only managed to see Aleena once as they rushed her to her chamber, and in that split moment, she managed to glance into my room and give me an exasperated, tortured look before the doors closed between us.

Frustrated, I turned to Janna and snapped, "Where's my mother?"

"In the kitchen," she said. "But you are to stay here. Tamar! Wait! Come back!"

I was running down the great stairs toward the kitchen doors, my wet hair slapping against my back and my robe wrapped tightly around me. Right as I reached the doors, they swung open, and my mother barreled out, shouting, "I want those finished in the next half hour."

"Mother!" I bellowed.

She turned to me, and her eyes went over my figure as if I had not just bellowed for her attention. "Good heavens! You live only to torment me! Where are your clothes? Everyone can see you here! Why are you not getting ready? Where's Digin Galia? Did I not tell Janna to keep you in your room?"

"Sh…she tried," I stammered against the torrent of questions, but I shook my head and continued strongly, "I want to prepare with Aleena. As her sister and closest companion, I should be in the room with her," I said, lifting my chin assertively.

"Akh, Tamar," she sighed, exasperated, and turned to a maid standing behind her. "Fetch Digin Galia." The maid bobbed into a quick curtsy and hurried off.

When I turned back to my mother, she had gone. I stood for several seconds, wondering if I had only dreamed of speaking and had stayed silent instead, or if she had ignored me that easily. Those last seconds that I could have used to run out of the kitchen, I foolishly stayed. The minute Digin Galia cast her discerning eyes over my shivering self, I was whisked upstairs to my chambers, where a frustrated Janna was waiting for us.

If I thought my preparations would be easier than Aleena's, I was terribly mistaken. Digin Galia called for five other maids, who all worked on me at the same time. I sat in an uncomfortable chair and was dressed in a thin white satin shift. I felt as fragile as a doll, cursed to stay still as they fixed and preened me into what they believed was perfection. Three maids, including Janna, set to work on my hair, brushing it in three long sections. I gritted my teeth as they brushed through the knots at my scalp, and I yelped when Janna yanked through one particularly large one.

"If you brushed your hair more often, this would not be happening right now."

I shot Digin Galia an irritated look but had nothing to say to that.

"What is this?" asked a maid, picking something out of my hair delicately.

"It is a thorn," muttered Janna. "It is a wonder she does not wake up with blood all over her head."

I turned my head to stick my tongue out at Janna, but the other maid pulled my chin back to center.

"At least you have nice hair," muttered Digin Galia. "Many girls would kill for what you have. If you cannot attract a man's attention with your abominable personality, use your hair."

I gave Digin Galia an exasperated look. "Then I shall cut all my hair off."

"Then you shall live with your parents forever."

"Make my hair pretty!" I cried.

Digin Galia smirked. She approached us and took over one of the sections, feeling its length with her bony fingers. My hair reached under my bottom, which was the usual length for a young girl's hair. To cut it short was punishment, and nothing short of humiliation, so I would most definitely not be doing that.

"What will I wear?" I asked, my voice straining when Janna pulled hard again with the brush.

Digin Galia walked away and, rustling inside my wardrobe, took out a dress and laid it across the table across from where I sat. I could not see clearly from where I sat, but I could tell it was not ball gown attire.

"Why can I not wear my fancy dress?" I managed through gritted teeth while the maids and Janna pulled and strained at my hair, getting it into a tight braid.

Before Digin Galia could say anything, I heard a loud commotion outside my doors. Instinctively I escaped from the maid's hands, spilling my hair and all their hard work over my shoulders, and ran to the hall, where I collided with Bedros. "Bedros?"

"Stop him!" cried a maid.

Bedros's wide eyes glossed over my wild hair while he stumbled past me, but before he left, he managed to wink at me and added a smart remark: "Nice dress, Princess!"

I crossed my arms around my shift, which hugged my body, but he was already gone. As soon as he rounded the corner, a large group of my aunts appeared, among Aleena and some of our cousins, who were all laughing. They were all in a comical state of undress, shifts and petticoats half put on and hair dangling across their faces. "What has happened?" I cried, a flush over my face at his sudden appearance.

"He stole my earring!" laughed Aleena. The glint in her eyes was refreshing and lifted my spirits to bring a huge smile to my face.

"They began to steal already?" I cried.

This was one of the more chaotic traditions of our marriages. While the bride was getting ready, the groom's side had to steal as many of her personal items as possible. Everything would be returned, of course, at the end of the ceremony, but the message was clear that they were taking her away from us.

"They are going to be stealing the entire time. Keep your eyes peeled, Tamar. And none of the fox stuff from any of you!" cried my aunt with a sharp look at Talin, who rolled her eyes and sent us all into fits of laughter.

As the women walked back to Aleena's chamber, I made to follow them, but Digin Galia grabbed me from behind. I struggled in her grip desperately. "Please, Digin Galia, let me go with them! They've begun to steal! I want to be with my sister."

"You are not decent. And to let Bedros see you that way was unseemly," she said and sighed, dragging me back to my chambers.

"Keep the doors open! I want to see."

They let me keep the doors open, but I kept up the steady whining about my hair and dress, aware that Digin Galia was slowly losing her patience. But she did not yell at me, which was unusual. I even noticed that her handy pomegranate branch whip was not on her.

"I shall have no hair left on my head after all this brushing and pulling, and then I shall look like a man, and you will never be able to marry me off," I said, sulking.

Digin Galia paused and had the maids stop working. When I glanced at her, she reached down and pulled me up from my seat, almost gently. For a moment, I thought she would beat me with her hands, so I moved away from her, but she only said, "Tamar." Something in her expression made me obey, and she led me to the window, which had been opened to let in some fresh air.

"Look out there, Tamar, and tell me what you see."

I tried to remember her lessons, so I could tie it in to this question and answer correctly, but for the life of me, I could not remember. I furrowed my brows as I looked out at the scenery. I saw the lake in the distance glittering like diamonds in the sunlight, and far off, the horizon held such mystery. Beneath me, though, I saw the village and the people bustling throughout it. There was more movement there than I had ever seen before. I could not imagine what Digin Galia wanted me to say, so I answered as truthfully as I could. "Villagers preparing the square for the ceremony and guests from the mainland."

"Villagers, yes. This ceremony, along with the traditional dancers, is going to be among some of the few times you lose your status as royalty for the day."

I glanced at her, puzzled.

"The village dances are circle dances. Do you remember what this means?"

"Unity?"

"Exactly. They all hold hands and join together for the dance. It does not matter *who* is dancing, but *why* they are dancing, what the purpose is; do you understand? Tonight, the maids are not maids, the baker man is not a baker man, the fisherman is not a fisherman, your father is not king, and you are not a princess. We are all dancers joined in unity under God. He is who we dance for and who we are giving ourselves to tonight."

I was quiet, as I processed what she told me. Together we solemnly watched the villagers preparing outside under the heat of the sun. They looked like ants moving about quickly. As we watched, we saw a young man stumble out of our palace, followed by several other young men. One of them managed to grab the man in the front and pull him aside, and I saw some trinkets fly out of the first man's hands. I knew it was Bedros being caught by my cousins. I watched in amusement as my cousin tumbled to the ground with Bedros, and they began to wrestle like little boys. I heard their laughter drift up with the wind toward my window. A small smile was on my lips, but I immediately wiped it off when I felt Digin Galia glance sideways at me.

She nodded slightly and turned around to walk toward the maids. I turned, my face flushed, and noticed that they were holding a piece of clothing in their arms. Digin Galia held up the dress. "You shall wear this, instead of your fancy clothing that you seem all of a sudden interested in. We dress traditionally for our most traditional events. This is what everyone shall be wearing today."

I nodded, and the maids set to work undressing me slowly, to make sure they did not disturb my braided hair, which coiled in two long ropes over my shoulders. As Digin Galia took away my shift and arranged it in the wardrobe, I called out, "Does this mean I can call you Galia?"

She turned and gave me a half-hearted glare, while I grinned cheekily. Before she could respond, however, I noticed movement and females squealing outside. "Get him!" I shouted, tearing away from the maids. I managed to grab a robe and struggle into it as I ran outside. The boy ran, and some of my cousins joined me in the chase, all of us shouting and whooping to scare away the boy.

And from upstairs, I heard Digin Galia shout, "Akh, Tamar!"

→⊨⊙ ⊙⊨←

Over the next two hours, Aleena lost both of her earrings, a bouquet of flowers, her coat (which was mine that I had lent to her), her right-hand glove, and many plates of desserts and crumpets (most of which were stolen by Bedros). We were already preparing to gather together and make our way to the church.

But before we left, a maid rushed to me and announced that Aleena wanted to see me alone before she left her room. I lifted up my skirts and went up the stairs to her chambers. Mother called out, "Tell her to hurry; we must leave soon!"

I approached her chambers and entered the room timidly. The room, which a moment ago was chaotic and full of a gaggle of women, was now empty and unusually quiet.

I saw only Aleena standing before her ornately framed mirror, smoothing her dress with slow, soft strokes of her hands. Her eyes caught mine through the mirror, and I saw how wide they were. "So?" she asked softly.

I closed the door behind me. "You look beautiful."

And she did, indeed. The dress fit her stunningly, the crimson red bringing out the red in her lips and cheeks. Her dark hair had been pulled together in two tight braids, while the headpiece was pinned on top of her head, like a crown. The lace and soft fabric from the headpiece came down the length of her back in soft waves, like a waterfall of clouds. Mother's brilliant ruby was nestled at the base of her neck, but her blue eyes sparkled like diamonds, and they alone were worth more than any jewel that could adorn her.

I, meanwhile, wore my dark beige dress of a slightly simpler cut with a dark brown belt and a lace shawl that I was to wrap my head in at the church. I was her shadow, and somehow I didn't mind.

I walked up next to her.

"I love you, sister, and only you," she said earnestly.

"I love you, too," I said, "only you."

"One day, you shall love me and another," she mused, feeling her dress again, with a small smile. I smiled back, but she turned smoothly and, with no change to her sweet voice, said, "And if that other is Bedros, I shall personally fling you off our dear old cliff. Yes?"

I laughed and took her arm. "Bedros and I shall kill each other before we fall in love."

She gave me a look. "If they are marrying me off to Vartan, do you perhaps not think that you shall follow closely with Bedros?"

I remembered anxiously Digin Galia catching my look at Bedros, and my face flushed. "Not if I have any say in it."

"That's my sister," she said and smiled. Before we left the room behind, she added, "Besides, you two will be related by tonight. I would not want you to marry your brother." And with a sly wink in my direction, she walked out of the room.

Oh dear.

Chapter 10

WE WERE GREETED extravagantly, coming down the stairs to many oohs and ahs, while several of the elder women had tears in their eyes as they kissed our cheeks, once on each side. The men puffed out their chests and glanced at my father with congratulatory smiles, clapping each other on the back, as if they had a hand each in arranging this marriage. I was fairly certain I hadn't seen my father in days during the preparations. Cries and exclamations from our cousins echoed: "Beautiful!" and "You're so lucky!" The attention made me feel uncomfortable, although I was not the one getting married. I watched as Aleena fidgeted with the long sleeves of her dress, so I took her hand in a tight grip.

My father came forward with a large, flat parcel wrapped in parchment paper, and I knew it was the painting. Normally the gifts would be presented to Aleena later during the festivities, but my father did not like the attention of strangers gathered around him. The guests crowded around as Aleena unwrapped the parcel, and the paper fell away to reveal Aleena's portrait. There were sighs all around us at her beauty. In the portrait, she sat very ceremoniously in her wedding dress. Her crystal-blue eyes were trained on my father, and it looked as though she was watching us through the glass of a window. Her lips were slightly pursed, and she had her hands clasped tightly in her lap. Father had a way of painting that was brilliantly unique. He could combine such contrasting colors and create the perfect hue. Her face was a smooth swirl of colors and emotions. The guests were enthralled. But only I noticed the shadows in her eyes. The smile faded from my lips.

Father had really captured her emotions in every way, but I did not think he realized what emotions those were. This wedding was a mistake—how could they not see that?

Aleena hugged him in a show of gratitude and turned her back on the painting to take my hand again.

And with this large procession, including our parents, our aunts, uncles, cousins, and two rather forlorn princesses, we walked amid great revelry toward the church, where the groom's entire family was awaiting us. When we arrived, our guests, cousins, aunts, and uncles first piled into the pews, where they sat on the left side, kept empty for our family, while the right side was already filled with the groom's guests and family.

They filed in slowly, leaving outside Aleena, father, me, Lilit, and two other female cousins of ours as bridesmaids, and three of Vartan's male cousins, who were waiting to escort them. We bustled into our lines, each of us anxious with hearts beating, when the traditional marriage music suddenly began from inside the church. The first couple, the bridesmaid holding a bouquet and the man taking her by the elbow, walked down the aisle.

Aleena suddenly clutched my arm in panic. I whispered to her, "It'll be over with soon; don't worry," believing her to be overcome by a sudden sense of anxiety.

"No, Tamar," she hissed, "where is *your* escort and your bouquet?"

I hesitated, my eyes widening while a flush spread over my cheeks. "Oops."

Her eyes widened. Lilit looked back at me, but it was her turn. Her escort took her arm, and they walked forward, slowly and agonizingly. I began to perspire. What would people say when they saw me walk down the aisle alone?

How could I have forgotten?

I was so unbelievably stupid! I felt as if *I* were the one getting married, instead of Aleena, and my groom had failed to appear. Tears pricked my eyes, and I struggled to keep them in. Aleena was made to go back to her spot next to our father as the third couple walked down. I could see all the guests now, glassy-eyed and smiling. Vartan stood at the pew, smiling at a distant cousin before resuming his expressionless stare toward the flowers that had been arranged around the church. He was no doubt wondering how much they had cost.

I was going to be sick. The music sounded for my entrance, and I hesitated a moment. But there was no other way to go but forward. As soon as I lifted my foot for my first step, an arm suddenly linked through mine, and a bouquet of flowers was placed into my hands. We walked down the aisle, not missing a step. There were excited sighs and gasps when we were seen. I glanced to my right and was greeted by a flashy smile and brown glittering eyes.

"You thought I would leave you alone up here?"

"I always hope," I muttered, my smile firmly on my face.

Of course. The brother of the groom and the sister of the bride—terrific.

I could just feel Aleena's gaze burning into my back. And I tried not to look straight ahead, as Lilit was winking at me and smiling mischievously.

"You look absolutely enchanting, Princess," he whispered. "And my flowers suit your dress."

I glanced down at the bouquet. They were a lovely shade of cream—cream roses. "You were so sure I would be alone up here that you brought me flowers?"

"You are rather pathetic, Princess. Who would want to escort you?"

My face flushed, and I pinched the inside of his arm. He winced, but his smile was steady. I shot him a look as I let go of his arm to go to my post next to Lilit as bridesmaid and him next to Vartan as bodyguard. He slightly bowed his head at me as I walked away, his eyes trained on me.

I turned my attention to my sister, the true beauty, walking down the aisle. There was a loud rustle as everyone stood up, as if hundreds of birds had taken flight all at once. She glowed with such beauty, and my father, who had linked his arm with hers, seemed a proud man with his chin up and a satisfied smile on his face. I watched my mother in the front row dab at her eyes, her perfectly embroidered handkerchief clutched tightly.

I glanced at Vartan, but his expression had maintained the same dull stare as before. It had not even altered when Aleena began her journey down the aisle. How could he have turned out this way? His father was a jolly man, but Vartan was a snob and his younger brother was much too confident and completely unlike him.

Baron Avedis, as godfather, was in charge of the entire wedding. He stood with the priest just near me, and when I looked at him, he gave me a little nod and a smile, making me feel slightly better. If Vartan were half the man Baron Avedis was, this marriage would not as much resemble death to Aleena.

I kept my eyes on my sister, who was not looking at Vartan, but at me. I grinned and discreetly sharpened my face into Vartan's prim expression. Her eyes widened, and she struggled desperately to maintain her calm composure, but I could see the laughter twitch at the corners of her mouth.

The music reached its crescendo as Aleena reached Vartan, and both turned to face the priest. He waited a moment until the music hushed before gesturing for the couple to kneel before him. The ceremony began as the high priest, accompanied by several other priests and young men, proceeded to bless the couple and the guests with the golden, ruby-encrusted cross he held in his hand. He was a large man, wearing a black-hooded slip over his body. A royal purple robe with a pattern of silvery crosses was thrown over his shoulders, clasped tightly at the neck. The hem and the sleeves of the robe were a lining of intricately crossed gold lace. Glittering over his chest with a sharp contrast against the black shroud was a golden necklace with a small-framed portrait of the Virgin Mary. In his right hand, he held the intricate golden cross with brilliant rubies and a red lace handkerchief. In his left hand was a large staff made of gold and silver, inset with many jewels.

The priest opened his mouth and began to sing the traditional verses in a bellowing operatic voice. I sighed inwardly. This was the longest part of the ceremony. I shot Lilit a look, and she gave me a look of utter boredom. No doubt she had heard this hundreds of times. At least he had a powerful and majestic voice. It filled the church like the incense that puffed up toward the ceiling. The priest broke off two small pieces of *nshkhark*, our flat lavash bread with the traditional holy seal stamped into it, and placed them into a large golden goblet, full to the brim with blood-red wine. He blessed them over and over in his loud bellowing baritone and then walked to the kneeling couple. He presented the golden cross in front of Vartan, who kissed it, touched his forehead to the cross, and then made the sign of the cross over his chest. Aleena did the same. Third was Bedros, and I was last, as siblings of the couple. Then, the priest dipped his fingers into holy water and drew a small cross on our foreheads.

Vartan's blank stare was mirrored by Aleena's.

Last, the priest lifted the piece of wine-dipped bread to Vartan's lips and put it on his tongue. He did the same to Aleena, and the couple was officially married.

All the guests, beginning with the family and bridesmaids and groomsmen, piled forward where we, one by one, bowed in front of the priest, kissed the cross in his hands, touched our foreheads to its cool metal, and ate a piece of nshkhark. When it was Bedros's turn again, he winked at me before kissing the cross, and a heated flush rose to my face. If anyone caught him making these faces in the church, he'd be reprimanded and forced to recite every line of scripture in the Bible. I turned away promptly so as not to encourage him.

As soon as the last guest had taken a piece of nshkhark, the priest stepped forward with a small box. He blessed its contents and sang a verse from our Bible, echoed by a woman who sang the chorus in a sweet voice from the back of the church, before opening the lid of the box. Two white doves flew out of the box, twisting together and flying out toward the one open window in the church, eager to escape into the vast sky. There was a sigh of awe that spread through the crowd, and I smiled at the shine in Aleena's eyes as she looked up toward the birds.

I knew what she was thinking. She wanted the same freedom that the birds felt; she wanted that same smooth flight toward the open window, which would lead her straight to the open sky and away from the stone wall she had been carved into.

The musicians, all at once, struck up a traditional fun tune that echoed through the night. One of them carried the *dhol*, a traditional drum hung by a leather strap around his neck. He beat on it with his hands and fingers, while two other men played the *duduk*, a long wind instrument made of apricot wood. The music was playful as they twisted their songs together and created a lovely harmony. We all gathered together, the formalities ending as soon as the music began. We headed out of the church and began to walk toward the village, some of us dancing and all of us conversing and making quite a racket. I kept my eyes on Aleena, who was walking ahead with Vartan, and I tried to near her by pushing through the crowd. Several of my relatives grabbed hold of me and urged me to dance, but I managed to slip out of their grasps, smiling apologetically.

All at once, two hands grabbed me by the waist, and I heard, "Maybe you shall dance with me instead?"

"Bedros, not now." I tried shaking him off.

"Later then."

"No," I asserted. He began to twist me around in a dance anyway, bobbing me up and down to the music, but I grew angry and snapped, "Let go; you are my brother now."

He held me tighter, to my absolute frustration. The group around us slowly went ahead, not realizing that two in their midst were not moving with them.

"I want to speak with you."

"Can't it be done later?"

"Before we get to the village," he insisted infuriatingly.

"Let go of me. I need to be with my sister."

"Fine!" he suddenly cried, surprising me with his outburst. He let me go, but I only stared at him. His face was red and brows furrowed. I suddenly remembered him as a child; that stubborn look on his face had not changed, and I saw it now, in the way his lips had a small pout to them. He was all of fifteen again. "Run to her. She obviously needs to be with you as well."

"What does that mean?" I asked, my face flushing. We were standing alone, but our families were still visible, and the music echoed along the road and mountains.

Bedros ran his hand through his hair with a frustrated sigh. "It means that she's moved on. Or she's in the process of moving on. You always chase after her. It's time for you to move on as well." I pursed my lips and turned to leave, but he stepped in front of me quickly, blocking my way. "All I am asking is that you don't stick to your sister tonight."

"On her most important day?"

"Yes, this is Aleena and Vartan's day, not ours."

"You only want me to stick to you," I snapped. A guilty smile spread over his face suddenly, and I looked away, refusing to give in to his charm. "I can do whatever I want tonight; I am not Princess Tamar."

"Then I am not Bedros, and therefore, I am not your brother." I sighed and he said, "Just tonight. You will have fun; I shall see to it."

I glanced at his cheeky smile, which was growing over his face, and I couldn't help it; I giggled. "*You* are the pathetic one," I sighed. He suddenly leaned forward and kissed me on the cheek. A fierce burning spread over my face. "What was that?"

"Just a kiss from one stranger to another," he said and shrugged.

I shoved him back hard, and he stumbled into a run toward the village, with me in pursuit, skirts pulled up to my knees. When we arrived panting to the village, we were just in time to see the beginning of the celebration.

A pomegranate was brought forth, wrapped in lace and tied with a satin ribbon. The villagers stood waiting on one side while our two large families and guests stood on the other. It was refreshing to see the similarity in costume; one could not tell who was royalty and who was not. The only colors that stood out were the colors of the bride and the groom, with their deep crimson and thin sparks of gold.

Aleena was led forward, and a child placed the pomegranate gingerly in my sister's hands. She carefully untied the string and let the lace fall from the pomegranate. Without a moment's hesitation, she lifted up her hand and threw the fruit down hard toward the ground. We waited to hear the crack, followed by the expected explosion of seeds, but there was just a wet *smoosh*. No seeds came out.

Silence.

She gave a small nervous chuckle and picked up the pomegranate again. She brought it down harder. It did not crack; it just smooshed into a heap.

I flinched. Aleena would have no children.

Low murmurs spread around the clearing. At my father's stern gesture, the musicians began playing the music, and our groups mingled, slightly forcefully, with many congratulatory remarks and exclamations.

Aleena stood frozen where the pomegranate was, gazing down at it as if it were scolding her harshly. I touched Bedros's arm in the universal gesture for him to "wait a moment" and went to her.

She looked up at me with wide eyes and said, "Oh God."

I muttered in her ear, "If they had scattered, it would have meant you would have many children with him. Now you do not have to worry about that."

She laughed breathlessly. "You always know what to say."

"Aleena!" called several voices. A gaggle of our younger cousins came forward, enveloping my sister in a great hug and all crying out happily for the occasion. They touched her dress and felt her tight braids and the soft folds of her headdress, their hands exploring her with no restraint. I stood to the side, smiling to myself. My poor sister. I knew she wanted to throttle the lot of them and hide in a corner until the night was over, but propriety tied her arms tightly to her sides as she was touched like a newly bought doll.

I walked back to Bedros, who was standing where I had left him, watching me with a measured look. "Let us find some of the dancers. I am desperate to see what they look like," I remarked, walking toward the raging campfire that roared in the square of the village. He stopped me with a hand on my elbow.

"The dancers are not gathered yet."

"But they are here, no?"

"Of course, they arrived an hour before we arrived here."

My heart skipped a beat in excitement and anticipation. "Let us find them!"

"For what?"

"I want to talk to them before they begin to dance."

"Let us get something to drink instead," he suggested, gesturing to the wine jars.

"I do not want a drink."

"Come with me then. I am going to find some friends."

"I do not want to see your friends," I said defiantly.

"Tamar," he asserted.

"Bedros, leave me in peace."

"Come on," he sighed.

"I want to see the dancers."

"You must stay with me."

"My *sister* married your *brother*. I don't know when you mistook the marriage for one between you and me. And I never actually agreed to spend the evening with you."

"Fine, go find your dancers! I can assure you, you will be disappointed. They are a filthy lot."

"You don't know anything," I snapped, walking away from him toward the campfire. He did not follow, and I slipped into the throng of people, happy to disappear from his sight at last.

The crowds were much larger and denser around the fire, and I felt my eyes stinging slightly from the great roil of black smoke rising from the fire. I lifted the shawl around my shoulders, so it covered my mouth and nose, and I walked among the people, reveling in the freedom I felt in being one with the villagers. The shadows of the night and the fire played across everyone's faces, and it distorted their expressions, lending them a darkness that would have frightened me had I been younger.

But tonight I found great comfort in their strangeness. The unfamiliarity of my surroundings was refreshing and made me feel invincible.

I could finally breathe without fearing that I would upset society's course. Not one person suspected my being royalty, and it felt glorious. I saw hundreds of people I didn't recognize and many I had seen vaguely in passing through the village. My heart beat fast with excitement. I could do anything; I could go anywhere.

I could be *anyone*.

Chapter 11

MY FIRST STEP as this new person was to ask around for the dancers. I asked several of the villagers standing in groups where they could be found. After all the failed attempts, I realized none knew where they were, and I grew frustrated. They made me feel out of place, as if it was not my place to ask where someone could be found. I was a young girl, in the end, and young girls were supposed to be seen and not heard.

Someone fell into step beside me, and I noticed it was Lilit, who saw through my disguise with no difficulty. She linked her arm through mine and lifted up her shawl as I had done so that only her dancing eyes shone through. We spent a while walking through the crowds and trying new desserts and pastries that the village women had made. Delicious jams made them sweet enough so that we could not stop tasting them. "We shall grow fat by the end of the night," announced Lilit, giggling.

But we were stopped when suddenly the musicians began to play a traditional dance song, a song I had heard numerous times from the cliff's edge. The crowd grew dense and formed a large clearing where the dancers, half of them men and half of them women, linked hands in a circle.

I looked around frantically and caught Aleena's eyes where she stood with Vartan. She rushed over to me and took my hand, her eyes wide. "This is one of the songs!"

It was a fast dance, and the dancers laughed and giggled but stayed perfectly synchronized through the movements. Their feet pounded the dusty ground in unison, and some of the men shouted out, whooping and yelling throughout the dance.

"This is called *tzaghkadzori*," said a voice from our right. Aleena, Lilit, and I looked over and saw a younger girl smiling at the dancers, but speaking to us. "It's from an area called Tsaghkunyats Dzor."

"Have you been there?" asked Aleena.

She shook her head, and a light sparkled in her eye. "No, but one day I will! I travel with the dancers, and they will be traveling there soon!" She traveled! I decided I liked this girl. There was a raw energy reverberating through her.

We watched the dance in silence, and when it ended amid loud applause and cheers, they began another one—slower, denser. The little girl grabbed Lilit's hand and said, "Come! We will teach you!" Lilit grabbed my hand, and I grabbed Aleena's hand, and soon we had entered the circle. More villagers joined the circle, all dancing in tune together. I stumbled a bit, along with my sister and Lilit. The little girl gestured to some of the dancers, and two of them stepped between each of us, separating us three.

My face flushed as the men intertwined their fingers with mine, as was customary. My head was down, my shawl covering my face, as I tried matching the steps with theirs. I found myself stumbling, unable to determine the next move and keep up.

"Put more heart into it. Don't think about getting the steps right; it'll come naturally once you become accustomed to the music," said a voice. I looked up to the dancer on my right. He was tall, his skin dark from spending time under the sun, his hair a mop of loose curls on top of his head. He had dark brown eyes and high cheekbones, and he was looking at me with such a *look*. "And also when you become accustomed to me."

I looked back down, flustered. He threw his head back and laughed, then whooped loudly. The people who knew the dances suddenly changed some of the moves, and I realized that the whooping was a sign to change the dance.

We went on like this for about an hour, changing dances, fast to slow, slow to fast. I managed to find myself back with Aleena and Lilit, and we were laughing and having the time of our lives as we swung through the dances. A few times I noticed the handsome dancer watching me, a curious grin on his face, but I was having too much fun to think more on it. I only reveled in his attention, tossing my head with a flirtatious streak that I did not know I had, while letting the music course through my body and move me through the dances. He was right: after allowing the dance to come from inside me and after becoming accustomed to the dancers around me, I found myself flowing through the dances as though I had known them all my life.

When the time finally came to eat, the dancing paused for a little while, though I could have danced forever. The clearing filled with people, and I noticed that the dancers disappeared all of a sudden, leaving a void where they once were. I separated from Aleena and Lilit, and I walked about, trying to look for them. It felt as though there was a string pulling me toward them; I was so eager to speak to them and learn from them. Finding an old man, I asked, "Pardon me, but I am looking for the dancers who were performing earlier."

He cast his eye over me and sipped at his drink, making a strained face as the drink burned down his throat. I would never understand how men could drink something that pained them so. "They are resting while they eat. They will dance more later," he said simply, his voice a husky growl.

"Of course," I murmured, but I was distracted by the drink in his hand, an idea forming in my head. I walked away, straight toward the tables set up where several older women were standing and serving out the drinks. I could smell the alcohol in them, and I winced again. I wasn't much used to the smell, as mother and Digin Galia made sure Aleena and I were kept away from the drinks. I shuffled toward one of the women respectfully and said, "Digin, I have come to take drinks to the dancers."

The woman glanced at me, as if trying to see who I was behind the shawl. Her eyes were dark and inky, framed by a face that resembled a weathered almond. Her hair was wrapped with a shawl, which tied under her chin in a tight knot. She smiled at me, baring teeth that had colored with age. Lifting the thick clay jar with surprising strength, she began to pour the blood-red wine into the thin glass cups, placing them onto a wooden tray. "You are his sister, then?" she asked in a cracked voice. I pulled my shawl tighter around my nose, knowing that this was dangerous.

"Yes."

"How is the lad?"

"Very well, thank you."

"I remember when he was this little." She gestured with her shaking hands. "Your mother gave him to me to hold. He was such a darling; I did not want to give him back!" She cackled. She gave me the tray and smiled, showing those ghastly teeth once again.

I quickly asked, "Do you know where I might find them?"

"They have gone to the butcher's shop, my dear."

"Bless you, Digin," I muttered.

"I am truly sorry for what happened to your eldest brother. Your mother must be in a dreadful state," she mumbled, her voice low, as if afraid anyone would hear her words. I nodded, feigning sadness. "I must come to call one day. Tell your mother I shall come."

"Yes, Digin. Good day," I muttered and hastened toward the butcher's shop with the wooden tray balanced in my hands. I hoped I did not place another burden on this poor family she believed I was a part of.

The crowd slowly thinned as distance was put between myself and the campfire, and the light from the fire dimmed, casting longer and thicker shadows over everything I passed. But I was not afraid, for I knew shadows could not harm me. Still my mind was constantly on the knife I kept in my belt, and my hands were ready to dart toward the spot. I kept my eyes open until I arrived at the shop, alert for anything out of place. I smelled the meat, still lingering in the air after a day of hard work. My family was well acquainted with the butcher and his sons, for they would deliver hunks of meat to our kitchen every other week. He was in the center of the village with the celebrations currently, so his shop was eerily dark.

It was silent; I could not hear anything, except the dim instruments echoing, while the lake splashed against the shore in the distance. The two contradicting noises danced around me, and I longed to dance with them. I put my ear to the door to hear any conversation occurring inside. Maybe they were rehearsing for the second round of their performance, or maybe they were discussing the trip here, or maybe they liked how the palace looked in the moonlight—

The door suddenly swung open, and I reared back, heat rushing to my face in humiliation and guilt. A young man looked down at me with a sly smile spreading over his face. "Drinks brought by a little mouse, lads!" whooped the man who had opened the door and was now staring at me with amusement.

"Enjoy," I muttered hurriedly, handing him the tray, which was taken from my hands unceremoniously by another man.

"Come inside and have a drink with us then," someone called from the inside. I squinted but could not see who was there. It was dark, and I vaguely saw a cloud of smoke, which had gathered densely in the small room. I wrinkled my nose. The man who took the tray disappeared into the dark with it, where I assumed he went to hand out the drinks.

"No, I really must leave, thank you," I stammered, flustered with the situation. Where were the women? They were only men it seemed. There could not be women in there, for men would never act this way in front of ladies. I could not see the handsome man who'd stood to my right during the dance, and I hoped he was not in there.

I walked quickly away, and only when I was a little ways down did I hear the door shut quietly behind me. Tears pricked my eyes from humiliation, and I struggled to keep the blush from off of my face. Why had they called me inside like that? I did not know what I had expected, but whatever had happened was disappointing, and I did not like it at all. I had half a mind to rush back and announce that I was royalty and that they should show me the respect I deserved. But I knew that the ending to that would be much more mortifying than this one.

I walked on slowly toward the campfire and music when a figure appeared in front of me—a small figure. The young girl from earlier! She was no more than ten or eleven years old from the looks of it.

She almost walked past me, but I stopped her with a firm touch to her elbow. "You are leaving the celebration alone?" I asked.

She glanced at me with her wide green eyes. "I remember you! You can be a very good dancer if you practice!"

"That is kind of you to say. But come back to the celebration with me."

"Oh no, I am visiting the dancers at the butcher's shop!"

"You shouldn't go there alone. It is dark."

She giggled and pulled away from my resisting hand. "I am not afraid of the dark. And don't be silly. Don't you know me? I am Aleek's sister!"

I froze for a moment. That name sounded so familiar. I tried to remember where I had heard it before. She saw the puzzlement in my face. "You are born on this island then?" she asked, her eyes lighting up with understanding. She was quite bright for a little girl.

"Yes."

"I thought so," she said cheekily. "*Everyone* knows Aleek."

"Not I."

"You danced next to him today. The dancers are all very sweet to me."

I paused for a moment. Aleek...*Aleek*. Like a flash, I suddenly remembered the little boy I had met years ago. Was this *him*? He was the handsome one who'd stood next to me? My heart beat faster with anticipation. I nodded slowly with understanding and put down my hand. She was who I had been mistaken for, perhaps. That old woman must have been blinder than I had thought. I wondered what had happened to her elder brother. I frowned when I remembered Kevork, the boy who had been standing with Aleek in the village all those years ago. I was afraid to ask. "Very well then. My apologies."

"What did they say to you?" she asked. "If they teased you, I shall hurt them."

I could not help it. I grinned at her innocence. She was a lovely little thing, with her bright, innocent eyes and chirpy way of speaking. "Oh nothing, really, I was silly enough to intrude."

"What did you want?"

"I wanted to learn some of the dances."

"I shall teach you!" she cried, a broad smile exploding on her face.

"No need, I will learn during the actual performance. I already learned a few that way."

"You will only ruin the line more. I will teach you now."

"I will not ruin the line; I am a fast learner, you said so yourself!"

"But why pass up the chance to master it?"

"Will you not give up until I say yes?"

"I have always wanted an apprentice."

We were silent for a moment; then I sighed. "Fine, you may teach me."

She reached over and took my hand. "I knew you'd come to your senses."

·→≡● ●≡←·

A few minutes later, we were in a secluded area where the villagers would not intrude. We were standing a street away from the festivities, between some of the closed shops. It wasn't so dark, since the light from the campfire was bright enough to steal into this area as well. We stood next to each other, intense with the project at hand.

She told me her name was Karin.

When she asked me my name, I said curtly, "Lori," and she took it without question.

"There are several ways to hold hands during the dances. One is just to hook pinkies. The other is to hold hands. The third is interlacing fingers—tight—shoulders touching. And the last is arms straight out, holding the shoulders of the people on either side of you. Of course there are many variations of this..."

And on we went, with Karin taking my hand and leading me in very simple steps.

"Are all the dances with these moves?" I asked incredulously, for our moves consisted of several steps and taps to the right, with one step to the left. It created a somewhat continuous move to the right.

"Nooo," she said, dragging out the word. "That is our easiest dance, but the usual ones they like to dance are harder."

"Can you teach me one of them?"

She nodded but stopped midnod, her eyes lighting up with an idea. "Can you come to the mainland, so I could teach you? It would be easier, because I can't really teach you well during the festivities. The music is too loud."

"What?" I gasped.

"Could you row over to the mainland? I could teach you how to dance."

"Why would you want to teach me how to dance that much?"

"Our dances are important. You must learn them," she said and shrugged, as if it were the simplest matter in the world.

I sighed. "I am sorry; I cannot."

"Why not? It is not too hard."

I hesitated. "I would have to come at night."

"You can't come during the day?"

"No."

"Why?"

"My parents would never allow it."

"Then that's even more exciting! Come at night! I like it!"

"Karin," I said, trying to calm her down, "it is dangerous."

"Fine." She raised her chin defiantly. Her eyes—full of challenge—locked on mine. "Stay here."

It was a simple two-word sentence: *stay here*. But it hit me hard, and I was taken aback. I suddenly felt as Aleena did all her life. With those two words, I finally understood everything Aleena had ever fought for: her desire to leave this island that we were destined to stay rooted to, her anger at the authorities and higher figures whose very goals in life were to keep us here and continue our line forever.

She never wanted to be a part of it. She wanted to leave. I saw in my mind again the way she looked at the white doves that flew up, up, toward the one open window, seeing their chance at freedom and taking it with no hesitation. And here was our chance—our one open window.

"Are you sure you want to go through with this?" I asked, my voice shaking.

"Are *you* sure you want to go through with this?" She grinned teasingly, knowing full well that I had been persuaded.

I was saved from responding for that moment because we were suddenly interrupted by loud cries of delight and shouts of excitement from the villagers. I was pulled out of this life-changing situation where I would finally make my own decision, and we looked across at the rising anticipation that had suddenly taken over the crowd. The music grew louder and more animated, and the people gathered into another large huddle around the campfire, creating a clearing in their midst. We heard suddenly from near us, "Karin, where have you been?" We looked up to the side and saw a young man approaching us, followed by two other men of similar age. I was startled and caught off guard. It was *him*! Aleek. I had never seen a more beautiful man. My heart skipped a beat, surprising me. This was finally him—the boy I had been looking for as a child. These rapid thoughts raced through my mind and I could only stare at him, dumbfounded.

Karin lifted her chin proudly. "I have been teaching her how to dance."

"You don't know how to dance?" he asked, his eyes resting on my form. He towered over us with his tall build and lean shoulders. "You were the one who stood next to me today, yes?"

I had to search for my voice, and I felt my face flush at the worry of looking like a complete ninny. I managed to say, "Yes, that was me. I do know how to dance, but your dances are different from ours. We only began with the basic steps today."

He narrowed his eyes, but a shadow of a smile played on his lips. "They could not be so different; most village dances are the same."

"You are mistaken. Village dances are quite different from one another," I said, trying to prevent my voice from shaking. I hated the way my voice sounded, weak and fragile.

"Who are you anyway?" he asked bluntly.

I blanched; my voice ran into some corner in my mind and hid out of sight. What would I say? How would I avoid this? Everyone in the villages was known by someone; he would know immediately that I had lied if he did not recognize the name. I opened my mouth to blurt something I knew I would regret, but loud voices called, "Aleek! Aleek!"

He turned abruptly, but before he walked toward the gathering crowd, he gestured for Karin to leave. "You can't stay here; go back and find mother and stay with her."

She nodded, and I was surprised to not see any defiance in her stance. "Why can't you stay here?" I asked quietly from behind my shawl.

"It's the *eznmortel*," she murmured. Before she walked away, she leaned in and whispered, "Tomorrow night, row toward the light on the mainland." Then she squeezed my hand and walked away to find her mother. I stood, puzzled.

What light? And what was the eznmortel?

Chapter 12

I WATCHED KARIN walk away, and when I turned back, I realized Aleek had stopped walking to raise his eyebrows at me. Again my heart skipped a beat when I glanced at him. Why was he looking at me in such a way? I assumed it was his reaction to hearing my low murmur to Karin and her swift whisper into my ear, because he asked incredulously, "You don't know what happens now?"

"Of course I do," I replied, a little harsher than I intended.

"Then why do you stay?" he challenged, for he knew I was lying.

"I will not hide behind my mother," I said, raising my chin, copying Karin's defiance.

"You are the mouse who brought us our drinks," said one of the men behind him with sudden realization. "I recognize her voice."

Aleek grinned knowingly at me. "It can't be. Mice are not brave. They scurry around in the darkness and bite you when you are not looking."

"I brought you your drinks," I snapped. "The least you could do is thank me."

"She has fangs!" laughed the third man.

"Perhaps you are a snake then," Aleek teased.

"It is better to be a snake than a wolf."

He straightened, his eyebrows raised. It seemed that I had hit a soft spot, but my pride prevented me from apologizing. But there was no hurt in his eyes. I saw a mixture of hardness and admiration. "Perhaps you would like a front seat for the eznmortel?"

I stayed silent, and he exchanged a look with his friends. For a moment I was afraid that he would try to get his revenge on me. Maybe I had crossed the line. I suddenly felt very small, a lone, young girl in the shadows with three men. Aleek turned back to me with a grin on his face, but he spoke to his friends when he said, "Shall we give her an experience she will never forget then, lads?" They hooted suddenly, growing very animated, while my heart jumped like a rabbit. I stayed rooted to my spot as they began to make their way toward the crowds, but Aleek gestured for me to join them, calling out in a singsong voice, "Will you be a mouse or a snake tonight, my mysterious lady?"

I followed, unable to back away. There was a danger in his voice that drew me in. I was led by uncertainty but encouraged by excitement. *My mysterious lady*. This was most definitely far more interesting than sitting with Bedros.

I gazed at Aleek as we walked, unsure what to make of him. He was a very handsome man, and I found my face flushing constantly when I looked at him, but he seemed not much better in arrogance than Bedros. There was a mocking tilt to his lips. But there was also a look in his eyes that Bedros lacked. It was a fire passion, and it seemed to burn its way into my soul upon every glance, as if he could read all my thoughts. It sent shivers down my back and a rushing through my veins.

As we entered the crowds, no one recognized me behind my shawl, save for three people. Aleena, Lilit, and Bedros stood together, both with wide eyes on their faces as they struggled to understand what I was doing with these villagers. I ignored them and stood at the edge of the crowd as the dancers entered the clearing boldly. The boys had increased in number, all the dancers coming together in similar village attire. Colorful vests and belts adorned them and set them apart from everyone else. Aleek's vest was a deep purple, and it made him look almost royal, though he was undoubtedly a village boy.

I had never seen or heard about this part of a wedding, and I was excited to experience something new. I thought for a moment that they were going to begin dancing, but somehow I knew it was not yet time.

One of the boys stayed with me, as if to keep me company. There were hoots and hollers everywhere, and I vaguely noticed the lack of children from this particular happening. When I glanced around, I saw that they were standing some ways off with some of the older women and men. I saw Karin among them, sitting with an old woman and speaking with her animatedly. I was not sure whether I should be afraid, but the feeling was there regardless, settling in my stomach like a heavy stone.

As I watched from my place, five small calves were led into the clearing with ropes tied loosely around their necks to guide them. Aleek strolled over to me and, gesturing to the animals, said, "Go on and pick the calf that you like best."

I smiled modestly under my shawl, a burn spreading over my cheeks. They wanted to know which calf I liked the best. All eyes were on me.

I felt powerful, knowing that my opinion mattered, and the proceedings would happen around my decision. I tightened the shawl around my face and walked around slowly, glancing at all the cattle one by one.

"Tamar!" I heard faintly from the din of the crowd, muffled among the noise. "Tamar!"

But I was not Tamar. No, not tonight. Tonight, I was Lori, a villager who was going to be freed from her cage, at least just for the night.

I walked slowly with measured steps. Something in my heart moved for the poor cattle, as I saw them restrained by the ropes. I stopped in front of one calf who looked particularly hopeless. I hesitated while he glanced up at me with his big brown eyes and floppy ears. I could change his fate. I could make things different for him. I had heard stories of other cultures that painted animals that they cherished as a form of sacred gesture. The animals were protected. I smiled, feeling such power at my fingertips. This calf would be protected by my hand. "This one!"

The shouts grew loud, almost to a deafening roar, and I stepped back, jolting abruptly out of my dreamlike state. The other cattle were led away, and the one I had chosen tried to follow his mates, but he was held back by one of the dancers whose face had brightened with a grin. The calf grew afraid at the sudden loneliness and extra attention and began struggling in his bonds, trying so desperately to free himself, and I began to doubt my decision. What had I actually chosen him for? Aleek stepped forward with the other boys and, with one deft move, tightened the rope around the calf's neck so he would not escape. "Wait," I said, trying to stop him, but I was lost in the crowd of dancers that gathered around me.

They steered the calf toward the fire, which roared and danced up into the black shroud that covered the sky. He struggled and cried out and jumped about to escape from the boys. "Wait!" I cried again, but no one could hear me over the roar of the crowd. The realization of what was going to happen dawned on me suddenly, and it felt as if I had burned myself with the flames. The stone that was first in the pit of my stomach rose abruptly and lodged itself into my throat, threatening to release itself.

I saw Aleek glance up, his neck straining as if looking for someone. As his eyes fell on me, I realized that someone was me. He reached forward to take my arm and tugged me to him, placing the rope in my hands and muttering into my ear, "Whatever you do, don't let go."

"Please," I pleaded, unable to finish. I could not find my voice. I held the rope to the calf's neck. *Let go. Let go.* I gripped it tight, panic paralyzing my muscles. I was surrounded by the dancers, who were half-heartedly dancing some of the moves, creating a vision of swirling bodies in my eyes; I could hardly recognize it as a dance. Aleek stood with a knife in his hand, making some loud, shouting speech that spread like fire among the crowd. There was no spark, no start, just the spreading of it, so swift that it destroyed everything in its path.

I could change this. *Let go.*

The people were yelling and shouting, the prayers fast on their tongues and the hunger roiling in their bellies.

Let go.

In the distance, all I could hear was, "Tamar! Tamar!" I saw the lake in my mind; I was standing on the shore—I was someone else, someone from a distant legend. I heard my name being shouted from the depths of the waters. Pain, such pain, filled my heart. Mind-numbing panic blinded me, so all I saw was a deep blue: Aleena's eyes, tormented and watching me with such broken sorrow. I couldn't find the shore; the storm was too strong. I was drowning in its depths, and I wanted to run to her, but she was calling someone else's name. *Tamar!*

I was not Tamar. Who was I?

Lori—that made more sense. Tamar would certainly let go.

Let go.

Aleek stepped forward toward the calf. I tried to say something; I tried to tug at the rope. The calf panicked and tried to wrap around my legs in an effort to escape. I twisted around, instinctively grabbing tighter to the rope, while Aleek approached him. I couldn't scream; I couldn't shout as he moved his hand in the swiftest of moves and slit the animal's throat with one quick stroke. Its bony knees wobbled and collapsed in on themselves, as if they had just snapped like twigs. Its cry of terror was cut short abruptly, and blood spurted out from its neck.

Tears ran down my cheeks and absorbed into the cloth at my mouth as its life's blood poured out of its body, pooling into the dirt ground and staining it red. My hands were covered in blood, and they slipped over the wet rope, which I still held gripped so tight that the whites of my knuckles appeared. The body convulsed and twitched at my feet, though Aleek held it tight against him.

Excitement reigned around me, and many people came forward to clasp their hands at my back and praise Aleek. The priest stepped forward and blessed the calf for providing us with food. I heard none of it. I stared at him, on his knees next to the quivering animal, his face clear and not bothered by what he had just done. He was praying as well, his head bowed over the animal.

As if he knew I had been looking at him, Aleek looked up at me and smiled cautiously, as though I were a calf as well. The minute he did that, the rope slipped from my fingers, and I stumbled back.

I finally let go.

My vision was blurred as shadows filled my mind, but before I collapsed next to both of them, both predator and prey, arms wrapped tightly around me and pulled me away from the clearing. Bedros murmured in my ear, "It's OK; you're OK. Damn them, putting you in there. Damn them!" Aleena was next to him, her face devoid of emotion, but I could sense the anger and concern rumbling beneath her skin.

And as they led me away, I looked back once more at Aleek, who was still kneeling on the ground, his hands covered in blood. But all I saw were his eyes—those beautiful dark eyes of his—riveted on mine and a frown pulling down his perfect lips. He rose to his feet, as though he was going to follow, but the crowd surrounded him, and I saw him no more.

I buried my face into Aleena's chest and cried and cried as she held me tight and both sister and brother-in-law led me away from the noise and revelry.

→⟶◉ ◉⟵←

The doctor said it was only a fever and I needed rest.

I knew it wasn't a fever, but I was grateful. I needed to be left alone with my raging thoughts and nightmares.

I was to have no visitors and no excitement until it passed. But I did not care. My visions were haunted with large dark eyes, rotating back and forth between the calf's eyes and Aleek's eyes. His smooth frown twisted in the vision until the image became one and the same: a deformed calf who called out to me with blood dripping from its neck and its body convulsing.

I saw Aleena holding the calf, blood crossing intricately over her arms and body as if it was henna, preparing her for an exotic Arabic marriage. She looked up at me with the saddest eyes. Those eyes. Blue turned dark, the mud rising up and covering it completely. The brown of Aleek's eyes. I looked into them, falling in, losing myself in them, until I was swimming hard for the shore. An endless ocean tossed me back and forth, as if I were nothing more than a broken doll. I opened my mouth to scream, but water rushed in, filling my throat, pulling me under. Black everywhere. My name...Someone was screaming my name. *Tamar...Tamar!* And then I saw the light: a red light, a pomegranate, glowing like a gem. I reached for it, breaking free from the waves, and it appeared suddenly in my hands, but as soon as I touched it, it melted into a hot congealing liquid.

I would jolt awake throughout the night, drenched in sweat and crying out, before falling back into a feverish nightmare that haunted me all night. But at some point in the night, I felt a rustling of my sheets that did not match my movement. I opened my eyes into slits, wondering if I was imagining it, but I suddenly felt a pair of hands take my right hand, which had been resting on top of the sheets.

Tilting my head slightly, I recognized my mother in the darkness, her face shrouded in shadow. She was meticulous, rubbing a rose-scented ointment onto my hands. It was exceedingly soothing, and I felt all the muscles in my body release their tension—could almost see the stress wafting away from my body. "Akh Tamar," I heard her murmur, her voice low, "I worry about you so."

In my feverish state, I remember being surprised at her worry and attentiveness to my health. She had for so long focused her attentions on Aleena that her sudden regard for me was strange. I fell back into a deep sleep, lulled into a numb calm from the ointment, and I was able to finally stay asleep for a few hours. When I awoke, I was alone except for Janna, who placed a palm against my forehead and pronounced the fever gone.

It was quick, vanishing as if it had never haunted me at all. The nightmares disappeared with the cool breeze that drifted in through the open window.

When my wits were finally about me, I began to fidget. Karin expected me that night. Would I be able to go? I must! I tugged at the collar that had stuck to me from the perspiration that had dampened the cloth. Janna sat next to me on my bed, wringing a clean white rag with cold water and placing it over my forehead and neck to help cool me down.

"Where is Aleena?" I asked.

"She has other duties she must attend to," she said, frowning.

I did not realize the importance of the wedding night yet, so I could not understand why she did not visit me. I only sulked and let Janna soothe my burning skin.

Chapter 13

DURING THE DAY, regaining my strength rather quickly from the horrid night, I spent most of my time reading a novel from my father's library. It was a simple way of turning my thoughts away from all that had happened. I was also forbidden from joining the family for breakfast, because of my last night's behavior. Unsurprisingly, my parents were appalled when they learned of my taking part in the eznmortel—though my mother never acknowledged her midnight's visit to my room.

I learned a day late that the eznmortel was the sacrificing of a small animal as the opening to a festival. No meat was to be eaten before the sacrifice. The killing of the animal and the blessing of its meat allowed for the food to be taken out and presented to everyone. It was a ritual that was highly respected and esteemed among the villagers, and I had taken a direct hand in choosing the sacrifice. I had missed the entire rest of the wedding celebration—the rest of the dances and the music that I had dreamed of seeing and hearing for days.

All because I had decided to talk to the damned dancers. Bedros's silent "I told you so" resounded in my mind, although he had said no such thing.

I delved deeper into my novel, trying to imagine myself as the heroine and escape the current reality that humiliated me. After half an hour of silent reading, I suddenly turned to Janna, who stood at my door quietly. "Might I have a pomegranate please?" She nodded and went off. I tore a slip of paper from inside my journal and picked up my pen. Dipping it in ink, I positioned the bright nib over the parchment and wrote in smooth strokes.

I have a surprise for you. Meet at the beach tonight. Dress warmly. Very warmly.

Janna arrived with a pomegranate on a silver platter. Next to it she had placed a small silver spoon and a dainty knife. I thanked her and said I wished to be left alone for a few minutes. As soon as the doors had shut behind her, I picked up the knife and carefully slit the pomegranate, spreading its lips with a crackle. The sweet smell wafted up into my nose, and I took a deep breath, letting it in. I took the spoon and scooped out about twenty of the seeds into the platter. I ate them quickly, shoveling them into my mouth with the silver spoon. While still chewing, I replaced them with the neatly folded letter. When I had once again shut the pomegranate tightly, I called Janna back into my room. "Would you take this to Aleena please?" I asked. She nodded and took the tray. She was surprisingly quiet today, but I thought nothing of it. Aleena and Vartan were still in the palace and would be until Baron Avedis fixed their rooms in Vartan's home. I was glad, for I wanted Aleena to stay close to me for as long as possible.

I wasted the day away, anxious for what the night would bring. I was glad and fearful that I had told Aleena. What if she told Mother? No, she would never. I was still angry with her for not coming to see me, but I still desperately wanted her to join me. Though she had changed in the last few months, I was certain her sense of adventure was still there. I hoped she could come. I couldn't row a boat all by myself, and I really wanted a chance to speak to Aleena and spend some time with her before she had to leave. Father took us out once on a rowboat, but he rowed by himself while I enjoyed the water. He took Aleena for a few times to teach her, but I never joined them, for Digin Galia made sure I always had something to read.

I didn't even know where I could find a boat. I walked around my chambers, fidgeting. I wanted to leave my room, but my mother had forbidden it today. I was afraid to face her, besides, after the horror and scandal of last night.

Sometime in the late afternoon, I heard a knocking at my door. Janna opened the door and my father walked in. Bobbing into a curtsy, Janna left the room, closing the door behind her and leaving me alone with him. I sat at the edge of my bed, waiting for a scolding.

To my utter surprise, a smile broke over his face. "You have great spirit, my girl."

What?

"Spirit is good, Tamar. You are bold of spirit and strong of heart, a rare combination in one so young as you."

"I don't understand," I managed to say.

"You are, no doubt, in a lot of trouble. Your mother will certainly see to that. But during the eznmortel, I saw my daughter in a disguise, led solely by curiosity and pride for her culture. It was foolish and I had to divert attention from your carelessness, but

Tamar, if you harness those traits of yours, you can be so powerful. The entire world can know your name!"

I felt as though my father was feverish, just as I had been. "Aleena will be Queen, not I."

"It does not matter. You do not need to be Queen to be powerful. A simple milkmaid can be powerful and change her fate. And so can you. I am proud of you, Tamar."

He placed a hand over my head and rustled my hair affectionately, before leaving the room and allowing Janna to enter again. I curled up on my bed, wondering what had just happened. He was proud of me? I had most certainly brought humiliation upon his head, but he did not seem to care. Mother would not be so kind.

There was another knock at my door, and I went toward it, but Janna stepped in front of me. "Begging your pardon, but your mother said you are not to go outside."

"There was a knock at the door. I am only letting someone in."

"I shall do it for you," she said, moving to open the door. But before she could, it swung open, and Bedros strode in boldly.

He paused, seeing my huffing maid, who was appalled at the sight of a man striding purposefully into my room, and my blank expression, as if this was a regular occurrence. After a moment of silence where he appraised us both, he said, "Both of you standing by the door, and no one saw fit to open it?"

"Sorry, Bedros. I am not allowed to touch my door," I said and sighed, walking toward my window. He followed, while Janna stayed near the door, rocking on her heels. I could see her wondering whether or not to tell Mother, but after seeing my withering glance in her direction, she decided not to.

"Princess," he murmured sarcastically, rolling his eye, "wouldn't want to ruin your dainty little fingers."

I stifled a laugh and turned to him, raising my eyebrows. "What brings you here?"

His expression turned serious. "I wanted to see if you were all right."

"As you can see, I am perfectly fine." I smiled.

He did not seem convinced, but I lacked the will to convince him. Before the thought to dismiss him crossed my mind, I had the sudden realization that I needed his help. How to go about it? My father had said that I had the potential to be powerful. Could I? I shot a subtle glance at Janna, who was unsure whether to look at us. The mere idea that there was a man in here brought a sharp blush to her cheeks, and she kept her head bowed and slightly at an angle away from us. "I do need something, though," I murmured, stepping closer so she would not hear us. He raised his eyebrows. "Promise me you will help?"

"I promise anything, Princess."

"Good," I smiled. "Can we go for a walk tonight?"

He narrowed his eyes. "Why?"

"It is just a walk. We can stroll in our clearing in the woods. I just need some fresh air; it is unbearably stifling in here." I frowned.

He thought about it for a moment. I saw the disbelief in his eyes, for he knew me too well, but I could also see that the idea of us alone in the woods on a cold night was appealing, and he could not resist. "Yes, of course."

"You must convince Janna that it's my mother's idea, or else she will never let me out of here."

"I will," he nodded, eyes glimmering.

"Thank you," I said, standing up on my tiptoes and kissing him on the cheek, before I turned my back to him and signaled the end to our conversation.

⇥⊨○ ○⊨↤

I could feel that something had changed inside of me. During the wedding, I'd tasted freedom so delicious and sweet; the flavor lingered on my tongue. The nightmares had stained me, and the visions echoed in my mind, turning me away from the timid Tamar that I'd once been. My father had seen it and I could feel it. I knew I would not be able to sit within the confines of my room anymore, content with books that told stories of other places. I had to see and touch these other places for myself. A worm of restlessness had nestled its way inside my heart, and I would not be content until I fed it. And what it needed was not from this island.

Though feeling this newfound fire rushing through my veins, I decided to sit back and let Bedros do most of the work in order to plan my escape from the room. I had hardly waited an hour before there was a knock on the door. I feigned ignorance and continued to work at my studies. Janna opened the door and saw another maid standing in the hall and holding a simple platter with a note on top. She read the letter and dismissed the other girl with a nod. Nonchalant, as if I had more important matters to think of, I asked, "What is it?"

"You are to take a walk with Bedros, as your mother instructs."

"A walk? With Bedros? I shan't go." I turned to my papers.

"The queen has instructed it," she scolded suddenly, as I hid my smile. "And you'd best dress warmly; it looks dreadfully cold out there."

"I suppose I shall," I sighed, standing. I began to dress appropriately, wondering how Bedros had bribed the maid to deliver the forged letter. My face flushed at thinking about what he would have said or promised to her. It was just like Bedros to do something of the sort—the rascal. I layered thick socks under my skirts and wrapped several shawls around my shoulders and neck. I took my thickest coat, the one I only wore during winter when our island was covered in snow and the sky gray with clouds and wind. I tried to ignore the inkling of fear in my mind that Aleena would not come and my plan would be ruined. To be truthful, my plan was already built on shaky ground, as I had no idea how I would rid myself of Bedros. And I still had no boat.

But I needed him now, and so that mountain would be crossed later.

It did not take long after receiving the letter when there was another knock at my door. Janna huffed, frustrated, and opened the door to reveal Bedros standing there, bundled comfortably in his warm outfit and smiling at me. "Ready when you are, Princess."

"I'm ready," I said, grabbing my gloves and sliding them on. I nodded coolly at Janna as I walked out. I felt a pang of remorse for my coolness, for she was my favorite maid and was only following my mother's orders, but I was angry all the same.

We walked down the silent halls and, after what seemed like an eternity, finally burst out into the cool night air. I breathed in the fresh, crisp night, letting it fill my lungs and course through my body like a drink of fresh water. "So," said Bedros, not wasting any time, "what is this really about?"

"I have been cooped up all day. I wanted a walk," I said.

"With me?"

I nodded.

"Don't play dumb with me, Princess. I know who you are, and you always have a trick up your sleeve."

"I never have tricks up my sleeve. Aleena was always the mischievous one."

"At some point in growing up, your roles reversed."

I said nothing but continued walking.

"Where are we walking?"

"Where is your sense of adventure, Bedros?"

"It is currently hand in hand with my sense of suspicion. I don't trust you, Princess."

I stopped walking and glanced up at him. He raised his eyebrows.

"That hurt," I said simply.

I turned to walk again, but he stopped me with a soft touch on my elbow. "I apologize."

There was a moment of silence between us. I nodded slowly, slightly uncomfortable, and turned to walk again, but his hand slid down and took me by the hand, keeping it in a firm grasp as we trudged through the cold. My mouth opened in a silent gasp, but I continued walking as though nothing had happened. I tried to ignore the way his thumb slowly rubbed back and forth along my finger, but I could not stop thinking of it. I knew this was wrong; I should not tempt him in this way. But my determination at escaping my chains outweighed any other concern I had.

"May I ask you a question?" he asked. Prompted by my nodding, he continued, "Who was that man yesterday at Aleena's wedding?"

"Which man?" I asked, knowing perfectly well whom he was talking about. A tingle ran up my spine when I thought of him—the mysterious dancer, my childhood fancy.

"The man who sacrificed the calf."

"I do not know his name," I lied, "but he was one of the dancers."

"I do not like him."

"Why not?"

"He is a dirty sort. To put you in that position," he said.

When I looked at him, I was surprised at the anger in his face. "You're just sour because I spent most of my time with him instead of with you."

"Did you?" He pulled me to another stop. "Did you spend most of your time with him?"

"We will never make it at this pace," I huffed, pulling him along. "Tamar."

I tore my hand out of his grip. "Look, if you can't take a regular walk with me, then just leave."

I hoped with all my heart that he would grow angry and let his pride take control, but he only squared his shoulders and set his jaw with a solid, "No."

I tried not to show the disappointment in my face and gave a curt smile instead. We continued to walk, almost oblivious to the falling darkness that surrounded us. I should not have told him that I'd spent most of my time with Aleek. That was unseemly, especially since I had had no chaperone. I hoped he would not tell on me, but I doubted he would. I held many things over his head as well, so he would not even think of giving me up to my parents. I tried desperately to find a reason to separate from him, but all my ideas were falling flat as I realized he would do everything possible to stay near me.

I had one idea left, and I decided to try it. The time was coming near where I would have to meet Aleena, and I feared what Bedros would say if he knew what we were up to. I wrapped my arms around myself and shuddered as if I was filled with a sudden cold.

"What has happened?" he asked.

"It is desperately cold," I muttered.

As I knew he would, he put an arm around me and slid his hand up and down my arm, the friction bringing forth heat to my body. "Is it working?"

I stopped walking and turned into him, my head burrowing into his chest. "Bedros, I'm frightfully cold."

"We shall go back inside," he said immediately, turning me back around.

"No!" I grabbed his arms, looking up at him. "I can't! I like it here; it has been so dreadful all day cooped up inside the palace. I want to walk for just an hour more. I just need my fur shawl."

"Your fur shawl? In your chamber?"

"Yes, but, alas, it is so far."

He was hesitant for a moment, and I could feel his head moving to survey our surroundings. Something flickered in his eyes, and I saw the suspicion.

He knew this was it. This was where I would reveal the trick up my sleeve, but he was caught at a crossroads. To accept would be falling into my trap, but to refuse would be risking everything he had built with me. I almost felt bad for him, but it was not enough to abandon my plan. He looked at me, straight in the eyes, hoping I would leave it be, but I squared my shoulders and challenged him with a glint in my eyes. For a moment, I thought he would refuse and get angry with me for trying to separate from him like that.

But to my utter surprise, he stepped back and whipped out of his topcoat, putting it over my shoulders. "Stay here. Sit on the side, out of the road's way, so no one sees you. I shall be back soon." He turned, hesitated, and then twisted back around, took my hand, and kissed my knuckles as a gentleman would. Then he ran off. He perhaps assumed that this small gesture would give me second thoughts about abandoning him.

"Bedros!" I called from behind him, but I didn't know what I would say. When he turned around, I blurted, "Thank you."

⋅→╾▣ ▣╼←⋅

It was a short walk from that point to the clearing, and I was intent on arriving soon, having wasted too much time in idle chatter. In the back of my mind, I vaguely worried about Bedros and what I would say to him after, but he would not be angry for too long. It was not his way. Lightly, I touched my knuckles where he'd kissed me, feeling the gloves that were cooling quickly from the suddenness of his warm breath. It was wrong of me to flirt with him in that way and to use him. I sighed and wondered when I would face the consequences.

The darkness was thick during my run, but I knew how to get to the clearing. After years of using the clearing as our sanctuary,

I could reach it with my eyes shut. When I burst into the clearing, I saw Aleena waiting, her eyes shining in the moonlight, the rest of her body hidden in the shadows. "Where have you been?" she asked.

"I was with Bedros. It took me a while to escape him." She nodded slowly. "I will answer all your questions on the way, but we need a row—"

She held up a silencing hand. "I already have the boat. It is on the shore."

I was quiet.

"I met your Karin," she explained. "After your disaster at my wedding, I sought out who the boy was, and I was directed to his sister. She told me you were to meet her the next night."

My eyes widened. "Did she see you?"

"No, I covered my face. I assumed you did not reveal to her your identity, or she would not be daft enough to invite you over there."

"Yes, I had covered my face," I muttered.

"Shall we go then?" She gestured extravagantly toward the shore.

"You are not opposed?"

A sparkle came to her eyes. "Do you not know me, Tamar?"

I smiled, and we ran down to the beach, where, sure enough, I saw the rowboat wedged into the sand. I uttered a small yelp of excitement. I did not ask her where she had found the rowboat and how she had brought it here, for Aleena usually had her way with what she wanted. With her on one side and me on the other, we pushed and thrust our weight onto the boat so that it slid smoothly into the water. We ran alongside the boat until the icy water reached our knees; then Aleena jumped into the boat and helped me in to sit next to her. The long wooden oars were in our hands in a flash, and we began paddling hard against the waves, so we would not be pushed backward toward our beach.

We rowed in silence, the only noise being the splashing of the water against our boat and our grunting as we strained against the waves. And finally, after what seemed an eternity, we passed the rough shallow waters and reached the calmness of the deep.

"How do we know which direction we are going?" asked Aleena, putting down her oar to massage her shoulders. I kept rowing slowly to keep us in one direction. Her voice sounded flat in the silence around us.

"We follow the light," I responded.

"Which light?"

I sighed with wariness. "I would assume that one." I pointed toward a spot right over her shoulder. She turned her head and saw the small light shining steadily in the distance.

"A candle?"

"What else would it be?"

She turned and looked at me, her back ramrod straight and stiff, and though it was dark, I could feel her gaze burning into me. The glow of the candle cast a dim halo over her head. "This is eerie."

"I know."

We were quiet after. The silence was incredible around us; I could almost see it drifting around our heads in a dense mist, ominous and imposing. The darkness only made it worse. The water was ink black, as if it had no end to it, the mouth of a merciless monster that was poised wide open, ready to swallow us whole should we fall in. The only light we could see was the shining light, and I kept my eyes on it, afraid that if I blinked, it would disappear, and we would be stranded with no direction and little hope.

"Why did you not come to see me?" The question escaped my lips before I could stop to think.

She sighed, the sound thin, like a whisper compared to the wind that blew around us and disturbed the waters of Lake Van. "There are duties that we must follow, especially the night of a wedding."

She was speaking in riddles again. "What duties?"

"You will learn soon enough, Tamar," she replied with a resolute firmness to her voice that stopped me from asking any more questions.

"I had terrible nightmares," I told her.

"Tell me about them."

I thought for a moment, listening to the water slap against the bottom of the boat. "I saw you—you were holding a calf and there was blood crossed over your arms, like an Arabic wedding henna design. Then when you looked up at me, I fell into your eyes, which was the lake, and I was trying to swim to the shore."

She thought for a moment, her face serious. "I suppose it could mean that we are both losing ourselves in the strangeness of my wedding."

I nodded, wondering if I should tell her about the pomegranate that I saw—the pomegranate that I believed alluded to the one she used before her attempt at jumping off the cliff. I decided against it. She would feel terrible if she knew that her actions worried me so much.

"Dreams are fascinating..." she said, musing. "We analyze them and pick at them, as though we are fortunetellers, but they are only our deepest thoughts disguised as visualizations. And when we unveil a meaning from it, we are surprised, as though we never expected ourselves to have such thoughts as those."

I nodded. "We are not often allowed to have certain thoughts, so I suppose I am not surprised that we have such vivid dreams. It is the only time that it is safe to have them."

She nodded, glancing over at me almost sadly. "At least we are safe in our heads."

"We are nearing the shore," I said, suddenly realizing that the light on the shore had grown clearer. "My name is Lori," I told her.

She nodded. "I shall be..." A small smile came to her lips as she thought about what name she could give herself. "Arpi."

I nodded. "Her name is Karin, as you know. Her brother's name is Aleek."

Her face was serious now. "About Aleek..." she began.

Uh oh.

"What do you think of him?"

"He was interesting; very different from people I have met." I was careful in the description, unsure of how far to take it.

"He was a handsome man," she said. I stared at her, and after a moment, she glanced over at me and grinned mischievously.

"Really, Aleena?"

She raised her eyebrows at me. "Love works in mysterious ways," she responded.

I scoffed. "I have met him barely for an hour."

She shrugged. "An hour is sometimes all you need."

I let her sentence drift into silence, as we both lost ourselves in our thoughts.

It did not take as long as I thought it would to arrive, for soon the light had become more defined despite the haze that fell over the water. I looked into the ripples underneath our boat and wondered how that boy felt in the legend, crossing this same lake on the same route, except from inside the cold water instead of in a dry boat like us. Chills raised on my arms as I thought of his will and determination to reach his true love.

The looming dark mountains on the mainland showed clearer now, and my heart beat faster for anticipation of what we would find there. But as soon as the bottom of the boat scraped against the sand on the shore, my anticipation gave way to excitement, and I fought the urge to whoop with victory at finally having escaped the confines of my island.

Chapter 14

THE WIND WHIPPED at our hair as we struggled to pull the boat up onto the shore. We had to pull it high enough, so the water would not steal it away in the middle of our dance lesson. The lake was notoriously moody at this time of year, and I hoped silently that tonight would be a calm one. The wind did not seem dangerously strong as of yet, so we breathed with ease.

While we pulled the boat, I looked around at the beach. Higher up away from us, I saw the shine of the light, and I noticed that Karin had placed the candle in an alcove among several overhanging rocks, so the wind would not extinguish it. As soon as I noticed the candle, I saw a small dark figure appear near the candle, spot us under the moonlight, and then bound over to our side.

"Let me help!" Karin cried excitedly, pulling the boat alongside us. When it was safely rooted into the dry sand, we dissolved into disbelieving laughter at the unspoken scandal that we were all committing.

"I was afraid you wouldn't come! After what happened at the wedding," she said breathlessly.

Slightly embarrassed, I managed a laugh and said, "I wouldn't miss a chance like this! I know you met each other already, but formally, this is my sister, Arpi."

"So you wish to dance as well?" asked Karin.

"Yes," my sister said and nodded, unable to disguise the excitement in her eyes. Our shawls were tight over the bottom half of our faces so that Karin would not discover who we were. They also kept us slightly warmer, and at this time of night, the cold was bitingly harsh. Karin had lifted up her scarf as well to cover her face, so we looked quite the trio as we stood on the beach in the billowing wind, wrapped tightly so only our eyes showed, glimmering in the darkness.

It was here in those dismal conditions that our dancing lessons began, around the small candle that Karin had placed in that alcove where the wind was unable to reach us as strongly. It whistled just out of our reach, eager to pull us into its swirling embrace. Karin stood between us, holding our hands, and began to teach us the steps.

Once I used to scorn our dances, for they all looked very similar in that we stood in a circle and danced in the general direction to the right. But I began to see the uniqueness and the stories that each dance held, and I grew excited with each step, even though we were still only learning the basics. One by one, adding more steps each time, we began to feel as if we were really dancing. We learned that the true dancing was not even in the steps that we knew, but in how the beat ran through our bodies.

It was in the way our knees slightly bent with the rhythm of Karin's humming and our heels popped off the ground subtly that made the dance so powerful. It was in the way we held on to each other firmly and the music ran equally in all of us that made the dance so uniting. It was in the way our chins were initially forced to stay up, proudly, that helped us learn the dance with our hearts, and not just our legs, so that eventually our chins lifted up naturally. And as women, it was up to us to make all those beats in the dance just fluid enough so that we were graceful and beautiful, even as the men would be rough and strong.

We came to the mainland for weeks, planning on spontaneous days so that no one realized our pattern if we were unfortunate enough to be followed one night. We learned so much from this little girl I had come to admire for her passion and her willingness to teach two strangers how to dance. I was so surprised at her knowledge and bitterly embarrassed that Aleena and I had not been taught this throughout our young lives. The stories and dances were passed down through generations in the villages. Karin's parents and village elders had taught her and her brother the stories. And she now passed this on to Aleena and me.

We also learned the spiritual and religious and romantic side of our dances. When I was home, I would disappear into our library and find numerous books on old village dances. I pored over them for hours, losing myself among the pages, finding the stories and origins of the dances, and filling my mind with the romance and inspiration I found there. When I went into the village sometimes just to walk, I would try to engage in conversation with some of the elders, gathering information.

I learned a dance called *Mayroke*, which represented the way village women cut wheat. The arms moved forward and back in repeated motions, making it seem as if we were slicing down stems of wheat. Another dance was *Msho Khr*, which originated from the region of Moosh, described as being very rocky and mountainous. I had never been there, but from the stories, it was made clear that the villagers had not enough open space to be able to dance elaborate and wide dances. Msho Khr was danced with the people standing incredibly close to each other and moving in very tight steps.

I loved these dances, but my favorite, of course, was Tzaghkadzori, the dance we first saw performed at Aleena's wedding. But I was not advanced yet to dance it fluidly, though I remembered the song so vividly and longed to dance once more to its tune.

On one of the days we met, Karin began to teach us a dance called *Tarsbar*, which translates to "backward dance." Instead of going to the right, this dance led us generally toward the left. Held together by our pinky fingers, we were a bit thrown off by the changes in direction. For every three steps to the left, there were two steps to the right. We were intent on getting all the steps right without bumping into each other, when Aleena asked, "Why are we always in circles?"

"For protection," replied Karin.

"I thought it was unity," I said. She glanced at me. I shrugged.

"Well, both. We unite against evil. We unite and make a wall, so the devil can't enter our souls and corrupt our lives."

We let our hands go and stopped dancing for a small rest. I rubbed my pinky, which was sore from Karin's strong grip. She smiled at us, thoroughly enjoying her job as our teacher. "We are safe and peaceful when we dance to the right; we are appealing to

God. But when we break that harmony, the devil can take over, because we have become weak. In Tarsbar, we dance to the left, yes, but our left legs must never enter the circle. We still step with the right leg. We dance this dance at funerals or weddings or baptisms, when the soul is most vulnerable to change. In this way, we are warning the devil to stay away from these souls. When we dance to the left, we stomp hard with the left leg, because we are stepping on the devil and casting him out."

We joined hands again, and she explained as we danced. "Three steps to the left, and on the third step, we stomp hard, bounding back to the right for the next two steps. On the second step, we step inside the circle with our right leg and raise our hands up to God, to call him down to hear us and to protect us."

I smiled; I couldn't help it. These were stories that spoke to me, stories that I could understand and relate to and really feel with every beat of my heart. We danced and danced until the moves were a part of us, ripping through our bodies with such fervor. Our stomps sounded louder and stronger with each set, until I truly felt as if I were stomping on the devil underneath the soles of my feet. I felt as if I were grinding him into the sand, and when I raised my hands to God, I felt a hope, such as I had never felt before. I was calling him down to me, and it was then that I learned also what else the dance was about.

It was about being cautious and about knowing the consequences of our actions. We stomped on the devil, but there is a reason the devil can take so many souls with him. He is strong. He knows our weaknesses. So we turn to God for his protection, just in case the devil should wish to get his revenge.

Most of the dances followed this theme of a struggle between dark and light, evil and good. What was beautiful about them was that, as long as we stayed together, good would always prevail. We were always protected.

⊷⊜ ⊜⊶

The weeks passed in a blur. Every few nights, Aleena and I would find ourselves scurrying out of the castle, hidden in shadows and secrets to hie away to our trusted boat. I was always excited, spurred on by a strong eagerness of the forbidden. I was living at last!

Aleena, however, began to show some doubts. She had greater troubles. In order to escape the night from Vartan, she would tell him she wanted to spend the nights with me. He would not ask questions at first, but as the weeks passed, he began to loathe the idea and slandered her for not being a dutiful wife. The nights they spent together consisted of her trying to fulfill her duty though they both hated each other. I knew he was angry with her because she would not conceive a child, and so he tried as often as he could, and Aleena had to bear it.

I learned what these "duties" were of course, and they disgusted me, but only because it was *him*. To think of Vartan using Aleena in that way, to think of her having to lie there and endure this, I understood her sullenness, for I imagined those duties would destroy the spirit.

While she was harassed by Vartan on one end, Bedros began to question me on the other. He knew we were up to something since the first day I gave him the slip. He came by often to my chambers, wanting to talk, but I never gave him any of the puzzle pieces to figure out my nightly adventures with Aleena and Karin. I changed my friendship with him, for it was too risky now. I could not let him—or anyone else in both of our families—see that I was interested in a relationship with him in any way. I treated him as a brother, hoping he would not see past that.

One day, I was sitting in my chambers with Lilit, and we were both sewing half-heartedly and talking of our days to come. I had told Lilit about what I was doing, but she could not join us, as she traveled back and forth often between her home and our island. She sat on a chair, while I sat neatly on the Persian carpet laid on my floor.

"When will you be leaving again?" I asked her.

"Soon," she pouted. "I wish I could just live with you."

"I know," I sighed. "Then you could come with us."

"You will teach me the dances though?" she asked.

"Of course, Lilit!"

But suddenly, Bedros strolled in. He glanced around and commented, "No Janna to scold me for my intrusion?"

"She is with her mother," I said, exchanging a look with Lilit.

"If you do not mind, Bedros, this is our time together and we would much rather be alone," she said. She knew of my aversion to him and aided in my endeavors to be free of his company.

He smirked at her. "You can have your alone time at any point later." She clenched her fists, but before she could speak, he pronounced, "I need to speak with Tamar alone."

She glanced at me, and after a second of hesitation, I nodded for her to leave. With a huff, she walked out. "I will come by later," she said with a warning look at Bedros before the door closed behind her.

Bedros walked over and sat in the chair she had been sitting in. He glanced at me. Yarn surrounded me while I slowly knitted a scarf for Karin in her favorite colors of blue and silver. He stared at me like this for some time, until he suddenly broke the silence. "Knitting?"

"Yes."

"Since when?"

"New hobby."

He was silent for a moment. "Are you meeting a man?"

"Heavens!" I gasped. "Is that a serious question?"

"You are sneaking off in the middle of the night to some mysterious place. I am sure there is a man involved," he muttered.

"If there is, then he lives in your fantasies, for I am not meeting any man," I said curtly, my fingers flying swiftly over the knitting. "Besides, how do you know I am sneaking off in the middle of the night?"

"Sometimes I come by to say hello after hours, and you are not here," he said, his face reddening.

I shot him an irritated look, but I was worried. He came to my chambers? At night? What if he told someone that I was not there?

"Who is that scarf for?"

"Aleena."

"She hates silver."

"Not when it is mixed with blue," I retorted.

"Why won't you tell me, Tamar?"

"Why do you care?"

He gave me a look. "You know why I care."

My face flushed, and I looked down. I dared not take the bait. Instead I said, "I suggest you stop asking me where I am going. I will not tell you anything."

"I will find out; you know that, right?"

My fingers paused only for a moment, but it was long enough for him to notice. "Not if I can help it."

There was a split second of silence; then he leaned forward with his cocky grin and said slowly in his typical mocking tone, "You can't."

⇥⊙⊙⇤

The dances were just as interesting as ever, but Aleena began to sit out of the lessons, brooding over whatever had happened to her that day. The first few times she did this, I begged and pleaded for her to come join us. After I was promptly refused, I continued the lessons with Karin, paying no heed to her quiet presence that watched over us like a disturbed spirit. She began to arrive late to where I waited for her by the boat, and we always got into little arguments at the shore before we set off. It all seemed superficial though; I knew her enough to know that her frustration was deeper than just lack of sleep from the dancing. It bothered me that she never told me what was running through her mind. I asked her over and over what Vartan had said to her—or done to her—but she stayed silent.

I missed her fire; I missed her bite.

It seemed as if Bedros was right: somewhere along the way, Aleena and I had switched roles. I used to be the one to sit passively by and watch the action from a distance. Aleena would bound around, her wooden sword brandished in her hand, howling war cries, despite the shocked gasps of the servants and relatives. Aleena was drifting slowly from the person she once was, and it seemed as though I was stepping in to take over.

The day finally came when Aleena did not appear at the shore. I had known this day would come, but I foolishly had not prepared for it. I waited for a solid hour, unsure of what to do. But I could not keep Karin waiting. I watched the dark water and the glimmering candle in the distance for a long time, trying to conjure up the courage to go by myself. I almost turned back to the palace. I was halfway back up the beach, before I stopped, squinted at the candlelight that beckoned to me from the distance, and decided I needed to do this. I needed to be independent. It took a long time, but I pushed the boat slowly down the sandy shore and jumped into it as soon as it was freed by the sand.

It was eerie being on the lake by myself. There was hardly a whisper of wind that night, and the water was icy flat around me, the stars from the sky shining in the reflection. It was so tempting to dip my toe into the water or even slip under the surface and swim for a bit, but I dared not stray from the boat. With my eyes set upon the candle, I rowed and rowed, only breathing a sigh of relief when the bottom of the boat scraped against the sand at the shore.

As soon as I arrived, I told Karin that my sister was ill and would not be joining us. She seemed to believe me and was in awe that I had managed to travel across the lake all by myself. Wasting no time, we set to practicing the dances as if nothing was amiss. I was proud to say that, at this point, I knew most of the moves. I only wished we had the actual music to dance to, instead of Karin's humming.

The next morning, at breakfast, I sat across from Aleena and tried to catch her eyes, but she would not look at me. After I was scolded promptly by my mother for clearing my throat continually in an unladylike fashion, I kicked my sister's shin lightly with my boot. Her eyes widened, and a breathless gasp escaped her lips. Vartan glanced at her, and she pretended nothing had happened, but she managed to give me a piercing look as soon as he looked away. I shot her an equally angry look and mouthed, "We need to talk," but she merely averted her eyes.

Bedros, who had watched the whole thing, leaned over and whispered in my ear, "Is everything all right?" I nodded, not making eye contact with him. "I told you she wouldn't like the scarf."

I nudged his side, invoking another withering look from my mother.

I could hardly wait through breakfast, for I had frustration in me that needed to be let out. Breakfast was generally very tedious for me, as it was our only meal that was formal, but today was exceptionally dreary. It was normally a small family affair, but since the wedding, Vartan's entire family was invited to join us in the dining hall for breakfast. The food was simple, but the company was not. I wished Lilit could be here, but she had gone back home with her father.

As soon as we were dismissed at last, I managed to corner Aleena in the hallway, not willing to go down without a fight. "Let me pass, Tamar," she said, almost tiredly.

"Why did you leave me there?"

"I did not leave you there."

"You left me alone, to fend for myself. What if I had died? What if I had drowned?"

"If you were going to die, you would have died whether I would have been there or not."

I paused at her chilling words. "What?"

She shook her head, as if her thoughts had not been her own. "Let me pass; I will not ask again."

"Good, don't ask again," I said, standing strong. I wished she would push me or slap me or scream, but she was as timid as a mouse. She tried edging past me, but I reached out and wrapped my fingers around her arm. "Aleena."

She winced, as though in pain, and when I removed my fingers, I noticed a deep blue bruise on her arm. "What is that?" I cried.

"Tamar," she warned, her eyes leveling me with a look. "What do you want?"

"To *talk* to you. I want you to tell me what is going on. What is Vartan doing to you?"

"He does not want me leaving the house anymore."

"Why not? Aleena, you have to fight him."

"It is not worth it, Tamar."

"And what, pray tell, is worth it?" She stayed silent, her face serious but her eyes holding such pain that it hurt to see. "Aleena, please," I said, my expression softening.

"You are a big girl now. You do not need me," she said softly, brushing past me.

I stepped aside, letting her pass this time. There was nothing more to say except, "I do need you," but she would never believe me. I turned and watched her walk down the long hallway, her steps light and cautious, as if she were a cat. But instead of hunting, she was the one being hunted.

She did not look back; she did not look around. I watched her porcelain figure grow smaller and smaller until the dark of the hall swallowed her whole, as if it were the waters of the lake, the hungry mouth opened wide to accept anyone into its empty belly.

That was when I knew that all those months ago, when Aleena almost jumped into the lake, she actually had. Her soul had left her that night. She didn't need to jump in order to die.

I hardly saw Aleena after that, except for breakfast, dinner, and supper. And being with the family, it was hard to maintain a conversation between us. Vartan demanded most of her attention, and Bedros, perhaps bored of the tedious family get-togethers, demanded much of mine. I tried to ignore the knowing looks that our parents gave to one another when Bedros came to sit at my side.

The only way I was able to get through these dismal days was the anticipation of the coming night, when I would steal away in the shadows and row along toward the mainland. I had become much more confident with the boat and the oars, my arms growing stronger with every journey that I made across the waters. It was on the mainland, hand in hand with Karin, that I made my first true friendship with someone outside of my family and learned how to express my passions through the art of simple dancing.

Chapter 15

I SAT IN my room, gazing out my window, eager for nightfall to cover the land so that I might be able to go to Karin. I was worried for the storms that would be raging soon, as winter approached. The lake had an infamous nasty temper and could erupt into violent rages with me caught helplessly in the middle. I wished Aleena would come with me, but the matter was closed.

The pomegranate that had signaled Aleena's attempted suicide—I cringed at the thought—sat in front of me, on the ledge. Its luster had faded, the red shell turning a darker shade. I had not touched it since that fated day, and it winked at me every night, reflecting the diamonds that glittered from the lake. I sighed lightly at the thought.

Such illusions—they could tempt the strongest soul into their poisonous arms. I imagined the pomegranate I saw in my dreams—the one that melted in my grasp, slipping through my fingertips as I tried so hard to hold it together. I closed my eyes, losing myself in my thoughts as the quiet breeze kissed my cheeks, leaving them tinged with a fresh red.

"Oh, were I a painter," said a voice from behind me. I turned, half surprised to see Bedros leaning against the inside of my door, regarding me with his glimmering eyes. He had entered my chamber without my knowledge. A flush worked its way up my neck.

"I must teach you how to knock one of these days."

He sauntered over to a chair not far from where I sat and made himself comfortable as if this were his room as well. "You used to be more charitable toward me."

"I've grown some."

He raised his eyebrows. "Yes, you have."

"Why are you in my room, Bedros?"

"I'm always here, and you never ask me that question."

"Today I would like to know."

"I wanted to talk to you."

"Well, *talk*," I said, regarding him coolly.

"Tell me why you are being this way."

As if his words triggered an unspoken emotion inside me, I stood suddenly, fierce and poised. "*This* way? Are you blind, Bedros?"

"Ah! There is the girl I once knew," he said with a glint in his eyes as he stood as well to face me directly. "Tell me why you call me blind."

"I am protecting us."

"From whom?"

"Everyone. The way you act toward me in public, Bedros, our parents will believe we have intentions to get married, and they *will* act on it; I can promise you that."

"Is that so horrible?"

I froze, his words filling me with a slick dread. "Yes. Yes, that is."

"Why?"

"Did you not hear what I said? You and I, bound together in marriage—we'd kill each other."

"It would not be a dull marriage; that is for sure."

"You are impossible," I said, turning my back to him.

"Tamar...Tamar, look at me," he said, his voice so serious that I had to face him. "Please don't shut me out. You are all I have."

Perhaps it was the soft way he said that or the expression on his face, but after a moment of hesitation, I lost my fight and sat down with an unladylike thump into a chair. His brother must have been abominable to him as well, just as much as Aleena was ignoring me. Bedros was not even in his home, but living in a palace he was just as uncomfortable in as I was. He stepped forward and kneeled on the floor at my feet, taking my hands in his. I tried to pull away, lightly, but he was firm. His eyes gazed into mine. "And I am all you have."

After a moment of looking at him wonderingly, I managed to pull my hand away, shaking my head slowly. "No. You are wrong."

I turned my face away dismissively toward the window, where the shine of the lake was slowly fading with the setting sun. I did not know for a moment if I was lying to him or if I was lying to myself, and I could not look at him to see if he thought the same thing. So I stayed quiet, willing the prideful war inside me to ease down into nothing as I watched the darkness fall. It was not long after that I heard his soft footsteps fading as he left my room and shut the door quietly behind him, leaving no trace that he had been in my room at all, except for the fast beating of my heart.

⋆►━● ●━►⋆

That night, hidden under a thick winter cloak, I made my way to the boat, which waited patiently to take me over on its usual route to the place where I could laugh and dance to my heart's content. But today the waves were stronger than before.

I had anticipated a storm, but my urge to reach the mainland was stubborn, and so I boarded the boat and rowed through the rougher waters. The waves were thicker, not always letting my oars break the surface to push on the boat. I panicked a few times when the boat was rocked about precariously, threatening to tip me into the watery depths, and I held on to the sides in fear, my fingers grasping the rough wood. I lost all sense of direction as my focus was completely on keeping myself alive. I was almost blindly rowing, trying desperately to steer the boat toward its destination. If it weren't for the light burning steadily on the horizon, I would have completely lost my way. The legend of Akhtamar entered my thoughts and I felt helpless as the lake threatened with its haunting promise. I looked into the roiling water beneath me for a moment, and in my state of delusion, I almost saw *him:* the nameless boy from the legend swimming underneath the turbulent waves, focusing on reaching the horizon and keeping himself alive for *her* sake, for Tamar's sake. I winced at the thought. There was so much pain in this world from people not being allowed to do what their hearts desired.

The image was gone in the water, and I was able to focus on the candlelight, my arms straining and chest heaving.

With my breath labored and my clothes almost soaked through from the splatter of the waves, I arrived at the mainland in a soggy mess. I was lucky it did not turn into a full storm, for that would have been my end, certainly.

When I saw Karin, her eyes widened, and she cried, "What in heaven's name?"

"There is a storm tonight," I managed wryly through chattering teeth.

Karin gazed across at Lake Van, and the look in her eyes made fresh goose bumps rise over my skin. "This is not a storm," she said. I cocked my head in puzzlement, and she clarified, "You would not be standing here if there was a storm. And that boat"—she pointed at my only means of transportation—"would not be a boat anymore, but a pile of splintered wood."

I nodded, my breath caught in my throat, but she came forward and hugged me tight, calming me with that simple gesture. "Oh, I almost forgot!" I cried.

I turned and grabbed a small parcel out of the boat, holding it in front of her bright face. The paper was darkened by water, and I hoped the gift was not ruined.

"What is this?" she cried, but I saw the glee in her eyes and heard the excitement lining her voice.

"For your birthday tomorrow!"

She glanced at me, silent for a moment. I thought she would be angry, and my smile faded into a moment of worry. But then she murmured, "You remembered?"

"Of course I remembered, Karin! Happy birthday, dear," I said, hugging her tightly once more.

"Is today the day?" she asked distractedly, as she opened the package with all the eagerness of the child that she was.

"Is today what day?"

"That I get to see your face."

I froze from the shock. Not once had she ever asked that question. "No, Karin."

As if that conversation did not just happen, she lifted the delicate scarf I had made for her with great excitement and wrapped it around her thin neck. "Oh, Lori! I love it!"

I winced slightly at the use of my fake name. I was such a horrible friend.

"I hoped you would. I used your favorite colors!"

"The material is so fine," she said in a hushed voice, her fingers running along the soft yarn.

"Come, let us dance!" I took her hand, hoping she would forget the material, but she tugged slightly.

"Actually I am to tell you that you are welcome to have dinner with my family tonight—for my birthday."

I froze in horror. "You are to tell me? By whom?"

"My family," she said, as she turned away to walk up the beach, gesturing at me invitingly with her hand.

"Karin! I am soaked! I am hardly ready for a social gathering. And it is midnight!"

She gave me a look, as if I were stupid for opening my mouth. "If you stay out here in this cold, you will catch your death. My house is warm; we always have a fire burning. And we always celebrate well into the night on the eve of a birthday."

"Karin! Karin…" I chased her as she continued to walk. "I mustn't! Your family shouldn't know about me. Oh, the scandal!" I cried, flustered.

"They think it is perfectly fine! I have never had a friend like you. Please, Lori. Come with me." I looked into the wide, pleading eyes of my best friend.

Damn.

My sigh hinted at my decision, and she yelped in excitement, pulling and prodding me with her toward her house.

I was a nervous wreck when we arrived at her house. It did not help that it was a run-down wooden building, blackened by the damp of the wind blowing constantly from the lake and the many years that it was standing. I tried my best to hide the nicer fabric of my clothes, which peeked out from underneath my cloak, hoping that they would not notice or question it.

Karin opened the door and flew in, leaving me stricken in the doorway. "Mother! Father! Look what Lori made for me for my birthday!" I heard the appreciative murmurs at the fineness of the scarf, and I almost regretted using the precious silk for her present. I had assumed our nightly adventures and associations with each other were kept a secret.

"Lori! Come inside!" I heard her call. Taking a deep breath, I walked inside to the modest house and immediately saw the table set up with a small feast, illuminated by two simple candles. There were different types of meat and salads and small pastries filled with cheese and eggplant. Wine was poured into small clay cups and positioned around the table, ready for use. No one noticed me walk in, and my face flushed for a moment. I could just imagine the sight I presented: a ragtag girl in a cloak much too big for her, soaked through, with lanky, wet hair dripping from her head, runny nose and red cheeks, with wide frightened eyes.

I saw a man at the table with a cigar between his lips, while a heavyset woman lifted the plates above everyone's heads to place them carefully on the table. There was a bustle of noise, and I noticed that other members of the family were sitting farther out in the living room, waiting to be called in.

But what rooted me to my spot was the young man seated near his father who stood slowly with respect upon my entrance, all muscles taut and waiting for my next move. Familiar eyes—eyes that had haunted my nights—watched me closely, measured, calculated. I felt a prickling throughout my body, as if cold air was hugging me close. His eyes. Those eyes—they peeled away the layers of my clothes, unveiling my face and revealing my identity to the world.

As if her voice was coming from underwater, I vaguely heard Karin make the necessary introductions: "Mother and Father, this is my friend Lori. Aleek, you remember Lori, I am sure, from the princess's wedding." Her voice was wry.

He nodded, his eyes fixed on mine, while I made my way to the mother and gave her the traditional greeting kisses, one on each cheek, and shook the father's hand. I could not trust myself to speak just yet, for my throat had closed into a squeak of a hole. Instead, I gave Aleek another lingering glance accompanied by a polite nod and turned to the mother, who said, "Please, make yourself at home. We are so grateful that Karin has made a friend!"

Karin blushed at that, her cheeks turning a sweet pink, as we positioned ourselves around the table. She leaned in and whispered, "I have other friends too."

"Me too, of course," I whispered back. She giggled.

The rest of the family pulled chairs up to the same table and, in a state of much agitation at the cramped state, they all smiled as if nothing else mattered. I was seated between Karin and her father, who was talking loudly to Karin's uncle over the table. I assumed it was his brother, for they were very casual and forward with one another. The conversation was unlike anything I had ever heard, and it was very abrupt and loud.

"How's the back, old man?"

"Still as weak as ever; how's yours?"

"Stronger than a bull's."

His wife cut in with a sharp, "Is that why you were complaining of carrying my rice the other day?"

"Rice is women's work. Men are built for hunting and working."

The women laughed and turned to one another to tease the men, and I watched them with a mixture of fascination and humiliation, my face red from the coarseness of their talk. It was so different than any gathering at the palace. There, we were watched and judged and picked and preened over, until one could lose one's appetite. I had no permission to speak at that table, and if I dared open my mouth, it was to be short and polite. We were quiet, careful not to make any noise, even if chewing a piece of crunchy food or laughing or sneezing. A "proper" lady was as quiet as a church mouse and as disciplined as Digin Galia's pomegranate whip.

But here, conversation spread through all the guests until I could not separate one voice from another. My head spun from the noise, as if flies were buzzing loudly around me. I tried hiding my ruddy cheeks, but the conversation as well as the body heat of all the guests brought the harsh flush to my cheeks. I wished that I could have pulled off my headscarf, for the heat had gathered inside and created my own personal sauna. In the midst of my struggles, I vaguely noticed Aleek glance at me with heated curiosity, and it almost took my breath away, but I maintained as calm a composure as I possible could.

In trying to lean over to catch his brother's attention, Karin's father suddenly moved his arm in a sweeping gesture, tipping over his cup and shattering it against the floor to spill its contents on the ground. The clay pieces flew in separate directions, while the wine splashed against the bottom of my dress, soaking it to my skin. I jumped up, sliding the chair across the ground in shock and fear, for my skirts would be revealed if anyone tried helping me. A great ruckus immediately ensued at his cry of, "Why are we seating so many damn people at such a small table?"

Karin's mother snapped back, "Make us a larger table, and perhaps you will not have to break anything and horrify our guests. Every day, he breaks something in this house."

"If you stop placing breakable objects on the edges of tables, I am sure I will not break anything."

"Oh, I have to do everything, don't I?"

"Lusine, have a drink and relax—come now." The uncle smiled, with a warm glow to his flushed cheeks. Instead of complying, she stood and walked over to me, taking my arm to lead me to the basin that was filled with warm, soapy water. I saw her grab a wet rag, and horrified, I managed to say, "If you please, I'd rather clean it myself."

She paused and looked at me. For a moment, I thought she would be angry, but her face softened. I saw she was a pretty woman, weathered in time by work and poverty. She had clear blue eyes set into her olive complexion, and there were early wrinkles that marked her face, like memories that one can never be rid of. "You have been raised well," she said only, handing me the rag.

"Thank you," I sighed, relieved. I slipped out the door into the welcoming darkness. The cool air was a refreshing change to the stuffy inside. A small room filled with a lot of people was bound to get warm fast. It did not help that the clay oven was still hot from the earlier cooking; it had filled the room with a heavy heat. I stood a moment, filling my lungs deeply. When I was able to breathe normally and the color of my face returned to normal, I looked down at my skirts. The red wine had spread up the dress, leaving a dark mark that resembled a violent gash, as if I had torn it on a branch. It smelled strongly, and I cursed the sticky spirits. I could never understand the appeal of fermented grapes. I rubbed the towel against the stain, hoping that it would make a difference. Mother would be furious if she saw. Digin Galia would be furious—more than furious. My skin tightened at the thought of her whip carving the punishments into my palms.

There was a movement behind me, and I whipped around. Karin stood at the doorway, her eyes wide at my sudden jump.

"You frightened me," I breathed.

"Sorry! Do you need help?" she asked.

"I think I'm just about finished. I'll just have to wait until it dries to see if this helped at all," I said, giving it another good scrub before placing the rag into her outstretched hands.

"Sorry about that," she said solemnly. "My father is very rough."

"Please do not apologize to me," I replied, making sure the smile showed in my voice. It was difficult to show emotions without the help of my facial expressions. My shawl stayed fixed around my face with the help of a wooden brooch. "I rather like your family. They are very interesting."

She appeared to like that, and all was better it seemed. We walked inside, heading to our places, but Karin's mother turned to her husband and said, "Come sit next to your brother, if you're going to bellow across the table the entire evening. Aleek, switch places with your father."

My heart suddenly skipped a beat, and I feared my legs would topple beneath me. Were they all planning to make this a difficult night for me?

I sat heavily in my chair, trying to ignore the feeling at the pit of my stomach. Aleek moved to the chair next to me, and I struggled not to touch my shoulder to his, but we were so close; it was so terribly difficult. There was an electric shock of feeling every time we came close to grazing shoulders. I sat ramrod straight, all previous comfort having disappeared with the appearance of this boy and with my wet skirts clinging to my legs.

Conversation continued as it had before, loud and chaotic, with no beginning and no ending. I concentrated on my food, aware of every move that Aleek made next to me. From his constant side-glances in my direction, I had a feeling he felt the same, and it gave me goose bumps knowing I held this power. Such shivers ran throughout my body; it was all I could do not to burst into giggling.

"How do you like the food?" asked Karin into my ear.

"It's delicious! Who made it?"

"My mother and my aunt," she said and smiled proudly. The dishes were similar to our dishes, except not dressed to look pretty. They were just made to be eaten, not to be seen, and somehow they looked more delicious that way. I especially loved a dish called *manté*. They were tiny dumplings with shredded meat inside and were very difficult to make. But Karin's mom had mastered it, and it was perhaps the best manté I had ever had.

I felt a nudge at my side, and when I turned, I saw Aleek regarding me with curiosity as he opened his mouth to speak to me for the first time that night. "You seem as though you are a thousand miles away. Where are you?"

"Right here at your table, celebrating your sister's birthday."

He grinned. "Your mind is not."

"You are wrong," I said, looking away.

"I feel as though your thoughts are deeper than Lake Van. Curious that none of those thoughts slip through your lips."

My face was flushed at his forwardness. "I am raised to respect the people around me, and spewing out my thoughts to an entire party was not part of my lessons."

"Lessons?" he asked. I cursed myself inwardly for my blunder, and he grinned when he saw my furrowed brows. He leaned in close to my ear and whispered, "You hold many secrets behind that shawl of yours. And I would bet my house that your name is not Lori."

I whipped my head around to look at him in horror. He gave me his lilting grin again. "Karin warned us not to ask you about your family or your past, because it makes you uncomfortable. But you are far too interesting and mysterious for me to obey."

I looked at him in silence, our eyes catching. I could not even think of anything to respond; my mind was in such disarray. I was completely and utterly focused on him, with all surrounding noise dimming to a murmur. Was he threatening me or teasing me? I could not gather any signs from him, and in my focusing on attempting to figure out his intentions, I did not realize the sudden tension that rose in the room. So it was a shock to me when Karin suddenly stood next to me, her chair toppling backward. We all whipped our heads to look at her, and I saw the rage in her face, her pursed lips and her flashing blue eyes. Her fists were balled at her side, and I feared she would turn the table over in her anger.

"I will not go," she yelled at her father, wheeling around and storming out of the kitchen. Her father stood and slammed his fist on the table, shouting nonsense after her, the sort of rubbish that parents say when their authority is challenged—"I am your father, and I say you *will* go"—as if her anger should dissipate with that phrase. Whatever had happened a moment ago I had missed in my fascination with Aleek.

"Stupid girl," muttered her father.

"You should not have said it tonight," snapped his wife.

"Ungrateful!"

"Think before you speak!"

"Children must obey their parents," he bellowed.

An argument began, much more animated than the half-hearted bickering from earlier. I sat still, my heart beating fast, wondering what I should do. All instincts in my body had rushed to my legs, begging, pleading, for my mind to give the orders to run. I knew I did not belong here. It took all my energy to keep from bolting out the door, to the treacherous Lake Van, which seemed so much calmer compared to this kitchen right now. But all disorder and panic raging inside my body suddenly went quiet when Aleek touched my elbow.

Reeling from the looming unexpected silence of my mind, I looked over at him, and his gaze stopped my breath once again. It was like a dream. The hush inside my head was a low humming, and I could not understand this new feeling. There were no thoughts. No feelings. Just emptiness, observing and quiet. His face, his jaw, his nose, his lips, his eyes...His eyes—I melted into them. They were brown orbs of amber, molten rock, burning through me.

He whispered in my ear, "You should follow her."

And just as suddenly, he leaned back and turned away, air rushing between us to fill in the void. Heat burned my neck, rising to my cheeks. I stood quickly, excusing myself, and followed Karin hastily as if I could run away from my humiliation.

I found her outside, a dark figure in the shadows, throwing stones into the distance. They flashed with a silvery glint each time they caught the moonlight and then disappeared into the darkness, their moment of glory having passed within a few seconds.

"Karin."

She hurled another rock. I heard it land and clatter across the ground somewhere in the near distance.

"Karin, what has happened?"

"Didn't you hear?"

"N…no. I was lost in thought."

"They are sending me away," she managed through gritted teeth.

"They're punishing you? For what?" I gasped.

"No, it is not punishment," she said. The fight left her body suddenly, leaving her hunched over, as if her life had been sucked out of her. She sat on the ground with a thump, and after a moment, I came and sat across from her. She looked at me with tear-streaked cheeks. "They are sending me away to school."

"What? Why?" I managed to say. Sending someone away to school was just as well as never seeing them again.

"They think I am too idle here. They want me to learn and be a *part of something*. My aunt lives in the city, so they want me to stay with her."

Angry, I stood up and turned away. I heard a muffled sob behind me, but I was much too worked up to lend her my shoulder at the moment.

Damn.

"I shall visit you," I said resolutely. She glanced up at me, wiping her eyes.

"Can you?"

"I will. And before you leave, we shall have a party here."

She nodded. "During the day?"

"Yes." I smiled. "I will come. I promise, Karin. I promise, I will come."

Chapter 16

THE NEXT MORNING came much too early. The rays of the morning sun clawed at my eyes, and I buried my face into my pillow, groaning in frustration. Sleep had sounded so lovely, but I had tossed and turned all night, falling asleep right before dawn spread her skirts out over the island. But wake up I must, or else I would feel Digin Galia's wrath along my backside.

Groaning to the walls, I dressed myself slowly, my muscles weak after rowing in the rough waters last night. Exhaustion weighed me down, but I moved through it like it was thick honey that surrounded me. After gargling with rose water and spitting it out into a basin to rid my mouth of its thick morning coating, I sat at my dressing table and began to brush my hair in long, slow strokes. I stared back at myself in the oval mirror, cocking my head slightly to one side. Upturned brown eyes, framed by dark lashes and thick arching eyebrows, I had full lips but a rather pointy face, like a mouse. My hair was brown and long, stuck between the never-ending decision to be curly or straight. It only resulted in lanky waves. I would never have Aleena's beautiful dark curls. I ran my brush through it harshly, as if punishing it for its treason. But it was half-hearted, for the way

Aleek had looked at me brought a flush to my cheeks. Did he think I was beautiful?

But how could I be beautiful if my face was always covered in front of them?

I slammed my brush down on the table. Foolish girl.

I was almost late to breakfast, as I was promptly reminded by my mother's piercing glance when I entered the room and sat next to Bedros at my rightful seat. I wondered how many times my mother cursed my existence per day. I was such a bother to her.

The food was brought out, a modest assortment of jams and breads and pastries. Modest for us, of course, this would be a feast compared to Karin's meals. There was no noise at the table, just the low chewing of food and a murmur between my mother and my aunt, or my father. Everyone ate with such restraint, as if it was a shame to be chewing, and no one spoke except for the adults. I cleared my throat, and they stopped speaking, glancing at me in surprise. "The jam is delicious today."

The disbelief in their faces was almost comical. I popped an olive in my mouth.

"Tamar," snapped Digin Galia. I glanced at her, eyebrows raised. "Did we ask you?"

"No, Digin Galia, but really, it is delicious. I really think the cooks should be—"

"Akh, Tamar," my mother groaned.

"We will resume your lessons immediately after breakfast. It seems your manners need to be worked on," said Digin Galia, patting her thin lips with a napkin. My skin tightened as I imagined the stinging whip slapping my back. *That's what comes of trying to be conversational*, I thought wryly.

My manners were impeccable, and my appetite was not as hearty as it used to be anymore. I knew what everyone around me was thinking. They thought I was hopelessly in love with the boy sitting next to me.

He flashed me a sidelong glance, and when I looked back at him, I did not feel the same puzzling mixture of heart-wrenching and blissful calm feelings I did when I looked at Aleek.

I looked away from Bedros.

"Actually, I think the lessons should be canceled for the day. How would you like that, Tamar, my dear?" began my mother, and immediately I felt like being sick, for when my mother used the words "my dear" in the same sentence as my name, the day would near be ruined. In fact, I could not remember the last time she ever said "my dear" to me. And when had she ever canceled a lesson for me? Even my father glanced up and shot her a quizzical look, before resuming his breakfast indifferently.

I did not know how to respond. Sullenly, I managed a "Hmm?"

"Asdgh has not been taken to stretch her legs. Do you not think a short walk would do her some good?" Coming from the woman who believed that a young lady should not be permitted to ride a horse.

"I shall take her out after breakfast."

"Bedros, my dear boy, would you be so kind as to accompany her? One can never be too safe." Ah, so that's what this was.

"Of course," he responded, smiling. Only I saw the wicked look behind that smile. I put down my fork, fighting the urge to shatter my plate into a million pieces. This was my punishment. Aleena was looking at me, and when I finally caught her eye, her expression seemed to say, "I told you so."

My anger only accelerated by the time the horses were prepared and I met Bedros outside. If he had been any other man, my mother would have demanded an escort be placed with us, but since he was our "dear boy," I was admitted to being alone with him.

Such honor.

"Stop that," I snapped.

"What?" he asked, his face brightening in a failed attempt to look surprised.

"That silly smirk. You are much too pleased with yourself."

"I see that the fresh air has no effect on your mood."

"The air is wonderful. It is the company that upsets me."

"Don't speak that way about Asdgh; you'll upset him as well."

I shot him a look, and he shot it straight back at me. Our horses walked slowly down the path, oblivious of the tension that lingered above their heads. All was silent for a while between us.

He cleared his throat. "How are you?"

"Good. And how are you?"

"Good. It is a beautiful day today."

I scoffed, knowing that talk of the weather meant despair in a conversation. He shot me a sidelong glance, and I saw the worry tinged beneath the look. It softened my heart for a moment. He had been my friend for a long time, after all.

"What was that display today at breakfast?"

"I liked the food," I said curtly.

"Yes, well, you do not need to say it and interrupt the breakfast."

"Why not?" I asked. "If something is on my mind, I would like the right to say it. And how does complimenting the food interrupt breakfast?"

"You are living in another world, Tamar," he said and sighed.

"Yes…" I sighed as well. "It is a much better world than here."

He gave me a quizzical glance. When I did not elaborate, he said, "We used to be different together."

"Things change, Bedros. It is the way of the world."

"You sound like Aleena," he said.

"She is never wrong; it is what I have come to realize."

He gave me a cryptic glance. "What else was she right about?"

After a moment of hesitation, I replied, "Marriage. Mine with you."

"We are not married."

"You know as well as I do that it is in the plans."

"Yes, so why don't we just…accept it and pick our children's names?" He shrugged lightheartedly.

My eyes widened. "Bedros!" Before he could respond, I reached over and grabbed his handkerchief from his pocket. It was in the dirt on the ground in a flash, and I dug my heels into Asdgh's side, spurring him on to leave Bedros behind us in the dust. I looked back once, to see him slowly picking up his torn handkerchief, fading behind the whirlwind of dust until he disappeared into nothing but a lonely shadow. I couldn't help but remember the last time that I had stolen his handkerchief, all those months ago. Time does indeed change things.

⇥══◉ ◉══⇤

That night was the most frustrated I had been in all my younger years. I was eager to reach the shore and row to the mainland to find Karin. I had not seen her since the eve of her birthday a few nights ago, where the terrible news of her being sent to school was revealed. That night would have been the night I could set her mind at ease with girlish laughter and much-needed fun. We would have planned the day of her going-away party. Regardless of what we did, I needed her company and the feeling of the dances coursing through my body. There was a certain feel to the dances that could change the entire constitution of the character, and I needed it now more than ever.

Perhaps that was why I overreacted when I reached the beach. The boat was gone.

The moment I realized this, a thick blanket of fear fell over my mind, smothering all logic and reducing me to a state of child-ish panic. My breath immediately cut short, a fast-paced wheezing accompanying my hyperventilation in a desperate race. I whirled around in the darkness, my eyes straining to see into the shadows, my hands outstretched as if grabbing a fragment of a dream.

There was no boat.

I ran up and down the length of the small beach, not seeing the boat anywhere. My legs felt weak, as shaky as a calf's, and I stumbled a few times. I called loudly, my voice desperate, as if the boat was a dog and could hear me to come running with its tail between its legs, regretful for its disobedience. But nothing came. I ran in circles, looking where I had already looked, shouting at rock walls and the waves that mocked my every move.

"You took it!" I screamed suddenly at Lake Van, my final resort. "You stole it from me!" Tears rushed down my cheeks in great torrents. Blindly, with hands shaking, I fumbled with a handful of pebbles and mud and thrust it at the churning water. "You have taken away my only happiness!"

I stayed on that beach for hours, restlessly pacing like a wild animal that had been deprived of food, water, and sleep. I saw the candle burning like a bright star in the distance, and I grew even angrier. It was so near but so far. I cupped my hands around my mouth and screamed Karin's name. "Karin! Karin!" But I was too far. She would not hear me, though my shout echoed loudly against the walls of the cliff at my back. I had lived on this island my entire life, but only now did I understand what being trapped felt like—how allowing someone to taste freedom and then taking it away is the worst feeling in the world. I heard that nameless boy screaming, "Tamar!" I felt as she did, trapped on the shore, with nothing to do but pace back and forth.

I kicked at the water. It took a long time for the feeling inside me to change. But finally, when my fight and anger had congealed into heavy weights that sat on my eyelids, I sat down, with my back against the rough wall, and stared at the light in the distance that danced back and forth in my vision. I waited and waited until finally the candle was snuffed, and a dark shroud fell over the mainland.

The next morning, I was in a foul mood. Breakfast was quiet, as it usually was, but I wanted to scream and shatter every plate to cause a ruckus. After breakfast was over, I went straight to Aleena's chambers, knowing that for an hour or so after meals, she would come here to rest before going to the rooms she shared with Vartan. I sat at the window, waiting, until the door opened and she entered.

There was a pause when she saw me. "I had a feeling you would be here."

"Why?" I asked her.

"You looked dreadful at breakfast, like you were going to vomit."

I put my head into the palms of my hands. "The boat is gone, Aleena; it is gone."

She crossed the room and sat next to me by the window, putting a hand comfortingly on my shoulder. "No one knows about the beach. I can't imagine that anyone took it."

"It can't have been pulled into the water. I had placed it well out of its reaches."

"I am sorry, Tamar," she said. She had pursed her lips, looking as though she was deep in thought.

"Aleena."

"Hmm?"

"Whose boat was it?"

"I do not know. I found it a long time ago and kept it just in case."

"What do I do now?"

She frowned. "We can try to find another boat. If not, maybe Karin will be able to find a way to you."

"Karin is too young to cross the lake by herself. It is dangerous. I will try to find another boat."

"Be safe, Tamar," she said, hugging me tight.

As I left her room, I was still troubled. Where had she found the boat? What had she been keeping it for? It stayed in my mind, like a stubborn melody.

I went to the beach desperately every other night for two weeks, each time sitting among the pebbles and watching the candle until it was snuffed. Karin appeared day after day. Her loyalty and determination pained me. The candle was her burning hope, and I let her down each day that I did not appear to her. I tried finding a boat meanwhile, asking around indiscreetly, but I could not ask too many people without raising suspicion. I had no way to cross the waters. Some days I shouted at the lake, some days I cried, and some days I just lay there, drifting off into a restless sleep.

Then one night, I decided to let her know that I was waiting just like her. I brought my own candle, the largest I could find, and lit the tip of it with a matchstick I had stolen from the kitchen. I placed it on a step in the rock at a good height so that she would be able to see it from her side. As soon as I had positioned it, I sat back and waited, watching her light flickering in the distance. Nothing happened that day, and as soon as I saw her light snuff, I did the same to mine.

But the next night, everything changed. I sat waiting, my candle burning next to me, but this time, her light never went on. Wide awake, I stared intently at the shoreline, but there was no candle at all.

Damn! Had she given up at last?

The seconds and minutes crawled by, while I sat quietly at my place, like an obedient schoolgirl. The waves crashed against the shore, and the wind whistled above my head as it skimmed the rock wall. I was frightened, my thoughts traveling to new and alarming places. Where could she be? What if she'd given up? But it didn't make sense that she would give up now. *What if they already sent her away?* I was restless, pulling at my hair in distress. It seemed to take days until I finally heard a new sound—a splashing that was different from the usual waves that Lake Van made. I sat up a little straighter, eyes straining. I saw a dark shadow getting closer, and when my eyes adjusted, I realized it was another boat, tottering toward the shore. I leaped up to my feet wildly.

"Karin!" I shouted, waving my hands, although my candle provided enough light for her to see me. "Hooray!" I ran to the shore to wait for the boat. "I'm so sorry, Karin! It's been so long; I missed you so—" I rambled, but as soon as I saw the boat clearly, I gasped and stepped back.

Aleek.

As soon as it was near enough, he bounded out lightly and splashed into the shallow water, pulling up the boat behind him until it was lodged in the sand at the shore. I had stepped back silently.

Finally, after what seemed an eternity, he faced me and gestured majestically toward the crudely built boat. "Your carriage awaits."

"Where is she?" I asked, my voice weak.

"Worried sick about you on the other side. There was no way I would allow her to cross the lake, so I offered to come in her stead."

He watched me as I stood completely still. My arms were crossed tightly across my chest as my hands clutched the fabric over my nose so that he would not see my face. I could not function properly under his gaze.

"Is everything all right?" he asked, raising an eyebrow.

"Yes," I muttered, coming out of my trance. "My candle."

I made to run to retrieve it, but he stopped me by holding out a hand. "I shall get it." Without waiting for my answer, he ran up the beach. I watched him wordlessly, my heart beating in starts and stops. The dark shadows of the rocky cliffs hung over him ominously, and only the light of the candle showed his presence. But when he leaned over and blew it out, the entire upper section of the beach was cast into darkness. For a moment, he was nowhere to be seen, and I grew afraid as I stood next to the boat expectantly. Then suddenly, as if he was a ray of light, he stepped out of the shadows, running toward me, his head bowed against the cold breeze.

He handed me the candle and stepped toward the boat, holding it steady for me to step inside. As I stepped gingerly into the rickety boat, he lifted a hand and took mine, making sure I did not lose my balance. My breath caught at his touch, and I realized I was trembling. I let go immediately when I stepped inside. As soon as I was settled, he pushed against the boat, sending it and me into the water. When the hull of the boat was free of the sand, he leaped in to sit across from me, taking both oars into his hands and rowing hard against the strong waves.

"Let me help," I said.

He shook his head, straining against the oars. The waves were stronger tonight, and a flush came to my face when I realized I was glad for the weather. His arms bulged underneath his sweater from the tension, and I saw how built and poised he was. They were muscles that had developed from hard work, and I could not imagine how many years of hard labor he'd had to perform. And dancing had created a wiry agility in him that I had not seen in anyone else.

Still flushing from my observations, I averted my eyes from him to gaze out over the water instead. It looked like a painting, a desperate swirl of dark blues and blacks, until I could not tell which color was which.

He rowed us to calmer waters, where he put down his oars upon his knees and treaded the water slowly to regain his energy. Finally, he turned his eyes upon me.

"Where were you this past few weeks?"

"My boat was gone."

"Someone stole it?"

"I believe so. Or it was taken by the lake," I said truthfully, though I would never admit that we had stolen it in the first place. "Where did you find this boat?"

"I made it," he said, smiling proudly. "I am not a builder, so that explains its crudeness. I had a friend help me."

He'd made the boat! To come get me? I dared not ask.

"Let me help with the rowing," I suggested again.

He gave me a look. "It is a man's weakness when a woman must help him."

I sat back, shooting him a look as well. "It is a man's weakness to not allow a woman to help him."

He was surprised at my retort for a moment; then a small smile came to his lips, accompanied by the raising of his eyebrows. "You are not the usual village girl, pining to be royalty."

"No," I muttered, looking off, "I suppose I am not."

"You have an aura about you," he said matter-of-factly.

"Doesn't everyone?"

"Yes, but something about you is different. Something I have not seen in anyone. Your entire person is unique. I find myself entirely fascinated by you."

"Is that good or bad?" I asked.

He grinned. "It is beautiful. And I have not even seen your face yet."

Yet.

I could feel his gaze linger on my face, but I had turned away, unable to speak for the beating of my heart. Instead I watched the candle that was lit in the distance while he rowed. I could imagine Karin waiting anxiously, torn by relief and anger. She would have thought I had abandoned her, left her to her fate to go away to school without dancing anymore.

I tightened the shawl. Would she still be my friend if she found out who I was?

Would *he*? Would he still think I was beautiful, even though I had betrayed him and his entire family?

I turned to face him again. He was looking at me with a slightly worried expression, and when we locked eyes, he gave a reassuring smile. I nodded in response, for he would never see my smile as long as I continued to deceive them.

Chapter 17

IN THE FOLLOWING days, I spent much of my time reflecting. I recalled the lazy days I would spend wasting time in the gardens or at the cliff or in my chambers, gazing out at the glistening lake. I remembered the peace I'd felt in those days, how what I most worried about was whether I would get flogged for disobeying orders, whether deliberately or unintentionally. I remembered how my idle thoughts were filled with images of unknown heroes and heroines living their own adventures, each time a fantastic affair even though I had read the same story over and over again. I remembered being envious of my sister, the fair Aleena, beautiful and wild of spirit, but also loving her with such admiring affection.

I remembered all this. But the memories were distant, as if in my childhood I had made them up. I no longer worried about my lessons, no longer wasted time reminiscing on strangers' adventures, no longer felt as though Aleena was a goddess, though I still loved her beyond belief. My mind now was entirely occupied by another figure; my heart was entirely stolen by someone who was *real*.

How does one live without *this* burning passion? How does one see when one is so blinded? How had I possibly woken up each morning before without this to wake up to? My heart felt strange as if it were trying to adjust itself to fit this new feeling of mine.

I suddenly understood those lovesick poems that filled my father's library, the ones I had pored over in my childhood, spending hours every day swooning over lovely words and impossible romances. I understood what had tortured and consumed poets' hearts simultaneously, so that their only possible binding to sanity was through poetry itself. All of a sudden, I wanted to write it all down, use words I had no knowledge of to describe the feeling I felt. I wanted to paint him with my pen, lock him into the pages of a cherished journal, and seal it all with permanent ink so that he would never escape my thoughts and memories.

I closed my eyes, letting his image fill my mind. I saw him so clearly; I almost believed he was really there. I could just reach out and touch him. But my hands were useless; I could only stare. I saw his soft brown locks falling over his forehead and tufting out as if he'd just woken up from sleep; I saw his brown eyes, staring as if he saw right through me. His lean muscles contrasted with the way he slightly stooped, as if afraid he would be noticed too easily. His grin crawled over his face, his nose wrinkled at the same time, and a rare laugh snuck out from his lips on occasion, resounding through the air and making anyone around him smile with contagious joy. His very presence changed the feeling in the air, as if he were an element that one could breathe and live on.

All this and yet so much more. Visions ran before my eyes, blinding me to my days and illuminating the nights when I could see him.

I loved him. I loved him wholeheartedly. And I did not care if anyone disapproved.

Aleek.

⊷⊨◉ ◉⊨⊶

After that first night, it was agreed that Aleek would bring Karin and himself from the mainland to my island. It was easier and much safer than two back-to-back trips across the lake to pick me up and take me to the mainland. I had no objection to this arrangement, for this meant that Aleek would also join us on the island and would have to stay there with us until the lessons were over. Those days were filled with bliss, with me waiting by my lit candle and seeing my best friend and my love appear out of the haze of darkness to the soft glow of my beach. There, we held hands, Karin between us, and all danced together. Sometimes, I would wish to be in the middle, but I knew that if my hand held his, I would forget how to dance.

Aleek knew the stories behind the dances, and he taught both of us as we danced, his voice narrating the story as Karin softly hummed in the background. Sometimes her voice stumbled over the beat, forgetting the rhythm, and he added his voice to hers, brother and sister creating a mesmerizing harmony.

I could hardly wait to come to the beach, which we had decided was to be every third night. Sometimes while Karin and I danced, Aleek stepped away, leaned against the cliffside, and appraised us with a small smile on his face. My nervousness at his gaze slowly faded into comfort as the weeks passed in this way. I began to laugh openly, letting the dance free my limbs as Karin and I eventually began to dance without having to pause to teach me the moves. With the humming of the song from Aleek's throat and Karin's singing, I already knew which dance was next, even before they said the name. It became second nature to me, as I spent as much time as I could learning the music and the dances.

Before I knew it, my birthday had snuck up on me, catching me by surprise. My father and mother surprised me at breakfast with a cake, and for a moment, I had no idea what the cake was for, until I heard, "Happy birthday!"

I had just turned fifteen. My parents gave me a new dress, pretty but very regal and befitting of my rank. It was a deep green, with an under layer of yellow beige that peeked out between the slits in the green. The pale pink sash around the waist was shot through with delicate golden thread, making it glitter brilliantly. It was beautiful, and I thanked them heartily, placing the dress gingerly upon an empty chair. Aleena gave me a new hooded cloak, black as midnight, and she winked at me when I took it. I hugged the cloth and thanked her passionately, for the material was not so fine that I would be questioned in the village. I knew she intended for me to use it on my nightly visits to the beach. It was perfect.

The rest of the day was tedious, for many family members and family friends visited us, each bringing some sort of gift for me. I received various gifts, ranging from jewelry to clothes to household items. I would have had no patience to sort through them all, but Aleena was fascinated by them. She sat on the floor, picking up each item and determining if we wanted it or not. I was eager for the day to pass, so that I would join Karin and Aleek when they visited the beach that night.

"Akh," I heard from Aleena. When I glanced at her, she held up a thick silver bracelet with bells on it. "We do not like this."

I feigned shock and took the bracelet from her, sliding it over my wrist. "You mean to say that you don't want me to look like an exotic dancer?" I danced across the room, shaking my wrist so that the bells made a loud ringing. Aleena laughed and shook her head.

"You would certainly make a great dancer."

"Lilit, you, Janna, and I can all leave the palace and make our way through the world as exotic dancers. What do you say, Janna?" I asked, grinning at her. Janna looked at me in dismay.

"I swear you learned nothing of politeness."

"This time, we would teach you, Janna," said Aleena, laughing as I moved my hips in a provocative way and brought a flush to Janna's cheeks.

"Well I would certainly come see the show," we heard suddenly from the doorway. We all turned in shock to see Bedros standing there with an amused grin on his face. Aleena groaned while I crossed the room and returned the bracelet back to her. "Hello, Princesses and Janna," he said, striding in and making himself comfortable on my chair.

"Hello, Bedros," we echoed, but Aleena's voice was an angry growl.

"I hear today is a special day."

"Oh? I hadn't heard." I cocked my head at him. Aleena rolled her eyes.

"Please do not lose your head on my behalf," he said to Aleena. She responded with a glare. "I got you something," he said to me, tossing me a small package, wrapped perfectly in silk.

I cast him a suspicious look. "I would bet all my birthday gifts that you did not wrap this."

"You are correct." He grinned, slightly embarrassed. "My mother helped."

I sat on the ground and opened the parcel. A small wooden box appeared, and when I opened the lid, I saw a glittering necklace nestled in a nest of satin. It was a delicate gold chain with emeralds spaced out every inch around the entire necklace. It was incredibly elegant and sparkled in my hand when I lifted it up out of the box to show Aleena and Janna. "Wow," I managed to say.

He grinned, pleased with himself. "Would you like help putting it on?"

"No," I answered immediately, smiling kindly at him. "I will wear it on a special occasion so that it will be more special. It is incredibly beautiful, Bedros; thank you."

He nodded, his eyes heated and watching me closely. "It is beautiful, yes, but I can assure you that it will look more beautiful against the skin of your neck."

I flushed, but Aleena snapped, "Get out of here before I wring *your* neck!" He bowed, his shoulders shaking from laughter, before he turned and left. Janna closed the door behind him with a resolute click, a frown on her face from his repulsive conduct.

"We should throw that necklace out with the rubbish," murmured Aleena.

"It is a lovely necklace," said Janna. "It is too bad it came from Bedros, that horrid boy."

"I agree," I said, shutting the box closed with the necklace tucked away inside, and bringing an end to our encounter with him.

That night, I wore the cloak that Aleena got for me. She had helped me wear it with a wink in my direction. Later, rushing to the beach, I let out an unrestrained laugh, excited to see the pair. As soon as I arrived at the beach, I wasted no time in lighting my candle and placing it on a safe alcove, away from the wind. I sat down upon the sand and waited, breathing in the cool night air and watching the horizon for any movement.

When they arrived at last, they both had parcels with them. Karin ran to me and hugged me, crying out, "Happy birthday!" She gave me a leather-covered parcel, and I grinned with excitement. When I opened it, I gasped. It was a small portrait of me.

"Karin! I didn't know you paint!" I cried. It was the size of my hand, and she had painted a small crown on my head, my chin lifted regally. I was wearing a pale pink dress with much lace at the neckline and wrapped around most of my face, with a pearl necklace hanging daintily around my throat. My eyes peeked out between the layers of lace, and they were solemn, with a hidden mischief to them.

"I made you into a princess."

My face flushed. It was beautifully done, but an ironic giggle wanted to bubble out of my throat. It was *me*: Princess Tamar. The true Princess Tamar, behind the mask named Lori that she had fashioned so carefully for them.

"It is beautiful, Karin," I murmured. I wrapped it carefully back in the leather and placed it underneath the overhanging rock where the candle stood. "Thank you," I said again, hugging her tightly. Over her shoulder, I saw Aleek, who stood quiet, with his own small parcel in his hands. He glanced at me and grinned, his eyes glimmering.

When I broke the hug, he came forward and handed it to me, almost modestly. "Happy birthday," he said. I opened it, and a large smile suddenly burst over my face.

It was a small dagger, fashioned almost crudely, but it seemed fitting for a dagger to be raw in that way. The hilt was made of strong wood and was carved to look like waves, curving back and forth. It fit perfectly into my grip. The blade was strong steel, with a pointy tip that looked like it had been sharpened to its utmost capability. "Did you make this?" I cried.

"Yes, he did!" blurted Karin before he could say anything. He ruffled Karin's hair in a brotherly gesture.

"I always see the outline of your kitchen knife at your waist. I figured it would be time for you to have a dagger."

He saw the knife at my *waist*. I flushed, unsure of what to make of that. "These gifts are brilliant. Thank you so much." And before I could stop myself, I stepped forward and hugged him. He hesitated only for a moment; then his arms wrapped around me tightly, one hand resting affectionately against the back of my neck.

I knew he could be everything to me. My passion for him was spurred by the fact that my life at the castle had quickly become a thudding bore. The only time I saw anyone was when I came down for meals. People began to talk about my absence from tea or family gatherings, and as with any rumor, the conclusion—no matter what it came to—was always false. Aleena usually tried to cover for me, but it was becoming more difficult.

Mother usually criticized me for my clumsiness—although I finally felt as though I walked on clouds—and demanded that Digin Galia put me back on track, but I never attended my studies anymore. They were worried; I knew that. Aleena was the only one who knew where I would disappear to, so she was not worried, but she also had her own affairs to handle. I could only imagine the dismay of the family. Both princesses seemed continually lost in their own minds.

But I didn't really care. I was finally happy. I finally felt free. They didn't like to see it, and it frustrated me.

Bedros began to corner me, desperate to catch me here and there for some quick conversation. I dodged him as best I could, but sometimes he would be one step ahead. Once, he stepped in front of my door, so I could not enter my chambers. He crossed his arms, blocking my way, and asserted, "I want to talk to you."

"In the hallway?" I raised an eyebrow.

"Would you like for us to talk inside your room?"

"You are not allowed in my room, brother. I have instructed Janna to tell someone immediately if you stride into my room without my consent."

"Do not call me your brother."

"Why ever not? That is what you are, isn't it?" I taunted.

"Tamar, what are you doing?"

I grew serious and pierced him with my gaze. "Living."

"You are throwing everything away."

"I was already thrown away. I found a place to go," I snapped.

His face softened. "You always had a place with me. I never abandoned you."

I watched him for a moment. I was waiting for that feeling, the feeling I felt with Aleek every time I neared him or caught him glancing at me from the corner of his mesmerizing eyes.

It did not happen. I knew it would never happen with him.

Softly I said, "But *I* will abandon *you*. Can't you see that?"

I walked past him, and he let me go, the fight having left his body.

⊷⊷⊷ ⊷⊷⊷

I awoke the next morning with a mix of excited and anxious feelings. Today was to be the day of the going-away party for Karin. The party was to be held in the early evening, and it would still be light out. I told my parents that Lilit was visiting the village with a cousin of hers, and I would spend the day with her. To my utter surprise, they allowed me to go, and excitedly I ruffled through my wardrobe, wondering which dress I should take. It needed to be simple but nice. Remembering the painting, I dug out a simple brick-pink dress, like the color of the tufa that built the church on our island. It would do perfectly! I took out a simple lace shawl and wrapped it around my shoulders and the bottom half of my face as though I were cold.

I left on foot and made my way toward the covered beach. It was a lovely day, and I was thrilled to be out while the sun was still shining. Once there, I lit the candle on the overhanging rock and waited. It was light out enough for them to see their way, but night would be falling soon, and I did not want to take any risks.

I saw the boat coming a few miles away; the golden rays of the sun shone down on the water, illuminating the arriving rowboat. I had never seen the boat arriving, because it would always happen when the light had disappeared from the sky. Now I saw it drifting on, cutting through the waves toward me. When I looked closer, I noticed it was only Aleek in the boat.

Hurriedly I pressed down my hair and arranged the shawl cleanly around my head and over my nose. Using my hands, I smoothed down my dress, which was billowing in the wind.

"Hello, princess!" he called when he was nearer. My blood froze in horror. *Princess?*

"What?" I called back when I found my voice.

The boat scraped along the bottom of the shore, and he jumped out, splashing water around his legs. As he grabbed the boat and tugged it up onto the sand, he explained, "Karin painted you as a princess, and now I can't stop thinking of you as one, especially in that beautiful attire you have on tonight. I wonder if I'll have to bow to you."

He can't stop thinking of me. He thinks my dress is beautiful.

I flushed and shook my head. "Don't be ridiculous; you do not need to bow, as I am simple me."

He stepped forward and took my hand to help me into the boat, saying at the same time, "No, not simple. Not simple at all." When I was settled in, he shoved the boat hard and sent us back into the water. "You know, we will convince you to go swimming one day, and you shall have to take your shawl off."

"I shall keep it on, if only to infuriate you even more."

"I have this image of who you are, and I fear you shall only disappoint me when you remove it one day."

"And what image, pray tell, is that?"

"Of the younger princess, Princess Tamar, the one they call a legend."

I was shocked. He thought of me as…me? Oh, the irony. A giggle bubbled up into my throat, but I kept it down. "Why do they call her a legend?"

"No one sees her," he laughed. "We have seen the Princess Aleena hundreds of times, but Princess Tamar is never around. They do not believe that she exists."

"Perhaps she is busy."

He shrugged. "Perhaps. I saw her once."

I struggled to keep my voice from sounding too interested. "Did you?"

"When I was younger. She had escaped from her guardians and bumped into me. We spoke only a little, but I remember her so vividly. The way she stood out from the common people, and shone like…"

"Like what?" I asked breathlessly. *An angel.*

He shook his head, ridding himself of the thought. "It does not matter. Princess Aleena came and took her away."

"Imagine that," I mused.

"So, I see you as Princess Tamar. You are as much shrouded in mystery as she is."

"What an honor then."

He was looking at me oddly. "You forget something."

"What am I forgetting?"

"When I first met you, at the wedding, you were dancing with the Princess Aleena." The words froze in my throat. Yes, I had forgotten that particular detail. He continued nonchalantly, "You know her well enough to dance all the dances with her and laugh as though you were...oh I don't know...sisters."

"Don't be ridiculous."

He shrugged. "Only stating an observation. Does Princess Tamar exist?"

"Yes, she does."

He nodded, but he said instead, "Ah, here we are." I looked back, and sure enough, the mainland shore was approaching fast.

"Where is Karin?" I asked, looking around the deserted beach.

"She is at the party already. They have begun in the village center. The entire village is attending the event."

My heart beat with excitement. When he had lodged the boat safely and helped me onto the sand, he gestured up the beach, and we walked up together. I heard the music in the near distance, and there was a slight spring in my step. A real village party!

When we neared the center, Karin saw me and shouted, "Lori!" I ran to her and hugged her tightly. "Come, dance with me!"

It seemed as though the entire village was attending. They had spilled into the center and were drinking, eating, talking, and laughing. The clearing in the center had been opened for the dancers, and oh, did they dance! Aleek left us and joined them at the front, grabbing a handkerchief from a laughing old lady and twirling it in his hands; he whooped and shouted while the rest followed his lead.

I joined them and held Karin's hand, with another young man to my right. We danced together, and while I stumbled a bit, I was much better because of Karin's teaching. We laughed and had wine for the first time. Both of our faces were flushed from sipping the spirits.

The music changed in tempo suddenly at one point, and all the women were hustled out of the clearing. I stood with Karin at the edge and watched the men, who were left in the center. They had paired off and stood across from each other, not touching each other. The music was a steady beat of the dhol and a single duduk playing loudly, as if charming a snake. The men began to dance, shuffling in their places and then turning abruptly and slapping each other's hands. One man fell to the floor in a squat and then bounded back up to his feet, as though resisting defeat. This happened in different sequences.

Karin explained in my ear that this was called *Yarxushta*, a war dance. The men were fighting with each other but with the great respect that was expected in a battle. When one man fell to the floor, the rest backed away, giving him space to leap back up. It was a synchronized, beautiful battle. I remembered when Janna told me about this dance—it was amazing to actually see it happening. I watched Aleek bounding about, laughing during the dance, when he caught my eye and winked playfully. "You have an admirer," giggled Karin, noticing it with her ever-watchful eye. I nudged her. "Maybe one day, you will be my sister."

"Karin!" I pushed her good-humoredly, and she bounced back, pretending to dance the Yarxushta.

The dance changed again, and I recognized this one, much to my delight. The women moved forward and made one straight line. Karin and I were in the center, and I was glad, for I felt secure between them all. Across from us was the line of men. The music was lilting and fun, and we danced the moves with much vigor, playful and flirting with the men. Aleek broke off from the line of men and did his own dance in the middle, much to everyone's excitement. They all shouted and whooped as he danced along the women's line, passing me with another wink. When he reached the end of our line, someone handed him a pair of shoes. They were high, stiff wooden heels, meant to be incredibly uncomfortable.

He danced with them above his head to the middle and showed them off to everyone. We all oohed and ahed in mock admiration at the fineness of the shoes. Then suddenly, he kneeled in front of me with the shoes presented in my direction.

There was much excitement and shouts and whistles, and I rolled my eyes, but I was secretly glad that he had picked me. Karin pushed me forward, and I toed out of my worn-out dance shoes, putting on the heels. But, as expected, they were much too small and uncomfortable. Aleek danced animatedly, twirling and skipping, and I tried, but I stumbled around—on purpose—to everyone's everlasting entertainment. The crowd clapped and cheered my name. "Lori! Lori!"

When Aleek whooped, indicating the change in movements, he fell to his knees, with his face up to me, and I threw off the uncomfortable heels with much ceremony and then proceeded to dance barefoot, as animatedly as Aleek, circling him while he craned his neck to keep his eye on me. It was quite a show, and I was having such fun. I gestured to Karin to join me, and she broke the line to come and join me, leading us into the next dances.

I threw my head back and laughed, such that I had never laughed before. I was having the time of my life, and I never wanted it to end. If only moments could last forever, I would be the happiest person in this moment right here.

But of course, it was to be my last day seeing Karin for a long while. When I grew tired of dancing, I sat a little ways off, to where I had a clear view of Lake Van. It was strange seeing my tiny island from this angle. It seemed so insignificant. I rubbed my ankle absent-mindedly, my chest still heaving from the rapid dances.

"You are a wonderful dancer," said Aleek, approaching to sit next to me on the bench. I shuddered at his nearness. "It seems as though you were made for dancing."

"Thank you," I muttered.

"You bring Karin much joy."

"I love her dearly."

"You bring me much joy as well," he said solemnly. I did not say anything. He reached out slowly, and I breathlessly thought he would touch my cheek, but he brought his hand down to the end of my shawl that had trailed down the length of my body and rested on my lap, half-heartedly running his fingers over it. I was afraid he would tug, opening the shawl to reveal my face, and I tensed, ready to slap his hand away if he dared. But he sensed my tension and retreated his hands back to his own lap.

"Karin is not to leave for another week. If you would like, I will bring you back to the mainland to see her for the last time."

"I would like that very much!" I exclaimed.

He nodded, smiling. "Now, come. I shall take you back to your home," he said, standing. He held out a hand to me, and I glanced at it with wide eyes.

"I must say bye to Karin."

"She is with our parents. You will see her soon; I promise."

I nodded and gingerly put my hand in his. He took it and led me toward the boat on the beach, not letting go of my hand. We were walking hand in hand, and I was in such bliss.

The whole boat ride back, we were lost in thought. I was so happy at his seeming affection, but frustrated that I could not just bring him to my father and announce our betrothal. I cast my eyes over him and my heart ached with the torment that churned inside it, for my joy at being near him was battling the agony of my not being with him. What did he think, I wondered. He was so difficult to read, for he seemed as though he cared for me, but how could he if he did not know me? We drifted toward the island, which loomed in the distance. The candle I had lit before I left was still burning there, awaiting my return.

When we arrived on my island of Akhtamar, he helped me off the boat and stood there, watching me from his perch. I smiled at him, and before I could react, he leaned down and kissed my temple, on the skin that showed above the lace shawl. "Sleep well, my lady."

Breathless, I nodded as he pushed away from the shore and disappeared into the darkness.

That night, I sat in my room, passively reading a novel. My mind was still at the party where I danced with Aleek, when he held my hand, and the boat ride where we were alone for those precious moments. And, of course, his gentle kiss. I could still feel his lips on my skin, and I could not concentrate on my novel properly. I was tormented, my brows furrowed. What would I do? I loved him so, but I had no way of knowing his intentions. Even if I did, I could not be with him. But if I could, would he want that life? I groaned inwardly. If we could just sit down and speak about it, this would rest much easier on my mind. My door suddenly opened and closed with a resolute click. Half expecting Bedros again, I turned in anger, my lips pulling down into a frown, but I saw Aleena, who had shuffled in quietly. I did not say anything but watched her as she approached a chair that was quite far from where I sat.

She sat, making herself comfortable, and I knew she took her time on purpose. When she had settled, she turned her cool crystal eyes to me. "I made a mistake. And for that, I am here to apologize."

"What happened?"

"It was Bedros's boat."

I sucked in my breath. "Do you think he took it?"

"I do not know. Tamar, this means he may know what you are doing," she said, a look of worry crossing her face.

"Why did he lend you the boat?"

She looked troubled. "I had asked him for it a long time ago. I knew he had one. I kept it just in case I wanted to free myself. I gave the boat to you because it is too late for me to be free. But it was not too late for you. And you've met a man whose very name lights you up on the inside. But Bedros notices it too, and I'm so worried."

I covered my face with my hands. "What do we do?"

She shook her head. "I don't know." I stayed silent, for she was looking at me with raised eyebrows. "Do you love him?" I knew she meant Aleek.

Tears pricked my eyes. After a moment, I nodded. "He's from the mainland, and I am from the island. And we are not of equal status. Oh, Aleena, what am I going to do? I am following the exact same steps as the very legend that killed an innocent man and condemned a young woman all throughout her life!"

"It was her decision to be condemned."

"But she was shamed. She was mocked by the people. She was called a whore and slandered by all who knew her. They took him from her, he who was not important. They did not even give him a name in the legend. If it was a story about true love, they would have given him an identity. No, it was not about love. It was about Tamar and how she broke the rules. *That* is the tragedy—not when he died."

Aleena approached me and sat next to me on the bed. She held my quivering shoulders and took one of my hands, gripping it tight. "Yes, you are right. The story is not to urge you to take the same path, but to stick to what *should* be your path. It is a warning for the young people in the future. But, Tamar, don't you see? That only emphasizes the truth of that kind of love."

"But how could I love someone from such a different place than I? Why can't I make this easier on myself and fall in love with Bedros?"

She leaned back on the bed, her long neck arching backwards as she lay her head on the pillow. I noticed how pale her face had become. Her skin looked more like porcelain than ever. "Perhaps the reason your heart opened to the idea of loving Aleek was because you can't have him. We are used to getting everything we want. We are the leaders—the rulers—the darlings of this island. I can stroll into the village and take whatever I want. But life dangled something unattainable in front of you. The juiciest pomegranate that always seems to be at the highest point in the biggest tree. And you want it."

I wrinkled my nose. "I am not a child—wanting a piece of fruit that she can not have."

"I never said a child behaves that way. Look around you; *everyone* acts that way. It is human. We want the thing we cannot have. And right now, you cannot have Aleek, while Bedros is so readily available and expecting you to be as well."

"Well how do I know if I'm on the right path?"

She smiled sweetly. "That, my dear, is the question. Until then, we must steer Bedros clear of you." She winked at me, but I was curious at her countenance. I put a hand to her forehead and she moved away from me. "What is the matter?"

"Are you ill? You look different."

"Merely consumed by the romance that is unraveling before me," she teased, and my sister rolled off the bed and danced out of my chambers, humming the tune to the song of Akhtamar.

It was only a couple of days later when Aleek appeared on the boat by himself again. He looked rather forlorn, which caused a heavy fist to grip my heart. "This is the day she leaves?" I asked, as he stepped out of the boat but did not approach me.

"Yes," he said and frowned. The wind whipped around us, and I was reminded of the coming colder days. "Karin will be leaving for school tomorrow."

I was shaky on my legs, but I managed to walk toward the boat, knowing that Karin would be waiting. He reached out a hand to help into the boat, but this time when I placed my hand in his, he pressed his fingers slightly to hold me there. I paused, glancing at him. He was so close.

"We *will* see her again."

I nodded, not because I believed him, but because he expected it.

The boat ride was solemn, both of us staying silent and surveying our surroundings. I half-heartedly wished there was a storm tonight, so we would not arrive quickly at the mainland.

But there was no such storm; the lake was unnervingly quiet tonight.

I watched the dim candle grow brighter and brighter as we neared the mainland, dreading the moment when I would have to say my last good-bye to my beloved friend. Besides the burning light, I saw the dark shadow of a person, unnaturally still against the cave wall. Usually she would be running down the length of the beach, excited for my return.

There was a sudden jolt as the boat scraped along the bottom. Without waiting for Aleek to jump out and lodge the boat on the shore, I leaped out, the water splashing up above my knees. Wading up the beach, I lifted my skirts slightly and ran to Karin, who had tears streaming down her face. We threw our arms around each other and held on tight, as if we would drown without each other. A small sob escaped her lips, and I was reminded of how young she really was, although I sometimes forgot that.

She was only twelve. And she was going on an adventure, while I would be stuck here.

I held on tighter.

"Will you visit one day?" she asked, her voice trembling.

I pulled her to arm's length to look at her. "I will try my best, Karin."

Aleek walked up the beach toward us, in quiet, solemn steps. When he reached the comfort and warmth of the overhanging rock with the candle, he sat on the sandy ground with his back against the rock wall. Karin walked to him and sat next to him, resting her head on his shoulder. The glow of the candle cast playful shadows across their faces, dancing around their prominent features and making them appear angry, happy, sad, comical, in quick flicks of movement.

I watched her, wanting to memorize her face so I would not forget her so easily. A person could have such a presence in someone's life and then disappear all at once. Such tears were spilled for Karin, until I almost believed that she had died, not just gone away to school. I wished to see her again, but it was so difficult. I had never left my island except for the dance lessons, and the thought of traveling farther was terrifying.

I could not imagine what my twelve-year-old friend was feeling.

We did not dance that night. None of us seemed to be in the right spirits. The final good-bye was difficult, and I had to tear myself away from her. It was exceedingly grave, and the atmosphere was heavy around us as Aleek rowed me back to the island. I wanted to run to Aleena's arms, pull her away from the castle, and fly away to a distant land with Aleek, Karin, and Lilit. These were the people I needed in my life, and I felt as though I was losing them all.

Aleek took a breath, and I glanced at him expectantly. He avoided my eyes, looking down at the bottom of the boat, as if hoping it would open up suddenly and pull him down into the depths of the lake.

"What is the matter?" I asked.

"I was just wondering…," he began, but he stopped abruptly and shook his head, frustrated. "Never mind. I am sorry Karin has to leave so early."

"Yes, I am as well. You were just wondering…," I prompted.

He gave a small, embarrassed smile, and I held my breath at the small dimples that appeared around his lips. "Well…I was wondering if you would…well…what I'm trying to say is…Would it be terribly unseemly to keep seeing you like this?"

My face flushed, and I turned to look out at the water. "I don't believe so."

"So you would like to continue meeting? There are so many more dances that you have little idea of. I could teach you the steps and the stories behind all of them. We don't have to end our meetings because she has left now." He was talking fast, as if trying to persuade me.

My hand gripped the wooden seat of the boat. "I would not want to be a burden on you."

"No," he said hastily and shook his head, a small smile rising to his lips. "I look forward to all of our meetings. I would find it an honor if you would continue them with me."

I took a deep breath, as if contemplating still, but my heart had already decided.

Of course.

Of course.

"Of course I will."

⊶═◉ ◉═⊶

The night was beautiful. The candle, perched on a small ledge, cast fantastic shadows all across the high walls. The flickering flame cast its warm glow over us, as if it was the smoothest honey that melted over our bodies. The lake seemed in better spirits, keeping at a reasonable distance from my beloved shore. Soft white foam gathered along the shore where the waves would break, as if preparing a bath that would fold us in its embrace. I recalled the stories Digin Galia taught me about the Greek myths of Aphrodite, the goddess of beauty and love. She was born from the white foam that was made by the crashing of the waves, and I could almost see it happening on nights like these, when the foam sparkled like crystals under the moonlight.

And there, sitting amid those crystals, was the rickety boat that brought the man I loved to me. He held out a hand toward me, palm up, and watched me closely with those eyes that I longed to see. His gaze, that gaze. I felt as if he could see right through my shawl to my face. He caressed my skin with his gaze, and shivers traveled up my spine at the very thought of his nearness. I could not trust my shaky legs to hold me up, but when I placed my hand in his, new strength and clarity shot through my body.

Fingers interlocked, muscles taut, the music rumbling deep in his throat, we began to dance. I had never felt the dance this way. There was such intensity, such a grip that made me feel as if I were a string being pulled tighter and tighter. His hand held mine so tightly as our shoulders grazed against each other with every move, but we kept in perfect rhythm together. Every small bounce I made, every hop and skip I had to do, was paralleled by him, and we moved in complete synchrony.

I had completely succumbed to this feeling, and I never wanted to lose it. But every night, when our dancing came to a close, he stepped back into his boat and, with a lighthearted salute of farewell, rowed away from my shore into the black of the night.

I knew he had managed to steal my heart, and every time he disappeared from view, I wrung my hands in such worry that the lake would take him that night, for my conversation with Aleena resounded in my mind. The legend haunted my every moment with him, and I ached for his protection.

So I prayed every night. I prayed that Lake Van would not take my love from me.

Chapter 18

MY DAYS WERE conflicted and torn. My joy came when I was with Aleena or every several nights at seeing Aleek and the dances and stories he would teach me. My sorrow was every moment that I was not with them and stuck instead within the confines of my walls, surrounded by the vast expanse of water that separated us. I sat at my windowsill, looking out at the lake, with these thoughts consuming my mind.

One day the roll of carriage wheels distracted me, and I glanced down into the courtyard where the carriage was pulling in. It was empty, however, and I remembered vaguely my mother mentioning that Baron Avedis would be leaving for home soon in order to put the finishing touches to the place for Vartan and Aleena. I turned away from the windowsill and slid off my perch, so I could go and bid Baron Avedis farewell. When I opened my front door to enter the hallway, I gasped in surprise. Bedros stood in the hallway, his hand raised to knock on my door, a similar look of surprise reflected on his face.

"Hello," he said.

"Hello," I replied.

"May I come in?" he asked.

I hesitated. I had not let him in for a long time. He looked like a timid puppy, with his big eyes and solemn expression. I sighed and moved out of the way to let him in. He walked in, nodding a thank you in my direction. He looked around the room, as if remembering every small memory we had had in that space. His eyes fell on the dagger that Aleek had made for me. It sat on my bed, where I had been admiring it earlier. I did not say anything, but only waited for him to speak. I was tense for the coming argument. Then, all at once, he turned to face me, and he did not look angry.

"I will not leave with my father tomorrow."

My heart sank. "Why?"

"I would like to stay."

"Yes, I know, but why?" I asked, frustrated. I was hoping I could be distanced from him a little when he left with Baron Avedis. I crossed to my perch by the window. The pomegranate that sat there, undisturbed, was pale now, a sick yellow sheen covering its once-vibrant skin.

"Aleena does not look well. I feel she needs people around her."

"What do you mean?" I asked, surprised at his unexpected answer.

"Your sister—her face is pale. She does not speak as animatedly as before. It is as if her soul went on a journey and left her shell behind. I fear she is ill."

I did not speak for a minute. I had certainly noticed her physical differences, but I imagined she had a cold of some sort. My eyes rested on the pomegranate. "So what does that mean?"

"I want to tell your mother to call the doctor."

"The doctor already has seen her numerous times," I said.

"They have no choice, Tamar. She is not well."

I stood and faced him. "My sister has not even had an actual cold in years; she gets better so fast. You are jumping to conclusions."

"Still—"

"Is that why you will stay here? To watch over my sister?"

He took a deep breath and said cautiously, "Of course, I also will stay here for you." I frowned, and he spoke quickly, his words rushing out, "I want us to be friends, Tamar; can't you see that? We were such good friends once; we understood each other and laughed together. You mean everything to me, and I can't imagine life without your friendship again. You are that fresh drink of water after a long day; you are the only real thing to happen to me. And I do not care if you never love me; so long as I could come to you at the end of the day and laugh with you and cry with you, I will be the happiest man on earth. I will never give up on you."

"They are going to make us marry each other, damn it; can you not see that?"

"Why is that so horrifying to you?"

"I would rather die than marry you," I declared.

"It is not as if you have a choice, is it?" he shouted angrily. He spun around and left the room, slamming the door behind him. I ran against the door and slapped the palms of my hands against the wood, feeling the impact sting my skin.

I turned and pressed my back against the door, tears filling my eyes. I tried to calm my breathing. I was more upset than angry, and I wished he could see that, but he was just as blinded as I was. Why could he not leave me alone? Of course I missed our friendship. But

I did not want him to have the same hold on me as Vartan did on Aleena. I did not want my spirit broken by Bedros.

After a moment, I heard a shuffle behind me, outside the door. He had come back, but he was quiet, just as I was. I felt a light push against the door, and I knew he was leaning against it, just as tortured as I was.

"I'm sorry," I heard him say.

How did he know I was against the door as well?

"Why?" I asked.

"Because I do not know how to express myself as you do. It is difficult for me to just say that I am here for you. I *am* here for you. But I cannot say it. I cannot even show it the way you would like. I never want you to feel alone." There was a heavy pause. "I will always love you. I am sorry I disappoint you so much."

"I cannot give you the part of my heart that you want," I whispered.

"I will not force you."

"Promise?"

"I promise."

I breathed a sigh of relief, the tears coming to my eyes. I did not feel alone anymore, for I dearly did miss his friendship. I opened the door to face him and found myself hugging him tightly, burying my face in his chest. He put his arms around me, resting his chin on top of my head for a brief moment.

I pulled away and smiled at him. "I want to bid your father farewell."

He nodded, and we walked downstairs together where the preparations were being made for Vartan and Baron Avedis to be on their way. When my godfather saw me, he opened his arms and pulled me into a great big hug. "Best of luck to you," he murmured in my ear. "Come and visit us whenever you want, my child; our home is open to you."

"Thank you," I said and smiled at him. I nodded coolly at Vartan, who nodded back, and they went on their way.

~⟫═⊙ ⊙═⟪~

That night was lovely when I met with Aleek. We did not stay on Akhtamar, but rather went back to the mainland, where his village was having another party. Most of the villagers knew me now, after the last party when Karin had thrust me into the center of attention. While they made teasing comments about my covered face, they never pushed me to reveal my identity, and they were satisfied with my simple first name. The women only focused on pulling me into every dance, and we laughed for hours, reveling in the moment. Aleek and I danced together for most of the dances, and we were cheered and encouraged by everyone. I was surprised, for there was not one person here who was not happy for us. His mother smiled at me when I went to help her with the food, and his father even danced a dance with me. They loved me, and they loved watching me with him. There was an unspoken attraction between us, and the entire village could feel it, but we had done nothing about it. We did not hold hands outside of dancing, and he did not kiss me. He was cordial, but his eyes were heated, and I longed to be in his arms.

Toward the end of the party, Aleek and I found ourselves drifting away from the revelries. We found a seat on a boulder near the beach, and watching the calm lake, we talked well into the night. It was a perfect night.

I found myself telling him about my sister's mysterious illness. He listened to me, watching me with his dark eyes, and when I finished speaking, he said simply, "You must spend some time with her, to talk to her and see what really is happening."

I was quiet for a moment. "Perhaps I should take her to get some fresh air. She has been stuck inside for a long time; I do not remember the last time we went to the cliff."

He smiled at me with encouragement, and that smile stayed with me all through the night, even as I lay curled in my bed, alone in the dark.

The next day, I went on a walk with Aleena. We had linked arms and were strolling through the lovely garden, rich with its delicious fruits and perfumed flowers. I had decided on the walk to the garden after my talk with Aleek the night before, for fresh air always brings a flush to the cheeks, and Aleena's pale face most definitely needed some flushing.

The sun was strong that day, despite the promise of winter, and it shone down on us with its bright rays. It was not long before I saw the perspiration beading Aleena's face. "It is desperately hot," she muttered, fanning herself with her hand. "Why is it so hot?"

"Maybe later we can swim in the lake to cool ourselves off," I suggested.

She smiled at that. "We could."

We walked on, comforted by each other's presence.

"How is Karin?" she asked.

I frowned. "She left for school."

Her eyebrows shot up. "Lucky girl…"

"I know. I wish I could go to school."

She smiled. "We have the largest library in the land."

"Yes, but it is the experience."

"I understand, Tamar. I spent years trying to open your eyes to that. And now you see it. I am proud of you."

She said it so matter-of-factly. *I am proud of you.* My life's purpose seemed to be to disappoint other people, and I had not realized how accustomed I had become to that.

"Thank you," I said quietly, overwhelmed by emotion.

She slowed her walking pace and sat down on a rock. "I must sit; this heat is unbearable."

I noticed that she sat under the pomegranate tree, the same tree she had always sat under when she had managed to escape from her lessons. While she dabbed at her collar and forehead with a hand-kerchief, I reached up and grabbed a pomegranate. I could not help but notice how pale her face was and how this simple walk had tired her, when she used to leap and bound all throughout the garden without slowing down.

She watched me as I cracked open the pomegranate and took out a seed, popping it into my mouth. I held one out to her, and she let me drop it into her palm. We sat together for an hour, eating the seeds one at a time, making small moans of delight every time the seed splashed its sweet flavor onto our tongues.

"I counted," I said finally.

"Counted what?"

"The seeds of the pomegranate you used the night before your wedding."

She looked at me solemnly. Her eyes were wide and shining.

"There were six hundred seeds, not three hundred sixty-five. Each pomegranate has a different amount of seeds apparently."

She nodded and looked down. Her hand fluttered to her chest, and she held it over her heart with her eyes closed.

"Aleena?"

She lifted a finger to me, shushing me until she composed herself. It did not take long, but her face had a sheen over it. I decided that it was time to go back inside. The heat was not helping her. I handed her to her maids and instructed them to bathe her well, with cool, scented water.

When I went back to my room, I was happy that I had managed to fix my friendship with Bedros and taken Aleena out to have some fresh air. I was satisfied.

It was a quiet night that night, and I was curled up in my chair, facing my window, which I kept open every night now to watch the water and think of Aleek. I wondered if he sat on the other side thinking of me. Did he ever think of me in his arms? Did he ever kiss me in his dreams? My eyes began to drift closed, lulled by comforting thoughts of his strong presence and the way he would gaze upon my covered face when he thought I was not looking.

I often look back on this particular night. It is hard to do so without cringing, but I force myself to face it. It seemed as if it was the perfect night for something tragic to occur. How did I not feel that as I lay there on my soft sheets, looking out at the calm lake? When was Lake Van ever just *calm*? When did my life ever just go smoothly? Either way, I was oblivious. I was happy, blissful;

everything was normal at last. But to me, it could not have been normal. Nothing was normal in my life.

That is why it happened.

It must have been sometime in the middle of the night.

I jolted upright, my sheets flailing wildly around my limbs. Through my heavy breathing, I remember how quiet it was, and I was wondering what in the name of heaven had woken me like that. The silence was too thick, too tense. It was as if a string was pulled tight over my skin, ready to snap at any second. I could not move; my entire body had become frozen with anticipation. Right as the thought to run crossed my mind, I heard it: a high-pitched, gurgled shrieking.

The silence shattered around me as the sound sliced through the night. I leaped out of bed, but the sheets wrapped tightly around me, and I fell to the floor with a hard thump.

Aleena.

I began to scream mindlessly, as I stumbled up and ran out of my room, my panic opening my mouth and lungs. I had to let her know I was coming, that she was going to be OK.

I ran as fast as I could down the halls, and I saw maids and servants with puzzled faces fill the halls, moving into action to follow me.

"Tamar?" cried Janna, as she hustled out of her room with her mother. I heard my mother somewhere cry out my sister's name, and I wanted to scream again.

I was the first to reach her. I burst into Aleena's room, ready to fight whoever was hurting her. But I froze in horror.

Her eyes had rolled back in her head until only the whites of them showed, and her back was arched unnaturally. She was shaking fast, and her arms flailed with no control.

I had never seen a seizure before, and yet here I was, staring at it convulse through my sister's body.

My mother arrived in a frantic state, and my father right behind her with his magnificent sword gleaming in the hallway. I was watching him now as he fingered the sword helplessly, perhaps hoping it had been an attack so he could kill the man with one stroke.

But nothing could be done about an illness.

⋆═◉ ◉═⋆

It is amazing how quickly a life can turn completely upside down. One could be lying there, dreaming of the future, and then be struck with terror in the next minute.

The seizure had lasted about a minute, but in that one minute, the entire palace had become a buzz of chaos. My parents argued about whether to call the doctor, for he had never been able to help before. My mother wanted to call him, but my father refused, his pride getting in the way. I never liked the doctor either and disagreed with his methods, but he was the only one we could call. The maids were all set to their duties, to bring fresh sheets, clean Aleena's room, and wash her quivering body.

I found out from the maid that Aleena had felt faint earlier rather suddenly during teatime. Her knees had buckled for a moment, but she had not lost consciousness. She had been fine but was unusually pale throughout the day. I remembered taking her out in the heat. Was this my fault? I shook my head furiously, to rid myself of that thought. *No.*

Everyone was gathered in the hallway outside her room, unsure of what to do. Bedros was there as well, keeping a reasonable distance behind me. I continually looked around for Vartan and Baron Avedis, though I knew that they had left already to prepare the rooms for the bride and would not hear about this incident for a few days at least.

Aleena was lying in her bed, unnaturally still. Her face was ghostly pale, her mouth open to gulp in air. Her skin was a sheen of sweat, and her lips were dry and cracked. "Bring her water," I ordered, although a maid was already seated beside her with the pitcher of water.

I sat on her bed at her side, grabbed a clean cloth, and dipped it into the water to mop her face and cool her as much as possible. I heard the shouting as my parents argued outside her room. Bedros hovered nearby. "Is there anything I could do?"

I ignored him. "Don't let them in," I hissed at Janna. She gave me a wide-eyed look; for a maid to give orders to the king and queen would surely mean harsh punishment. Before I could say anything, they walked inside anyway, angry and heated.

"We need to call him in; she is sick," demanded the queen.

Aleena grabbed at her covers tight, her skin stretched tight over her knuckles.

"I will not have that rat sniffing about my castle."

"Your daughter will *die.*"

Aleena made a noise, a small gasp as she struggled for breath. She fidgeted in her bed, her body unable to lie still. I pressed the wet cloth to her forehead, murmuring, "Shh," hoping my parents would be quiet soon.

But they did not, and I noticed Aleena becoming more and more distressed by the second. It was too much to handle. The noise escalated, the maids shuffling back and forth, barking orders at each other, opening windows, bringing in water; Bedros lingering too close above my shoulder; my parents shouting terribly; and Aleena gasping with a sharp wheezing sound.

I could not handle it anymore. I turned and screamed, "Hush!"

And in the shocked silence that followed my shout, Aleena had her second seizure that night. Her body convulsed, her eyes rolling up again.

I held her tight, her body moving hard against me, as my face froze in a shocked look. Unbidden tears rolled down my cheeks as I sobbed, "I'm sorry, I'm sorry, I'm sorry," over and over again, like a broken mantra. I should not have taken her to the garden. I should not have let her sit under the sun for so long. This was my fault. It was entirely my fault.

They were all silent in the room; no one knew what to do. She was quiet this time during her attack, and it seemed like a horrible nightmare. When Aleena finally stopped moving, her eyes closed, and she lay still in my arms. She looked like an angel, peacefully resting her eyes.

My mother turned to my father's personal servant and barked, "Call the doctor." The servant ran out of the room immediately, eager to escape the horror in the room. I turned back to see why my father would not counter her anymore.

He was watching Aleena, a pale and terrified look on his face, as if he was losing everything and did not know how to stop it. And just that look was enough to bring such a feeling of fear into me as I held my sister, who was caught between two worlds, just as much as I was.

Chapter 19

AND JUST LIKE that, the heaviest of burdens was put onto my shoulders. I became sullen, sorrow pulling the emotions out of my body until I became numb with lack of feeling. My sister was ill, and I could do nothing about it. The helplessness I felt overpowered me, and I sat for hours in my room, staring out my window.

They told me that Aleena had a weak heart. They had known since she was a child and tried to keep her composed at all times, so as not to excite her. That was when I knew that Aleena had known about this. All those times she had hinted about her condition to me, and I had been too foolish and wrapped up in my own affairs to realize. Her words rushed back to me, cryptic and mysterious at the time, but so clear now.

That is not why I am dying…

It is too late for me to be free…

One day you will understand…

I cringed and put my head in my hands. Aleena was on the verge of dying of a broken heart.

The doctor told us to keep her out of the heat. Apparently it was the heat that had triggered the first seizure, though her heart had been weak already. She was not allowed any excitement, any drama, anything that would possibly upset her and strain her heart even more. She could not move anyway, her breath coming in fast, laborious gasps and her body lying completely still.

She could hardly speak more than a few words without running out of breath. She was so pale.

The doctor put her on a strict diet and medication he had procured from the East. He charged an enormous amount for it, but we did not care.

He said, "She should not have been under the sun."

I should not have taken her under the sun. It was my fault. It was my fault.

My face was swollen from crying, and my mother and father were in a tense state. Nothing seemed to make any of us feel better.

News traveled quickly of Aleena's illness, and we received small gifts from distant relatives, silk and lace and household items, to make it easier on us. My mother put the gifts to good use, being the practical woman she was, but they angered me. Gifts would not save her. Mother secretly believed that as well, for she did not even scold or beat me when I accidentally dropped and shattered a dozen engraved plates sent from the East. I could not understand why she kept them. Once, I had taken a vase in anger and thrown it outside, where it rolled away on the grass. I stormed up to my room and sat at my window, gazing out at the waters of the lake, hoping the breeze would soften my temper. But from my view at the window, I noticed movement beneath me. I looked down into the gardens and saw my mother walking slowly through the path, gazing around her quietly, until she found the abandoned vase lying sideways in a muddy patch. She sank to her knees, picked up the vase delicately, and used the bottom of her dress to wipe the mud from its surface. I could not see very clearly from my height, but from the way her shoulders were hunched over and trembling, I knew she was crying.

I never broke any of her gifts again, for I knew she saw some sort of rebirth in them. Both her daughters were drifting away from her, and she found solace in her material objects.

On one of these nights, it was my time to meet Aleek at the beach. I waited there for him, eagerly watching the dark waters for his arrival. It felt like I'd been kept away from him for forever. My candle flickered nearby, guiding him through the darkness.

It was my first joy that week when I finally did see him, churning the waters with his oar. He had a grin on his face as he saw me stand up and near the shore.

"Hello," he said.

"Hello," I replied.

He leaped out of the boat and pulled it up to safety on the wet sand. When he turned to face me, his expression changed abruptly. "Something is wrong."

"No."

He watched me for a moment, narrowing his eyes. I turned away from him and tried to brighten my eyes a bit. "I am all right, Aleek."

"Let me tell you something," he said suddenly with passionate vigor, taking a step toward me. "You think you can cover your identity with your shawl—I don't know what your reason is, but I have come to accept it. But you do not realize that you are revealing the most important part of a person—the eyes. They reflect what is in the heart. And you are talking to the one person who craves to know you the most. I have memorized your eyes and the feelings that shine through them. And in them, right now, I see pain. And they have dulled the beauty that I usually see. Your 'no' isn't going to push me away. Unburden yourself to me, and let me take away your pain."

My breath was caught. I had to turn away, so he would not see the emotions that ran through me. There was silence as his words rushed through me. I shut my eyes and murmured, "My sister is not well."

"In what way?"

"Her heart is breaking."

He sighed. "Just like the eldest princess."

"What?" I asked shakily, turning to him.

"The Princess Aleena—surely you've heard. Her heart is ill as well. It seems you are more similar to Princess Tamar than we previously said."

It took me a moment to remember that I was still in disguise. "Oh, yes. Odd."

"I am sorry to hear of her illness," he said, coming to stand next to me. He put his hands on my shoulders and squeezed comfortingly, but the touch just brought me torment. It was painful to feel the little touch, but not be able to have his love.

"I do not feel like dancing tonight. I apologize for having you come all the way here for nothing." I turned away from him and slipped out of his grasp, heading for the cliff wall behind us.

He scoffed slightly and gave me a look from the corner of his eyes, walking alongside me. "I enjoy your company. My trips here will never be for nothing."

We sat down with our backs against the rock wall, the candle lit between us. It was comforting being able to sit next to him and watch the ebbing waves of Lake Van. He glanced at me and asked, "What are you thinking about?"

I gave a wan smile. "How much I look forward to our meetings."

"I do too. There is something about you that draws me here. I told you once it was your aura. But it is so much more than that. You are different from anyone I have met."

"How?"

He sighed. "We live in a world of people who have small minds—one-sided, stubborn people. But there is so much to the world, and few people open their eyes to it. I feel as if you are one of the few, like me, who want more. You are intelligent, bright, passionate. It makes me want to know more about your mind."

"And will you?"

"As much as I can, yes."

"I wish I could understand myself," I said and sighed.

"Why don't you?"

"My heart is troubled. I feel as if *I* am the one with a broken heart, instead of my sister. But that is so selfish of me to say."

"You are not selfish. You are her sister, it is no wonder you feel her pain strongly."

He was right, but I still felt foolish. I let the conversation drift— allowing silence to take the reigns for a few minutes. We listened to the waves that crashed along the shore and felt the breeze caress our faces. It was soothing, this silence, and I felt truly comfortable, as I hadn't in a long while. There was no obligation for me, no expectation I had to fulfill. It was refreshing.

"If you could be anywhere in the world right now, where would you be?" I asked him softly.

I heard his steady breathing, and his eyes turned up to the dark skies, as if searching for the answers among the stars. I couldn't help but to watch him, to see the shadows that ran along his jawbone, the way his expression was unreadable but also held so much emotion. His face was roughened from years of hard work, but I could see places where it was still soft, untouched by labor: underneath his jaw, behind his ears, right over his eyebrows where the skin smoothed out, his soft lips that had a certain firmness to them. He pointed up to the stars and said, "I'd follow that star—the really bright one. And I'd see where I'd end up."

I smiled. Such a lovely answer.

"And you?"

"Anywhere but on this island."

"Why?"

"I feel trapped. I long to escape it, but I am held down by the thickest chains."

"What are they?"

"My mother, propriety, duties."

"What duties?"

I gave a frustrated sigh. I wished I could tell him, but I was trapped in a cage I had fashioned for myself. And the cage was named *Lori*. "I don't know…chores, lessons, guests."

"You have money, don't you?"

I did not speak. It was an unexpected question. I only looked at him with eyes he believed to be beautiful. "I wish I didn't."

"I wish I did," he said. I scoffed. "No, really. But not for the reason that you would think I would give."

"And what reason is yours?"

"I want to be free. And I'd use my money to be free. But then I'd use the rest to help others, others who are like me, now, who need all the help."

"You cannot save everyone."

"Yes, but I can save a few. I don't *need* money. But I know that I would use it well. I would spend it on others: build comfortable homes, give food, take people to school."

I nodded. I vaguely wondered what I would do if I had free rein with the wealth in my family. Would I ever use it to help others in the way he was describing? I tried to find a charitable thought in my mind, scouring my brain for any possible ideas. I was ashamed at the answer that was whispering in my mind, not willing to back down and let kindness forward. I would not do that. I would somehow rid myself of the burden and still go after my life. To be free. He wanted money and good deeds to reach freedom. I wanted escape.

"Ever heard of the legend that surrounds your island?" he asked, giving me a cryptic glance.

"Akhtamar."

"Yes."

"Of course."

He was still watching me. "We have a rather similar situation I think."

My face was flushing, so I looked down to fidget with my cloak. "In some way." *You don't even know.*

"Akh, Lori," he said wryly. I winced at the fake name. It sounded so wrong with the other name—as if it had no right to be used in that way.

I noticed his eyes lingering over my face still, but after a moment, he turned away.

"Are you comfortable with me?"

I smiled wanly. "You would not ask me if you believed I was actually comfortable with you."

"True," he said.

"You would better ask me if I am happy with you."

He paused. "And are you happy with me then?"

I looked straight at him when I said it. "Undeniably."

"So why are you not comfortable with me?"

"I do not know. I feel there is tension between us. We are doing what we shouldn't be doing."

"We are doing nothing wrong."

"We are meeting at night, with no escorts. If anyone knew, they would slander my name."

"Your name that is not Lori."

I frowned. "Yes."

He shifted his position, so he faced me more. "May I ask you a question?" I eyed him warily. "It is about the princesses."

I hesitated for a moment. "Sure."

"What do you think of them?"

"They are misunderstood," I said immediately.

He leaned back and shifted again to look out at the dark water. "You have royalty in you, am I right?" I did not reply. He was digging too much tonight. "I wish I knew who you were, but at the same time, I am glad I do not. I feel as though by not knowing your details, I can only know your soul. And of course, that is the most beautiful part of a person."

"Would you ever hold my identity against me?"

"How could I? You have no intentions to harm me."

"How could you be so sure?"

"I have a hard time trusting people. So my trust in you is not just foolishness. It is a rarity."

I remembered here, on the night of Aleena's wedding, the conversation I had had with the old woman. Something had happened to his older brother. And I had met the boy when I was very young. I was surprised that both Karin and Aleek had never mentioned it. I looked away, wondering if I should say anything.

He leaned over to catch my eye. "Where are you?"

"Wondering why you have a hard time trusting people."

"And?"

"I am connecting it to the mystery of what happened to your brother."

He leaned back, stiff-backed. His lips were pursed, but I saw no anger in his eyes—just caution and pain that had been covered up over time. "It is no mystery."

"What happened?"

"He was killed—several years ago. It was a fight between some of the lads from my village and Turkish soldiers near the border."

"What were they fighting about?" I asked, my eyes wide.

He looked down at me, amused. "You must really not be a village girl if you do not know about the disputes between the Turkish and Armenian people."

"Surely my—the king must be able to do something about it," I said, tripping over the word.

"Not really. These disputes happen quite often. I hope it ends sooner than later. I fear the worst for our people."

I put a hand comfortingly on his shoulder. "I am sorry you lost your brother. Maybe our people will one day reach an agreement with them, and the conflict will stop."

He nodded, resting his hand over mine and looking straight at me. "That is the hope."

My heart was beating fast as we sat there, gazing at each other, his hand atop mine. I was playing with fire. I pulled my hand away and gave a nervous laugh, saying, "Until then, please be safe. Or else I shall lose my dance partner."

He grinned. "I will be safe. But I should be leaving now; dawn is about to arrive."

"Already?" I frowned.

He nodded and stood. I stood as well, wondering how time had passed.

We walked toward the boat, taking our time, for we did not want to leave each other's presence. When we arrived, he put a hand on the wood to push the boat toward the water, but he hesitated. I watched him, wondering what was on his mind. But I did not need to ask. He turned to me suddenly, and I was surprised at the look on his face. It seemed slightly tortured. "I wanted to apologize."

"For?"

"What I did…the day we met."

I did not speak.

"I had no right to play that trick on you. I understand if you were traumatized, and I was incredibly worried and angry with myself. I cannot forgive myself, but I hope that you will be able to."

"I do forgive you," I said softly. I had already forgiven him a long time ago.

He bowed his head slightly, his eyes closing for a brief moment in relief. "Thank you." He turned again to hop into the boat but paused and tensed. Without warning, he turned around fast and hastily kissed me on the cheek.

He left, disappearing out onto the water with a look over his shoulder and a farewell wave.

My breath was still caught in my throat at the swift kiss. I felt dizzy with exhilaration. But all I could do was wring my hands in despair and pray once again for Lake Van to stay quiet tonight.

Chapter 20

BEDROS WAS AVOIDING me. I had assumed our relationship would have been better after our conversation, but it seemed as if something had frightened him. He was skittish, like a horse that was afraid of its own shadow. When we bumped into each other in the hallway, he would slide past me without looking into my eyes. I tried to talk to him once or twice, but he hardly said more than a word to me. I dismissed it, believing it to be just another dramatic thought going through his mind.

I busied myself by going often to Aleena's room, watching her still form on the bed. She was awake, but hardly. Her eyes would flutter weakly, and her mouth was open to help her breathe easier. Her chest moved up and down rapidly and with no particular rhythm. If it was really quiet in the room, I could hear the faint wheezing rattling in her chest.

It hurt to look at her, and I felt such an aching pain in my heart when I sat next to her and watched her as she watched me, unable to say anything without it hurting her. It was as though her soul had been trapped in her body, which was caving in on her. The only way I could make myself feel better was by talking to her. I talked to her about everything, telling her what ran through my mind and how there was tension between Bedros and me. She listened quietly, her eyes watching me, her lips dry and unmoving.

Throughout the days, I grew more comfortable talking to her. She became a sort of verbal journal to me. The doctor told me that my voice soothed her, and she always seemed to be doing well after my visits. So I tried to go as often as I could, and I talked and talked until my throat cracked.

I told her more about Aleek, describing in detail our interactions and how I felt. "It is so hard for me to be near him sometimes," I said, resting my head against her hip. She had a hand resting on my hair. "I want to tell him how I feel, but if I do, then our interaction will be so different. Would he still want to see me? Would he push to see my face?"

Aleena took a breath, and I waited for her to find her words. "If you love him..." she paused to wheeze, "then seeing your face...will not be so...horrid."

I nodded. "You are right. I wish you could speak to him. He is so very interesting. The knowledge and passion that rest in his heart are very like mine, and we could sit for hours and talk about all of it. And he helps me dance; he is so very good at it. He understands me."

She smiled lightly.

"Sometimes we don't even dance; we just talk. He asks me questions about myself, Aleena. He waits to hear the answers, and it is so rare that someone does that. He wants to hear the full truth, not just bits and pieces like we've been taught to do all our lives. I want to tell him everything, and I know he will never look at me differently. But I still have not told him who I really am and I am in such torment."

She blinked.

"Aleena...Do you think he will die?" I asked abruptly, my own question taking me by surprise. She did not seem surprised to hear it, however.

She moved her hand slightly and opened her palm to face me. I put my hand in hers, but she did not hold it. Instead, she rubbed her thumb lightly against the scar that ran across my skin, the scar she had put there when I was fourteen.

She ran her tongue over her cracked lips, and I leaned in slightly to hear what she was going to say.

"Akh, Tamar..."

⟶⟫⊙ ⊙⟪⟵

That evening, I sat at my window, looking out at the lake. I was alone, for in the past week, Janna had been at Aleena's side, helping her when she could. The lake glistened so beautifully, and I could feel a light breeze blowing in at me. Why could it not always be this beautiful? I was feeling sick inside at what had happened earlier today when I told Aleena about Aleek. She believed he would die. That was certainly clear from her expression and her short comment. I was following the legend of Akhtamar much too closely, and I was frightened for what would happen to him. I looked down at the pearly scar on the palm of my hand. It shone like the moonlight reflecting off the surface of the water. I did fall in love, just like the princess in the legends. I fell in love just as strongly, though

I was so certain at the time that I wouldn't. I was playing with his fate.

But he had a boat! It was the biggest difference between him and the mysterious man in the legends. He had strong arms, and the water would have to destroy the boat before reaching him. He would always be able to prevail against Lake Van's treachery.

He was strong. He was ambitious.

I should not worry. *But I did.*

I put my head against the wooden window frame and wondered why everything was made so difficult. I wondered why life had to be dictated for everyone and why we could not live our own lives, to discover our own joys and be able to fly with our own wings.

My heart ached for Tamar in the legend. What really happened to her after he drowned? Did she marry another man? Did she die from a broken heart? Did she kill herself? Or did she refuse to be with another man and lived her days alone, cast away from her family and in shame?

What would happen to me?

I wondered this, and every minute that passed, my lips pulled down into a deeper and deeper frown. I closed my eyes and tried to relax my breathing. When had I become such a sad ghost of a girl? I had turned into Aleena, sporting that same frustrated and tormented look. I realized what the look was. It was knowledge and desperation. The knowledge of life's cruelties can show in a person's mere expression. There is no ignorance, no silliness.

I felt the wind lift a strand of my hair and envied its brief moment of flight. There was a knock at my door, and I turned my head away from the lake.

"Yes?" I called. My voice made me wince slightly. It was so cold.

The door opened hesitantly, and I saw Bedros standing, fidgeting with the wood at the doorway. I waited.

"Your father would like to see you in his study."

I nodded. He remained standing. "Is anything the matter?" I asked.

"No."

"Then I shall be there shortly," I said dismissively. He nodded, and after another moment of stalling, he walked away. I heard his soft footsteps disappearing down the hall, and I remembered the days when he would pound through the halls, the mischievous glint shining in his eyes and a sly smile spread over his face.

When had we all changed?

The echo of my footsteps in the hall was loud and hollow. I wondered what my father wanted. Aleena and I were hardly ever allowed in his study.

I knocked on the doors hesitantly. "Come in," I heard. I walked in, gliding into the room and standing in front of his desk. He was sitting behind it, watching me with an odd look in his eyes. I noticed for the first time the wrinkles and hard lines that spread over his face. Somewhere along the way, he had grown older, and I had not noticed.

"I have some news for you."

My eyes widened. "Is it Aleena?"

"A little bit," he mumbled, a troubled look crossing his face.

"OK," I said, urging him to continue with a nod.

"As you know, Aleena was very well loved by our people. They greatly looked forward to her ruling the kingdom alongside Vartan.

We spent quite a large part of her life showing her off to the public and making sure she was almost worshipped as a ruler. The people keep her name in their hearts."

"Yes."

"The people like you as well. Of course, they know less about you than Aleena, because of her exposure. We always assumed she would...she would rule the kingdom. That is why you were kept inside, away from the people. They know you as Aleena's sister: the beautiful young princess, the mysterious legend. They never thought of you as the ruler."

"Aleena will still be the future ruler." I winced. I did not like this talk. I felt such disappointment rolling off his voice. I knew I could never be as perfect as Aleena.

"Yes, well, we do not know that."

I sat down on the chair across from the desk. It was an ornate wooden chair, with intricate engravings carved into every inch of the chair. The seat was embroidered by hand, with beautiful colors shot through it. I remember when I was little, I had sat on the chair to run my hands over the carvings. There were grapes, clusters of them all across the wood surface. And each grape had textured lines cut through them. But I remember when I ran my hands over the grapes, I had noticed that they looked like little heads clustered together. Each one had the most sorrowful look on its face, and I would feel so sad for them. I wanted to free them, but they were stuck, frozen there forever in the carvings.

"Aleena is not going to make it for very long." A lump lodged itself in my throat, as if I had just swallowed one of the wooden grapes, but I stayed still. "We need a distraction for the people, to show them that hope lies in you."

Marriage.

He ran a hand through his hair. "Marriage."

I saw the portrait that father had painted of Aleena on her wedding day, leaning against the wall on the floor. She was so beautiful, but pale, a ghost in a crimson wedding dress. Somehow I knew my face would be the same, but I would have no portraits painted of me.

"Your name has spread over the countryside and the mainland since Aleena's illness. Mother has seen to that. Several dukes and lords have asked for your hand in marriage already. I did not believe they made suitable matches, however, so I rejected their offers."

My back had straightened. My eyes were wide, and my lips parted in a desperate silent call. I managed to utter, "What if a man with a perfect character came forth? But he was not of noble descent?"

My father gave me a look. "Don't be silly, child." I gripped the edge of my chair. "Besides, luckily for us, one of your offers was suitable. I have accepted it on your behalf."

I remembered the sidelong glances and the timid looks. I heard his voice: *I will never give up on you.* I remembered how much he had avoided me the past week. He was afraid. He had been afraid of me. He had known. I felt as though I were underwater. The grip I had on the chair loosened, and I felt the blood rush from my face. I knew my expression mirrored my sister's in the painting my father was so proud of.

"We will begin planning the marriage immediately between you and Bedros. It will give the people something to focus on. We will announce it publicly on my birthday, which, as you know, is in a few weeks."

There was silence.

"Tamar." There was warning in his voice.

"Do I have a choice?"

"Tamar."

"Yes, sir."

⊶▬ ◐▬⊷

I walked out of the study and shut the door quietly behind me. I began to walk aimlessly, my eyes staring straight ahead but unseeing. I was numb, focusing on my breathing, thinking of nothing else. Before I knew it, I was standing in front of Aleena's door.

Walking in timidly, I stood in the doorway, watching her still form. She was looking at me, almost as though she had been expecting my visit. "Tamar?" she managed to say.

I shuffled to her bed and lay down next to her. As soon as I put my head onto her shoulder and felt her arms rise around my quivering body, I began to cry. She held me as tight as she physically could.

"I am to marry Bedros," I sobbed.

"Akh," she muttered.

"I don't know what I will do. I cannot marry him—I am in love with Aleek. How could I walk away from the man I love?"

"You don't..." she said. Her chest rose with a ragged breath. "Tamar...if you truly love someone, nothing would stop you from being with them. Nothing, Tamar...do you understand? Circumstance...people...mountains...a lake...nothing."

I nodded heavily. "But there are so many obstacles to us being together."

She shook her head and gave me a weary smile. "No, Tamar... there are not. The obstacles are only in your mind...think with your heart and you will find no obstacles."

Her words resounded through my mind as I left her room. I had calmed down considerably, my rage turning into a cold stone that rested in my stomach. The walk to my chamber was dark, as the sun had been slowly setting during our talk. None of the maids and servants had bothered to light the candles that lined the walls. The entire palace seemed a tomb, its echoing hallways cast in ominous shadows.

I walked as if I were a ghost that haunted these halls. But when I reached my room, I saw the only other ghost of this palace, standing across from my door. He was sullen, shadows covering his eyes, so he looked like a skull. I longed for Aleek to be standing at my door, watching me with such affection. With each step, I felt Aleek slipping through my fingers as Bedros's chains around me tightened.

The whites of his eyes flashed as he glanced across at me, and the look on my face seemed to frighten him. I stopped in front of him and looked up at his face.

It would have been all right, I suppose. I was not feeling particularly vicious. I had not planned to act out.

But a smile appeared on his face, and he put his hands on my waist. Those gestures seemed to say, *Everything will be all right; you will be mine soon.*

But it wouldn't be; and he had the audacity to promise that with a selfish smile. So I slapped him once—hard, across his cheek.

I waited for a moment and saw the shock register on his face. The smile was replaced by a wide O.

"You broke your promise."

And only when I was sure that smile was gone, I turned, entered my chambers, and closed the door with a resolute click.

Chapter 21

THAT NIGHT, I would be seeing him again. I needed to. I had to. I felt as though I was falling apart, and I needed for him to put me back together again.

But as soon as I stepped out into the night, I felt a chill go down my spine. The wind was blowing stronger than it had last time—much stronger. It billowed past me as I began to run toward the shore. My head was ducked down as I fought against it, and I struggled to pull my black cloak around me for protection. The branches whipped at me as I ran through the trees that lined the side of the hill. They reared up like restless souls and quavered in fear at the wailing wind.

It was desperately cold, and I was terrified at the way the wind beat at me, but my worries lay with Lake Van. My mind ran wild with toxic thoughts, as I began to envision where this night could lead. "Please, please, please," I muttered under my breath. "Please, please, please, don't take him from me."

I reached the shore and paused in horror, for the tide was much higher than usual. Where we typically had a large bit of land to walk around on, this time the beach was only a few feet wide. I wasted no more time. I ran across the pebbles, ducking the spray of the waves and slipping over the slick ground. I fell a few times, my knees slamming into the rocks, but my fear had numbed me. With drops of blood dripping down my calves and ankles, I finally reached the overhanging rock. With trembling fingers, I tried to light the candle, but the wind was too strong. I lit match after match, crying out in frustration, until finally the candle came to life with a sputtering hiss. I placed it on the overhanging ledge, where it was protected from the storm, and I turned to look at the churning, angry waters.

There was such a violent howling as the wind screamed across the surface of the water, while the waves reached up in great arches to touch the sky. The roar that erupted when the waves fell back to the lake frightened me out of my wits. I remembered Karin's face as she had once looked out at the water and announced that if it had been a storm, my boat would not be a boat anymore.

The tears ran down my cheeks as I placed my palms together and prayed over and over again for him to reach my shore safely. "Please, please, please," I kept pleading. "Don't take him from me; don't take him from me." I almost heard *her* wails—Princess Tamar's wails—echoing against the cliff walls from so long ago.

I waited for an hour. It was the longest hour of my entire life. I dug a trench in the sand from how much I had paced back and forth, wringing my hands together, until I feared they would fall off. I was drenched from the spray of the water, my hair coming down in damp ringlets around my face. All my senses were on alert, as I tried to hear for any change in the waves to indicate his arrival. I squinted against the wind to try and see the silhouette of the man I loved. But there was nothing except darkness.

I couldn't help it. I opened my mouth and screamed, "Aleek!" My voice was shrill, as if it was an arrow that pierced the night. I hardly recognized it. "Aleek!" The echo against the cliff walls sent shivers down my spine. But I listened quietly.

It was a few seconds later when I heard it.

Somewhere in the distance, I heard an echo, "Lori!"

It almost sounded like it was part of the howling wind, but it was clear that it was a name. I didn't even care that it was not my name. Tears of relief ran down my cheeks. I ran to the water's edge and looked out into the darkness, while the waves licked at my feet and sprayed into my face. Where was he? My clothes were soaked through.

That was when I saw him.

But instead of yelping for joy at his appearance, I yelped in horror for his boat was nowhere to be seen.

The waves picked him up and tossed him on the shore at my feet as if he were a rag doll. "Aleek!" I cried out, falling to my knees at his side. I grabbed a strong hold of his arms and dragged him up the shore away from the angry waves. He was soaked through, and I had no way of knowing how long he had been in the water without his boat. He coughed hard, his chest heaving, and he hung his head as water streamed down his face. His usually wild hair was flat and dark against his head. I threw off my cloak and covered him with it, but he shrugged it off, sitting up.

"No," he said simply.

"You'll freeze," I insisted, but there was a hard look in his face. Angry. He was looking at me with such an odd look, as if the storm was in his eyes and not billowing around us.

He got up to his feet, stumbling a little, and I did the same, but I stepped away from him, fearful of that look in his dark, dark eyes.

"What happened?"

"My boat was destroyed halfway through."

"You swam the rest of the way?"

"Yes," he said. He took a few steps toward me. There was lightning in his eyes.

"Why did you not go back?"

"I had to see you," he said.

And that was when I noticed that I had forgotten to cover my face with my shawl. I gasped in horror and covered my face with my hands, but he reached up and took my hands in his. He held them tight while I tried to look away, but he pulled me back to face him. "No! Please!" I cried.

"Why? I have never seen one so beautiful as you. Would you take away that pleasure from me?"

"Pleasure? I will be found out, and it will be the end of me! It will be the end of you!" I cried, twisting my head.

"Look at me!"

I shut my eyes and stepped forward, burying my face in his chest and trying to hide. But he stepped back and cupped my chin in his hands. He looked at me—*really* looked at me—for the first time since we had met. I could see how beautiful he thought I was in his eyes. I could see how in awe he was.

But that look that I had anticipated never came: the angry, you-lied-to-me look. I knew then that he did not recognize me. How could he? He had never seen the youngest princess after his chance encounter with her when he was a little boy. I could not be sure whether the tears that ran down my face were from relief or from heartbreak.

"I would make that journey a million more times if I find you waiting at the end for me each time—just like this," he said, holding my face in his hands. My heart pounded with such feeling when he finally brought his lips down on mine with all the hunger that had led Lake Van to swallow his boat. His arms wrapped around my waist, his broad hands flat against my lower back, pulling me closer to him. I let my hands rest on his broad chest. I wasn't surprised at his touch. It seemed natural, as though we had been touching each other all along, but without using our hands. It was irresistible, this feeling, and I wanted more. He wanted more. There were no thoughts in my mind, no doubts, no fears—only his eyes, his lips, his hands, his hair, soft under my touch. He pushed me backward, and I found my back pressing into the rock wall behind me. I could feel the roughness of the rock digging into my back, but I did not care. It was as if his kiss had unleashed all the emotions from a cage inside me, and they were suddenly loose inside my body, bouncing against the walls of my skin. The fear of losing Aleena, the guilt I felt for her seizure, the love I felt for Aleek, the anxiety at being betrothed to Bedros, the joy I felt in this very moment—everything tumbled out, and the same seemed to happen to him. His kiss was desperate, and he grabbed my face like he could consume me.

The wind beat around us, and the spray of the lake washed over us. But we did not separate from each other.

"What is your name?" he breathed.

I tried to shake my head, but he kissed me again, and I fell under his touch. He pulled me away from the wall and, in one deft move, put his arm under my knees and lifted me up easily to cradle me in his arms. I felt his muscles tense underneath my body as he held me tight. Our kiss did not break, even when he walked over to the light of the candle and placed me on my back on the sand. Our kiss did not break even as the wind shrieked and swore, as the waves of the lake struggled to reach us and slapped us with their spray. The only time it broke was when he pulled back slightly and murmured again, "What is your name?"

I took a deep breath, and he let his kisses slide down the arch of my neck. He stopped at my collarbone, and I could not keep silent any longer.

"Tamar," I breathed. "Tamar."

His hands, which were on my waist, tightened and gripped me with such passion. "Tamar," he repeated. He looked at me once, his eyes searching my face. There was some confusion writ in his eyes, but he seemed to put it away. Then we both went under.

And it was there, on that shore, under the watchful eyes of the blinking stars, that we shared our love and became one with the raging wind that surrounded us. All the fear and sorrow I had felt earlier in the day disappeared with this new feeling, and all I had left was pure bliss. And I could see it in his eyes—those dark eyes—that he felt the same. He watched me with such care and held me with such tenderness, knowing this could hurt me. But it did not hurt. It felt right. We were one with the lake, giving and taking with every beat of its waves, sometimes soft and gentle, sometimes passionate and wild.

I *felt* as I had never felt before, and I wondered why such feelings were repressed in our days. This was the feeling that caused utter joy; why were we not allowed to experience it unless with a husband not of our choosing?

I was so lucky. This man—this soul—contained within the bursting seams of his skin, gave me life as I had never known it before. I was completely his that night, giving myself to him with no thoughts of doubt or hesitation.

I was his.

He was mine.

⇥═◉ ◉═⇤

The stars stretched out over us, a canopy of protection. I lay in his arms as he held me close. His heart beat steadily under my ear, as we looked up at the vast and glittering sky in silence. The sand was comfortable underneath our bodies, and my cloak was pulled over us to keep us warm against the cold night. The violence of the storm had ended, and the lake had resumed a calmer rumble.

"Tamar," he mumbled, letting it play on his tongue. "It seems fitting that it is your name."

I was quiet. "Do you think less of me now?"

"Why would I think less of you?" he asked, a tinge of surprise in his voice.

"That I would give myself to you here, like this."

He sighed. "It is not possible for me to think any less of you, Tamar. I am not just passing the time to be with you. It feels so natural to have my arms around you. It feels so...*right* that we are together. You know me too well by now to know that I have much respect for you and cherish you dearly."

"I have heard so many stories of girls being scandalized."

"Do you think I would scandalize you?"

"No."

"I want you to know me as well as I know you. I want you to let yourself know me. Can't you sense our connection? From the day I met you, I had a rare connection with you, and I knew I would not be whole until I could be with you."

"Even through my deceit?" I muttered.

"Even so, for I believe you have your own reasons to be mysterious."

I smiled and looked back up at the stars. He followed my gaze.

"They are happy for us," he mumbled.

"Who?"

"The stars." He gave a small smile, while his eyes wandered from each gleaming orb in the darkness to the next.

"They are so beautiful," I sighed. "But *they slandered at impudent, shameless Tamar,*" I recited.

"I don't think so," he whispered. "I think they were happy for them too. But the story was not written by them, was it?"

This was what Aleena had always told me.

"No, it was not."

Her words came back to me, as they always did. *It is a warning for young people in the future.*

"They will save us, you know," he said into my hair. He gave me a light kiss on my forehead.

"How?"

"They are our candles. We will take one of the stars and follow it and see where it takes us. And wherever it is, it shall be far away from here."

We. Us. My heart sighed.

"You are making it a habit to follow the light," I said and smiled.

He nodded. "It leads me to you. It will lead us to freedom."

I nestled into his shoulder. He took my hand and pressed my knuckles to his lips softly. Then he pulled his arms tighter around me and stroked my hair gently until I drifted off slowly to a content sleep.

Akh, Tamar.

Chapter 22

My heart had such raging emotions in it. It was confused as to how I should feel. It made me sick with its torment. A part of it rejoiced with the love that Aleek had shown me. I felt as though I could fly with his love and his sweet words that echoed inside my mind. My nights were made better when we met, and I always found joy with him. His soft touch soothed my very soul, and I had the pleasure of living in the moment with him—such a rarity. But the other part of my heart was in anguish at the confirmed marriage that was to take place between Bedros and me. And the last part that was left of my heart ached and broke just as Aleena's heart was breaking and aching.

Bedros had laid his claim on me, and he would win. I felt what little freedom I had slipping away through the spaces between my fingers, and I could not grab hold.

We did not speak to each other. Breakfast, as usual, was wearisome, as we all sat around the table in silence. My eyes were trained on the chair across from me that sat empty, where my sister should be. It was as if we had already lost her, and seeing the empty space was unbearable. Vartan and Baron Avedis were still not here, so their spaces were empty as well. My father and mother ate forlornly, not glancing in my direction once. I had always been invisible to them, but I felt more so now. Even the idea of me marrying Bedros was not a source of joy for my mother.

I visited Aleena as often as I could, for it was the only place in our palace where I felt at ease. Her eyes always somehow lit up when she saw me. She listened to me, and if she did not like what I was saying, she would rub my hand. If she did approve of my words, she would smile; it was a weak half smile, but it was a smile nonetheless, and it lit up my day. We were connected through her suffering, through the agony we both felt at this desperate situation. She could speak sometimes, but it was labored and painful to hear her.

I feared the nights, as I am sure she did as well. Somehow it was always in the night when her seizures would strike. It would be in the middle of the night, when we would least expect it. Then we would hear a shuffling, and the maids who were watching her would come running, crying for us to follow quickly. I was frightened when I would visit Aleek, for I feared that I would miss a terrible attack.

They were small and short seizures, however, each one finished by the time we arrived at her room. But they worsened her condition. Each seizure seemed to take away another part of her. Her body was smaller, the bones protruding from her frail skin, as she could not eat without vomiting everything back up. Food, water, fruit—they all disgusted her, and she turned her head when we brought them to her lips.

Her skin had become a pallid color, a slick sheen of sweat constant on its surface, no matter how many times we washed her. Her hair was greasy, hanging lanky about her shoulders. And her lips were dry, cracked, and peeling. Every chance I found, I would dab at them with a wet cloth, and she would blink in relief.

The doctor pronounced it a miracle that she was not dead yet. "Here is one girl who does *not* want to die," he said, turning his gray eyes to me. "She is holding on for you." I vowed that I would not let her down. I went to her every day, reading to her from her favorite books or talking to her or just lying next to her and looking up at the ceiling she was forced to look at every day.

The only thing that still shone with Aleena's soul was her eyes. They were calculating and thoughtful and pained, all at once, but they were *her*, and I found them a comfort to look at.

Once, I sat with her whilst reading the book of the world that she had left in the garden so long ago. We looked at the maps and she ran her fingers over the etchings, wonderingly and sadly.

"You said you never left with the boat because it was too late for you. Why was it too late?" I asked her.

She took several breaths then opened her mouth to speak. Her voice was a cracked whisper. "I could not escape...because my heart would not let me..." She gave a ragged sigh. "I had the spirit...still do. But my heart would have stopped me...which is so ironic," she gave a cough of a laugh, but it was tinged with sorrow. "All this time I thought...I thought the battle was between the heart...and the mind...but my heart has given up...and my mind is the only one that is...still pushing me along..." She coughed, trying to catch her breath. I winced and looked down at the book, wondering where I would go.

I was so afraid, and I finally understood mortality. Aleena was not ready to die, but her body was failing her. Fear completely consumed me, wrapping around my neck and cutting off my breath, as I watched her struggle to breathe.

Our father walked in once while I was with her, and he began telling us about his birthday plans. I was quiet, for his birthday merely reminded me of Bedros's betrayal, but Aleena's eyes managed to look happier. It made me feel better, as I listened to him asking about what we thought would look better on him: his royal-purple cloak or his crimson-red one. He spoke more than I had ever heard him speak, and I assumed it was due to his nerves, though I could not say why he was nervous.

"So what do you think?" he asked me. I was snapped back from my brooding to the matter at hand.

"What?" I asked.

"Purple or crimson?"

"Purple," I replied without hesitation. "It is the best color on you." Aleena managed a faint grin in response and nodded in agreement.

He nodded absent-mindedly. "Yes, yes, you are right. I shall do that. Oh, and the priest and his family are arriving tomorrow."

"Lilit!" I smiled. "I will be happy to see her!" Aleena's lips curled up into a tired smile as well. She was watching me, as if she was a child who had seen a smile for the first time and was trying it for herself.

My father's eyes were wide as he watched his eldest daughter smile. It was a moment I wanted to cherish forever, and in that rare moment, I had the audacity to believe that everything would turn out for the better.

In the next few days, I convinced my father to give me some of his brushes and a tray of paint. When I visited Aleena, I would bring with me a tall ladder I found in the servants' quarters, and I would place it in the middle of the room and climb the ladder with the paints. I began to paint, and although I had no skill as a painter, I managed to draw a swirling whirlwind of clouds and birds. I drew a tree coming up the side of her room as well, with the branches spreading their tendrils over the ceiling above her head. I put some pomegranates on the tree, although the tree was not a pomegranate tree. I added some apples to the tree, as well as apricots and figs. She found it all very amusing and smiled almost constantly. While drawing, I talked to her for hours, telling her about what happened during the day and my thoughts. I told her about how our father's birthday planning was going. He had spent days making sure his suit was perfect. I pulled another smile out of Aleena with that.

I always left her room with spatters of paint on my dresses and on my face and fingers. My mother saw me pass once and did not say anything at my disgrace. I almost missed when she would yell at me.

My father, meanwhile, had many meetings with the doctor during this time.

One day the doctor came and tested Aleena again. After an hour or so of tedious testing and listening to her heartbeat, the doctor pulled my father into his study, and they spent an hour behind the door. I paced back and forth in anxiety, my nerves becoming a mess inside of me. What was he saying to him? I am ashamed to say that I tried to eavesdrop, pressing my ear to the door in hopes of hearing something. But the doors were thick, and all sound was muffled, much to my incredible frustration.

When the door finally opened, I pounced, attacking them with questions and demanding answers. My father looked pale and stopped in front of me at the door. He put a hand on the top of my head, almost affectionately. But I knew it was not affectionate. I knew that simple gesture helped him stay on his feet, for he looked ready to faint. "Father?" I asked.

"Your strength, Tamar," he said shakily. "It is what we all need."

Then he walked away from his study and away from me. I watched him go, but when he turned back, he managed a nod at the doctor, giving him permission to speak.

The doctor pulled me into the study this time and sat me down at the desk. It seemed wrong that the doctor was in my father's study, sitting behind the desk as though this were his office. I chose my favorite chair again, feeling the curving wood beneath my fingertips. He was watching me carefully, as if afraid I would break into a million pieces.

I feared I would as well.

He took a deep breath and ran his hands through his hair. He spoke cautiously, as if he were tiptoeing down a long and narrow hall, the walls lined with fragile cups and plates. "Your father initially did not want me to tell you anything. He says you will not be able to handle it well."

"I can handle it," I managed after a moment of silence, but my vision had already blurred with tears, and my voice was hardly identifiable because it shook too much.

"Your sister's heart is very weak—much too weak to be saved. The next seizure could burst what is left of her heart. Then there will be no saving her. There *is* no saving her."

I nodded, unable to stop crying. My face was twisted; I could feel it, and it hurt, but I could not stop.

"I am deeply, deeply sorry."

I curled my legs up to my chest and buried my face in my skirts as I let myself cry. He stood after a few moments, and then he let himself out, closing the study door behind him softly and leaving me to my misery in the chair that held the crying grapes.

⊷▰ ▰⊶

I watched the waves caress the shore that night as I lay in Aleek's arms. He was still wet from his swim to my island, but we did not mind. The cloak and our body heat kept us both warm, although the beginning days of winter were upon us. We were quiet, listening to the comforting sounds of the wind and the water dancing with each other.

He knew I was upset, but he had not pressed me for answers. He just held me close, giving me a shoulder to lean my head on. My eyes were swollen from crying earlier, and I was a bit embarrassed for him to see me this way, but he only held me closer when I tried to pull away.

He kissed me so tenderly that night, and I just knew he had assumed the fate of my sister.

"I wish Karin came back," I said.

He smiled. "Yes…but then we would not be able to see each other like this."

I managed a small smile, but it felt wrong to smile, as if I were betraying Aleena with that gesture. I sighed instead.

He took my hand in his and touched my knuckles to his lips, as I had learned he loved to do.

"Do you feel guilty?"

I did not know if he meant for my sister or for being with him. "Yes," I answered truthfully. I was answering both questions.

"Why?"

"I ruin everything," I said, my voice choking on the words. I cleared my throat quickly, blinking away fresh tears. How could I still have any tears left?

"You cannot say that, Tamar. Everything happens for a reason. Do you believe that?"

I shook my head, unable to speak. He glanced down at the lines on my palm and stopped when he saw the scar, which he had never seen before. "Where did you get this?"

"My sister."

He raised an eyebrow. "I had not assumed that you and your sister were the violent type."

"Passion and violence have a blurred line between them."

"How did she give this to you?"

I glanced around us, my eyes searching the sand. His eyes followed my gaze and widened when I held up a shard of sea glass. "One of these."

His eyebrows were raised. "She stabbed you?"

I chose my words carefully. "We made…a pact."

"That…," he urged.

"That…I would fall in love before my fifteenth birthday."

"And you are fifteen now."

"I am."

"So have you fallen in love?"

I stayed quiet; my heart beat in starts and stops. Of course I was. Couldn't he see? I dared not say it. I looked away with a frown on my face, and he let me avoid the question, though he seemed amused.

"She has a scar too then?" he asked, with a hint of a smile on his face. I nodded, but he was not finished with asking questions. "Why did she make that pact with you?"

"She wanted me to be free. *Wants*," I corrected quickly, flinching at the way it sounded as if she was already gone.

"And are you?"

"Not yet."

"Why?"

I rested my head on his shoulder and closed my eyes. I really was going to answer him; I thought I had an answer ready to say aloud, but when I opened my mouth, the words surprised me.

"What if she dies?"

He was silent for a minute. Then he shrugged slightly, the movement jostling my head a bit. "I suppose a part of you shall die as well." Before I could burst into tears again, he continued, "But it will make way for a new life. You shall fly with the knowledge that she is free. Her escape will make *you* free."

It was easy to think about it that way. But I feared that I would be unable to live again when she left my life.

She was my island. I would have nowhere to rest my heart if she disappeared.

Chapter 23

THE PREPARATIONS FOR my father's birthday were underway. I had learned early on in my life that the villagers celebrated our birthdays as well, but on their own, as if it were a holiday. The largest festivities were for the king, of course, which meant that the preparations would take a much longer time than for a regular birthday. All the royalty and nobility would be invited to our palace, where our ballroom doors would be opened, and we would celebrate to our heart's content. Every maid and every servant was put to work to ensure that the castle was in perfect condition and ready to be viewed by all our family and friends.

I knew they would put me to work as well, for no hand should be idle during a time such as this, so I tried to stay out of the way. I found my refuge with my sister.

"They shall expect me to dance with Bedros," I told her. It was the night before the party. I was curled on her bed next to her legs, with my head resting against her hip. Her hand, as usual, lay weakly on my hair, which was spread out over her covers. "How could I dance with him, knowing what he did?"

I closed my eyes and listened to Aleena's heavy breathing. I wondered how she was feeling. It hurt to wonder that, but I couldn't help it. I hated that she felt any pain, and I knew she did, in the way the veins stood out on her forehead and the way her chest rose and fell rapidly. She would not speak of her pain, for she knew it would upset me.

I held her tight. "I wish you could come. We would dance and frolic all night, then run off to the beach and dance with the waves instead. They would be far better partners than the men. No one even cares anyway. All they want to do is one-up the other. Competitions, competitions. The women!" My voice rose in pitch. "They always have to look lovelier than the other, and if they don't, they slander the other's name. And the men are worse! They prance around with their chests puffed out like they are roosters, always looking for a way to be the bigger man. I can't bear it."

She gave a chuckle, nodding in agreement. "Peacocks."

"Exactly!" I said. "My dress *is* lovely I shall admit." I grinned finally. "Mother helped sew it. It is blue! My favorite color. I will come and show you before the party. I do hope you like it. I wish Aleek could come and see as well."

While I had to dress as simple as a villager for weddings, this was the complete opposite. All care was put into how I looked, for I was the only princess that was to attend the party and, as such, had to look the most presentable and noble. Digin Galia and several maids spent hours over me, poking and prodding and pulling me into perfection.

My mother was not there to oversee this, as she was surrounded by her own maids, instructed to make her look extravagant. She was the queen, after all, and the wife of the birthday king.

After several hours of tediously getting me ready, Digin Galia faced me to look in the mirror, and I hardly recognized myself. The dress fit my form beautifully, the deep blue hue bringing out colors in my eyes that I never knew were there. My long hair was braided, and it hung down my shoulders like two long coils of rope. I had golden tassels and lace lining the bodice and hems of the dress, to make certain that anyone who would see me would know that I was of royal blood. I was quite the vision.

Even Digin Galia was pleased. She had tears in her eyes, as she put a hand on my shoulder affectionately. "He will not be able to keep his eyes off you."

My face flushed, for I immediately thought of Aleek instead of Bedros. She took it as a good sign and turned away to prepare herself in a more modest fashion, for she would be attending as well.

I wished Aleek could see me tonight. I smoothed my hands over the folds of the dress and wondered what he would think of me, dressed in all this finery instead of the coarse clothing I would usually borrow from the maids. Would he still hold me in his arms the same way? Would he still look at me with that same twinkle in his eyes and the smile pulling at his perfect lips?

That thought rang through my mind as I made ready to walk down the hall toward the ballroom. But before I left the room, Digin Galia called out, "Make sure you are comfortable in your shoes. There will be dancing tonight. Your father thought it necessary to invite those dancers from the mainland."

I paused, my heart jumping to my throat. I coughed roughly, and she gave me a wry look. "When did he invite them?"

"This morning, after Aleena gave him the idea last night."

Aleena? I couldn't move. The dancers were to come? Aleek would be here? Hysteric panic ran through me like a lightning bolt. He would see me. He would learn of my identity. What would I do? My wish earlier felt like a curse now. I had not thought this through. I knew what Aleena meant to do: she wanted to cut away the obstacle I had created in my mind—that of my identity.

But today was to be the big announcement. Bedros would be there. Aleek would be there. I felt faint.

My heels clicked against the floor rapidly, and my skirts whirled around my legs as I hastily made my way toward Aleena's room. When I arrived, I was surprised instead: she sat up a bit in her bed, as Janna slowly fed her soup. She smiled at me when she saw me. "Aleena! Are you feeling better?"

"A bit," she said, though her voice still sounded faint. Her brows furrowed when she saw my expression. "What is the matter?"

"You told father to invite the dancers."

"Oh yes..." she began. Then she looked at me slyly from the corner of her eye. "Everyone loves a good dance."

I shook my head in disbelief. "You live to torment me, sister."

"It is because I love you," she said. She opened her arms to me. As Janna stepped away from the bed, I wrapped myself in Aleena's arms and hugged her tight.

"I love you too, sister. Come to the party if you can later."

"I shall try."

A servant chose this moment to walk into the room and bow politely. "Begging your pardon, Princess Tamar, but His Majesty has asked that you wait in his study until he comes to take you into the ballroom himself."

"Why?" I asked.

"It is for him to tell you," he said. I exchanged a look with Aleena.

"Go show them all who you really are," she said, with a gleam in her eyes.

I kissed her cheek and left her room. The study was empty, save for a beautiful tabby cat that a guest had brought. I crossed the room and sat in the chair with the crying grapes. The cat watched me curiously for a moment and then slowly meandered to me and rubbed against my legs affectionately.

I busied myself with petting her, taking pleasure in her small purrs of delight. I found myself giving a small smile, surprising myself with the gesture, for how long had it been since I had found joy in such a simple thing? I wished I could stay in the study all night, locked away in my secrecy. I was not ready for Aleek to find out who I was. I was not ready for Aleek's pain when he found out I was to wed another.

"I wonder what your name is," I muttered, scratching the cat behind her ear.

"Shamiram," said a voice from behind. I turned and stood abruptly at the same time, scaring the cat, who went dashing under a table.

Bedros.

"Shamiram?"

"It is the cat's name. It is my aunt's cat."

Shamiram—a beautiful but odd name for a cat.

I nodded and sat back down, snapping my fingers for Shamiram to come back to me. "You frightened her," I said, aware of Bedros watching me from the door.

"We are to be led in together," he said.

"Why?" I asked, as if I were stupid and did not know. I wanted to make him more uncomfortable than he already was.

A small act of torture, in return for the rest of my life. And the pain and heartbreak of my lover.

He shifted on his feet. "Your father wants to announce…our news."

"Ah, yes, our news," I echoed, "our exciting news."

I turned and pierced him with my eyes. It was not a glare, it was not an angry look, but it nevertheless made him wince as if I had cut him with a knife.

He opened his mouth to speak, but the door swung open, and my father strode in, his face bright red from having had already too much to drink. He seemed jolly, but I knew it was the alcohol that made him seem that way. My father had nothing to be jolly about.

He nodded at me and then turned to Bedros. "Well? Did you give it to her?"

"Not yet."

"Give what to me?"

"Hurry up; the guests are waiting," said my father. Bedros walked to me hastily and put something small in my lap and then turned around and walked out the door to wait in the hallway. I looked down and saw that it was a ring. It was encrusted with jewels and gems, reflecting the light extravagantly. "When you've put it on, meet us in the hallway. Please hurry," said my father, walking out after Bedros.

I picked up the ring and slid it onto my finger. It fit perfectly, and I knew it was made *for* me, although I did not know how they knew what my finger size was. It was heavy—a constant reminder of what it meant. I would rather have had a crudely made wooden ring from Aleek than this dazzling bribe.

I stood, the emotional weight of it making it difficult to achieve that feat, and I walked out into the hallway where they stood, both averting their eyes from my suffering.

Cowards.

I felt a difference inside me, after Aleena's words. I needed to be strong—I had no obligation to be with Bedros. Even without Aleek, I did not need to be with Bedros. *Go show them all who you really are.* It was time to figure out myself who I really was.

My father said, "I shall walk in with your mother and announce your betrothal. You shall follow and wave and walk to the front where we have the separate thrones for the princesses." The seats for Aleena and me. "They shall rejoice for you, and then we shall introduce the dancers, and they will dance, and all will be merry. You two will dance as well," he said, as if ordering us. *Dance or you shall regret it.*

When my mother joined us, she gave me a once-over followed by a satisfied smile when her eyes rested on the ring at my finger. Then they both turned and faced the doors to the ballroom. My father looked like a true king, dressed in finery and dripping with gold. Deep purple adorned him, and an elaborate golden crown sat atop his head. My mother looked beautiful in a gown of cream and purple adornments. My father lifted his hand to prepare the servants to open the doors. But before he could drop his hand, I said, "Father." He paused and turned back to look at me. "Happy birthday." He could hear the disdain in my voice, so he did not smile. He turned back around to face the doors of the ballroom and dropped his hand.

With much flair, the two servants threw open the doors, and the king and queen strode in flanked by more servants. I heard everything as if I was in a dream. It was hazy, in the background. His voice bellowed and echoed. "Welcome to our beautiful island of Akhtamar! We thank you for coming to this special occasion and hope you all have a merry night! We have dancers from the mainland and food and drinks for everyone! But we also have a second reason for celebration today. My youngest daughter, the fair Princess Tamar, the legendary beauty, is newly betrothed to my dear friend's youngest son, Bedros!"

Exclamations of joy went around the guests. "Finally!" shouted one woman from the crowd, and the people laughed. Baron Avedis walked to my father and clapped him on the back, both beaming with joy. I was surprised at seeing him. I had not seen Baron Avedis in ages, but the familiar tug to run to him was replaced by a feeling of dread at seeing his sons.

And here was one of them next to me, ready to take my life away.

But where was Vartan? Should he not be trying to see Aleena?

The servant behind us touched both of our backs, urging us forward through the doors. I felt as if I were walking into the room naked, as hundreds of eyes turned and beheld their future rulers. There were sighs of awe as they took in our appearance. I tried not to look at the people. I knew he was in the crowd. I could not look. The crowd erupted into applause. I looked over their heads, but I felt it—I felt his eyes, his burning dark eyes. As if drawn by a magnet, I looked down into the crowd and immediately locked eyes with him.

He saw me as he saw no other. He watched me as if I were a candle, shining bright amid the darkness that surrounded me.

Aleek.

Everyone else continued as they were. They did not notice that Bedros and I stood stiffly next to each other. They did not notice that I did not smile. They clapped their hands and rejoiced, as we approached the chairs and sat on the smaller thrones. I looked back into the crowd, but he was gone. My mother, who was sitting on her throne, smiled at me. It was a forced smile, for I knew she wished to see her other daughter in my place. I noticed Baron Avedis giving me a smile, but it had become strained. He, no doubt, realized how much everything had changed since he had left. I averted my eyes.

The musicians began playing the traditional music, and some of the guests began to dance. It was here that I noticed the difference between the royal dances and the village dances.

The royalty were so…contained. The dances were tame and calculated, while the village dances were wild and free-spirited.

The dancers were fitted with new outfits for the occasion, tight, restraining outfits that shined golden and sparkled as if they were actually dipped in gold. They danced with slower and more calculated movements. I tried not to find him again.

Bedros leaned over and asked if I liked the ring. I nodded. He smiled, pleased that he had done something right.

"Where is Vartan?" I asked suddenly.

"What?" he asked, taken aback by my question.

"Vartan, your brother, where is he?"

"He had a...duty to finish back home."

"While his wife lies dying here?"

"He will come back as soon as he is able to."

I scoffed. "Of course."

I turned away dismissively and saw someone waving to me in the crowd. My heart caught in my throat for a moment, but upon closer look, I recognized Lilit.

I glanced across at my mother and realized she would not even notice. She sat, glassy eyed, on her golden chair, and I knew she saw Aleena's face in her vision. I didn't care anyway. What more could they take away from me?

I stood and walked toward my friend, opening my arms to hug her. "There is much you need to tell me," she whispered into my ear. I pulled back and appraised her with a smile. She was beautiful with her long dark hair and dark eyes, contrasting against the porcelain smoothness of her skin. She was wearing a lovely pale-yellow dress, and there was a sweet glow to her cheeks. I had not seen her in so long, and my heart ached with the sudden comfort I felt in her presence.

I nodded. "Yes, there is."

She glanced around and began to walk with me toward the edge of the crowd, but Baron Avedis approached us. We waited expectantly, but he suddenly seemed at a loss for what to say. "Your ring is very glamorous."

"Thank you." I nodded.

"How are you, Tamar?"

"I am well."

"No, Tamar, *how are you?*" he repeated, emphasizing it intently.

"How do you think I am, Baron Avedis?"

"You are not the little girl I used to know. You are not the girl who used to run to greet me."

"All my life, I have been scolded for laughing or speaking or running too much, and now that I am finally acting as an adult, there is something wrong with me?"

Lilit linked her arm through mine comfortingly.

"I never said there is something wrong with you."

I smiled sadly. "Then you really do not know me."

He seemed confused.

I wanted to explain, to sit him down and tell him how wretched I felt and how my heart was tearing apart with all that pulled and pushed at me. The expectations and duties and masks I had to wear were cracking—falling apart—and I could only stand and stare. But I could not explain it to him, for he looked at me as if I were a stranger. He did not recognize me anymore. *Go show them who you really are.*

He opened his mouth to say something, but I lifted my hand abruptly, and he shut his mouth. "I do not wish to hear what you have to say. Now if you would excuse me, I am very busy."

I left him standing behind me as I walked to the edge of the crowd with Lilit. Her eyes were wide. "Wow, you really put him in his place."

"Lilit, I am in love with someone else." The words burst out of me as though she had pricked me with a sharp needle. Her eyes widened.

"What? Not Bedros?"

"Heavens no. I love someone else, and he is here tonight, and I do not intend on marrying Bedros. And Aleena is dying. Lilit, I do not know what to do or how to go about this."

She put a hand on my cheek. "Talk to me."

"I met him while meeting Karin on the mainland—you remember her: the little girl who taught us some dances. He is her brother. He is amazing, Lilit; he is everything I have dreamed about. But Bedros has been *infuriatingly* stubborn in trying to marry me."

"Who is the man you love?"

"His name is Aleek. He is…" I looked about us, craning my neck. I saw him immediately. He stood out in beauty and strength, his back ramrod straight and chin lifted defiantly. He was facing me with burning eyes. "Him."

Lilit had seen him as well. "He is very handsome. Is he angry with you?"

"I do not know. I had not told him that I am betrothed." Or that I was the princess.

She pursed her lips and then took my hand and led me into the crowd toward the dance circle. The crowds slightly parted for me, and smiling faces congratulated me with much enthusiasm. The music was playing, and I stood at the edge of the circle that formed to start dancing. Lilit grabbed my left hand, and I turned to smile at her, but then another hand took my right hand firmly. I did not need to turn to see who it was. The roughness of the hands and the passionate way they held on could only mean they belonged to one person.

I heard him say, "Your Highness." Lilit squeezed my hand.

From a distance, I could see Bedros watching me. The dance was a slow one, and we moved as though we danced through honey. His shoulder brushed mine. "Aleek," I began. I turned to look at him, but my breath was taken away at his look. The pale gold of his outfit shone and sparkled in contrast with his olive skin. His dark eyes looked even darker as he looked across at me. "Please," I said, begging him with my eyes, longing for him to not be upset with me. Bedros stood up, and I could see him wondering if he should approach. I knew he remembered Aleek from Aleena's wedding. I knew he did not like him.

"I offer my sincerest congratulations for your happy news."

Tears jumped to my eyes. "Aleek," I hissed.

He looked down and squeezed my hand tight. I could see the muscles in his jaw working tightly. "I must inform you that my feelings have not changed. You have always been a true princess in your heart. I am somehow not surprised that you are her—the angel I met in my youth, the girl I fell in love with, the girl I would swim across the lake for."

My knees almost buckled, and I stumbled slightly from the overwhelming love I felt for this man. But he steadied me. Lilit whispered, "Be careful; Bedros is watching." I turned my head, so Bedros could not see my face. But it was too late. He made up his mind and began to walk toward us. "We need to leave. I cannot marry him, Aleek. Save me."

He nodded. "That can be arranged, my love."

My love.

I opened my mouth to respond, but I closed it again suddenly.

Something was wrong. A feeling in the air, an electric charge, that suddenly struck fire. I felt sick suddenly, and the room swam in my vision. I saw Bedros pause midstride and look to the side, away from us.

And it was during this moment when it happened.

From the corner of my eye, through the throngs of people that would normally have blocked my vision, I saw a door open at the back. I knew it led to the hallways that went to the bedrooms. I saw the doctor enter the ballroom like a restless phantom, his face pale, frantically searching for my father.

But I was already running. I tore my hand from Aleek's and Lilit's grip and pelted across the floor. I had pulled my dress up to my knees and was running toward the doctor as fast as I could. Eyes turned to me while my mother cried out in horror. My father came running after me, followed by his servants and Bedros. The guards had jumped up with their weapons, unsure of who to attack and what to do.

I passed the doctor without giving him a second glance and burst into the hallway, not stopping until I reached her bedroom. I could tell from the rustled and twisted sheets that she had had another seizure, and from the doctor's expression, I knew it was *the* seizure.

Her fists gripped the sheets, and I crumpled onto the bed, crying out her name. My blue skirts spread out around us softly, as if an ominous cloud had enveloped us into its embrace. I hugged her to me, and I felt her heartbeat against my chest. It beat roughly, with a ragged and confused rhythm.

My mother and father burst into the room, the doctor and Bedros keeping at a respectful distance behind. Baron Avedis managed to arrive as well, with Aleek and Lilit behind them. He looked out of place in his golden outfits, as though this was all part of a dance that he did not know the steps to.

My sister had gone limp, unable to keep herself up. I could feel the energy leaving her muscles, and I held her tighter, pulling her into my arms and crying out desperately for the one person who understood me most behind my mask.

I pressed my ear to her heart, trying to comfort myself at the thought that it was still beating, though weakly. I held on to the noise with all my sanity. *Thump…thump…thump.*

It was such a feeble noise, but I heard it although my mother was crying loudly near us; my father was hissing with sobs that came from deep inside his chest, and Lilit was whimpering like a hurt animal. And still the heartbeat. *Thump…thump…thump—*

I waited. And waited. Nothing.

Then I broke.

There was a thick silence in her chest, where her heart had just been beating against my ear.

I could not believe it.

"Aleena! Aleena!" I screamed.

My mother was crying, as she held my sister's hand tightly. My father held my mother and murmured, "She's gone, she's gone."

Aleek and Lilit broke through the small crowd that had gathered and approached me. He sat at the edge of the bed boldly and put his arm comfortingly around my shoulders, while Lilit sat on my other side and rubbed my shoulder.

"Her heart stopped," I cried into Aleena's stomach that moved no more. Lilit held me tight.

"Tamar," whispered Aleek, also pulling me into a hug. Lilit on one side and Aleek on the other, I could feel the sharp intake of breath at the door at what transpired between us. But I did not care. I did not care.

"She is not gone. She is free," murmured Aleek into my ear.

She is free.

Chapter 24

NIGHT WAS FALLING. It was silent.

As if a tear was falling and your heart stopped beating for a moment, waiting for it to land somewhere, and when it did, it was a small splash bursting with one final damp plea and ending its life on the hem of your shirt. A small moment—meaningless—as what is one splash of a tear in a world of sorrow? It will dry in a matter of seconds and the moment shall pass. But it is the weight of that tear. It is the collection of ingredients that creates that single tear, the thoughts that mold and shape it to make it weigh as heavy as a boulder. And so I have learned with all things.

I watched as the lake in the distance turned an iridescent orange, as it reflected all the light that burned in the village. It looked as if the island of Akhtamar was on fire, as the flames of the bonfire licked the sky. There was a great sorrow that rang throughout the village, the name *Aleena* whispered from mouth to mouth, accompanied by disbelieving tears.

Once Aleena would have wished her name to be remembered with pride and joy. I wondered where that Aleena was, trapped inside a body that could not sustain her.

I hated funerals. I had never even been to one, but I had decided right then and there that funerals were not for me, but then, I suppose, who *did* enjoy them?

I followed my family down the beaten path from the palace to the village. We were sullen, quiet, a different group from the rowdy crowd who had made the same journey for my sister's wedding only a season ago.

We followed the priest, his black cloak swaying ahead of us. I saw him through the spaces between my family members, a shining beacon, beckoning the way. My mother and father were behind him, looking small and frail as they had never looked before. I was with Lilit, walking in front of the coffin, and in front of me were my cousins, relatives, and everyone else.

I wanted to be with Aleena. I gave out a shudder, and Lilit tightened her grip on my arm.

Some of the stronger men held Aleena's casket and had propped it up at a certain angle over their heads, so all who passed could gaze upon her peaceful face. I gazed back every so often to torture myself more by looking at her face.

I wanted to shake her, to tell her to wake up, but she looked so serene, with her pale face and dark hair haloed around her. She still looked beautiful, even in death. When I looked down, I saw Bedros, his face pale, grimacing underneath the weight of the casket. He stood next to Vartan, who had made the journey down for the funeral.

How thoughtful of him.

I turned my back on them. I knew the next time I spoke to any of them, I would be severely punished for allowing Aleek to touch me. For all they knew, he was a random villager. I could tell that Bedros knew there was more to it. I could see it in his eyes.

We paraded through the streets, moans and wails passing from person to person as we passed. They had gathered on the sides of the path, some on their knees, as if the sorrow weighed too heavily on their shoulders. The priest murmured prayers over and over again, an orb of incense swaying back and forth in his hand. I kept my eyes trained in front of me, seeing nothing, feeling nothing. I could not crumble in front of my family, in front of the villagers.

I would not crumble. They needed me to be strong, and strong I would be.

As we neared the clearing where the largest bonfire raged, I heard something familiar: music.

It was slow, a song I knew the dance to. Tarsbar, the backward dance, where the dancer stomps on the devil to forbid him from entering the circle and corrupting the soul. It seemed so long ago when Aleena and I had learned this same dance with Karin on the mainland. Now it was to be danced at her funeral.

Our small parade split up, each retreating to a corner while several villagers went to the center, linked hands, and began to dance mournfully, their bodies moving as if they were dancing in congealed stew. It was slow and tense, each step taking such effort to lift off the ground. It was eerily beautiful.

I could not cry; the tears would not come. What I felt was a numb burning, spreading through my veins coldly like ice. I have heard anger is not much different than fire, but as Aleena always said, do not listen to *them*. They are wrong. They are always wrong.

Anger is not fire. Anger is water, fighting in a battle against the mighty cliffs, furious and hateful.

The lake was inside my heart.

I watched with dull eyes as people filed by, dipping low, very low, in front of me, murmuring their condolences. I said nothing, but I was almost disgusted. I knew it was unfair of me; they were mourning for someone they looked up to. But they knew nothing of her. They did not know her fire and the light that shone in her eyes. They did not know how hard she fought against everyone who tried to suppress her, including her own body. I stayed underneath my hooded black cloak—her gift to me on my birthday—wanting to disappear in the shadows.

But a moment later, I felt it—that familiar tingling when someone is looking at me. I glanced up over bowing heads and froze. I stayed rooted to my spot, for I had locked eyes with a man who stood across the clearing with his people: Aleek.

After he had consoled me in front of my family, my father had pulled him up by his scruff and kicked him roughly out of the room. I hadn't seen him since. I watched him now as he paced restlessly around the bonfire, his eyes watching me like a predator, the fire casting dark and twisted shadows across his face.

Without another moment of waiting, he entered the circle to dance, pulling with him some of his friends. I watched him dance; every move he made was so familiar and beautiful to me. I wanted to cry, for fear of losing him. Was he angry with me? Would he give me another chance? I could not follow him when my father threw him out. But he must have understood that.

He was at the part of the circle nearest to me, and his back was to me as I stood in the shadows. I watched his wiry back—his muscles bulging with the tension in the dance. I wondered if he knew I was right behind him. I was going to look away, but then I noticed his hand suddenly hang free from the person to his left. Before that person could react and wonder why Aleek had let go, I was already there, grasping both their hands tightly and joining the dance as one with the villagers.

It was silent between us for a little while, and I could feel more than one person watching me: Bedros, Lilit, my mother, my father, Digin Galia, several villagers.

I glanced sidelong at him and saw his jaw working. He was angry and upset. His grip was strong on my hand. "I am…*so*…sorry for the loss of your sister. I cannot imagine what you are feeling at this moment, and I wish—" His voice broke. He tried again. "*I wish* I could make it all better. I wish I could take you away."

"You can," I hissed, my voice close to breaking. "Take me away. Please."

He squeezed my hand again. I could see him thinking it through, allowing the seriousness of the situation to settle in his mind. He nodded firmly. "I will."

"Thank you," I whispered, as I stomped on the devil that wanted to corrupt my sister's soul.

And when I lifted my hands to the heavens, I saw Aleek's hand joined with mine, and I prayed more than anything for our safety: my safety, Aleek's safety, and Aleena's safety.

I tried to ignore the way Bedros looked at us, making the connection immediately that it was no coincidence I had chosen to stand next to Aleek. I saw the anger in Bedros's stance. He whispered something to Vartan, and Vartan immediately pierced us with his eyes. They were going to come forward.

But at that moment, when the dance ended, Aleek and I immediately separated because we had to, though we did not want to. I walked toward my parents, and I stood with them quietly. Lilit came and stood next to me. "Be careful, Tamar," she whispered in my ear.

"I cannot," I managed. My eyes scanned the crowd for Aleek. I saw him with his friends, solemnly talking.

But as I watched them, another form entered my view, and I focused on Bedros, who was walking toward me. Over his shoulder, as if in a haze, I continued to watch Aleek. But as Bedros neared me, Aleek turned and walked the other way, his back facing us. He was leaving.

My heart began to sink, but still I watched him, until Aleek turned around for a split moment, looked straight at me with his penetrating eyes, and jerked his chin subtly toward the lake. I knew he was going to the beach.

Without any hesitation, I walked forward, straight past Bedros, who had opened his mouth to speak. Bedros reached out and grabbed me by the elbow. "Where are you going?"

"To see my friends. Let go," I snapped, pulling away.

He let go but watched me as I disappeared into the crowd. When I made sure he was not behind me, I turned and followed Aleek at a safe and considerable distance.

It was dark in the winding streets, and I continually looked back to make sure I was not being followed. I made my way to our secluded beach, and sure enough, I saw him standing on the pebbles, looking out at the water.

I walked over and stood next to him.

"Tamar," he murmured, looking at me at last. We had not been alone for such a long time. He held my face in his hands and touched our foreheads together. "Akh, Tamar."

My real name sounded so beautiful in his voice. But it made me wince. "I forbid you from ever saying that phrase."

He gave a bitter chuckle. "Need I ask why?"

"You know why," I said, shuddering.

His smile slipped from his face, and he pulled back to regard me seriously. "I notice your new item of jewelry."

I took his hand in mine without a word and led him up the beach to the overhanging rock where we always found ourselves. We sat underneath it, and I nestled into his shoulder, while he put an arm around me protectively.

"His name is Bedros," I said finally. "He is my godfather's son. His elder brother is Vartan, Aleena's husband. They hate each other. Just as I hate Bedros now."

"Then why must you marry him?"

"I shall lose everything if I do not."

"Like what?"

"My home, my family—"

He scoffed, interrupting me. "So you would sacrifice your entire life and future for that security?"

"Well, no! Heavens no! It is why I have continually asked to be free from this place. It is why I wish to run away with you!"

"And you think running away will help?"

"Yes! I will be running away with *you*. I will start a new life with you. And Aleek, even if you do not come with me, I shall find a way away from this place. I do not belong here—it is not who I am."

He shifted and grasped me gently by the shoulders. I saw the hurt in his eyes. "Tamar, you are a princess on this island, betrothed to a wealthy bore and sneaking behind everyone's back to meet a village man who lives on the mainland. Do you see the parallel of this story? This has happened before. We are in the same legend that named this island."

"I did not ask for this."

"No, you didn't," he said softly, reaching up and gently tucking a strand of my hair behind my ear. "But you have a heart filled with passion and adventure; no matter whom you marry, no matter where you live, it will always *fight* to show itself. It will kill you if you stay with Bedros—just as Aleena's heart killed her when she stayed with Vartan. But if you leave…" His voice trailed off. "If we run away together, you think our fate will be so different from the legend?"

"Yes. *Yes.* By staying here, they subjected themselves to the criticism and consequences of that around them. We *must* leave, or the same fate will fall over us."

He looked into my eyes. "We will leave. As soon as we can, we will leave. I have money saved up. We could go find Karin in Yerevan and stay with her for a little while, before deciding where to go."

My eyes widened with sudden excitement as the plan suddenly became a path ahead of us, and he pulled me close to hold me tight in his arms. I buried my face in his chest, breathing in his smell. It smelled like the lake, wild, unpredictable, everything in one.

"I wish you could have met my family under different circumstances. I wish they could accept you," I murmured.

"Regardless, I am grateful for them," he said lightly. I sat up and raised my eyebrow at him. With a smile, he continued, "I am grateful for them because without them I would not have this beautiful person in my sights. I appreciate them because I appreciate you and everything involved with you. There is not a single thing that I do not care about you—family included. I am not afraid of them because I have nothing to fear," he said, his lips set in a determined smile. "They can try to scare me, but my love will not waver. They can try and fight me, but I will not fight back. They are your family, and I must respect them. But I am yours, and they must respect that as well."

I held him so tight then, unsure of what I had done in my life that could be deserving of such a man. We were silent then, both of us lost in our own thoughts. We watched the lake, which shifted in front of us like a living beast, always watching, always waiting. It blinked at us.

Aleek gently stroked my hair.

It seemed expected, perhaps, so I was not surprised when he said it, but my heart still skipped a beat when I heard the words being murmured into the night.

"I love you, Tamar."

I heard the waves and the wind battling together in the distance while the villagers and my family buried my sister in her casket. I heard it all, but all I focused on at that moment was his voice, and mine in response.

"I love you too."

Chapter 25

SHOW THEM WHO you really are. Aleena's soul seemed to have entered my body and rested there, for I thought like her, acted like her. It was ironic—she gave me the permission to be who I really was, and I became Aleena. Our similarities shone all at once and I felt then that I was like her all along—I just did not have the courage to show that spirit. I gave no attention to anything that demanded attention, and what seemed such an important matter to everyone else was insignificant to me. What did clothing and jewelry and the quality of tea matter when there was so much more to see and experience?

Bedros was a nuisance, and Aleek's words haunted my nights. I felt as though they were going to confine me to my rooms, and I would not be able to escape and see Aleek. Would I really have the courage to run away and escape this marriage? My parents' wrath frightened me. They would do everything in their power to find me. And if they did, I would be imprisoned within these walls. They would force the marriage to happen. I would never see Aleek again.

I reveled in my time with Aleek, holding him close when I could and listening to him speak with all my attention. I loved his passion; I loved his wildness.

I loved him.

I felt pure joy and immense relief every time I saw him rise out of the waves, dripping with the lake water that would gladly pull him back into its depths. But I would always run to him and jump into his arms, happy to see him, not caring that water seeped into my clothes from off his body.

We grew closer on that beach, exploring the limits of our love for each other. We spoke words we would never think to say to our families. We felt each other as we would never feel anyone else. I found a home inside his heart, and I never wanted to leave. All this while he prepared for our upcoming journey.

Watching him swim away into the darkness of the water, toward the rising dawn, was torture. I always believed it would be the last time I would ever see him.

I told him this one night, and he smiled at me, giving me the *look* that I knew him best for. It seemed to say, "You are incredible," and it always made me feel invincible and beautiful, as I had never felt before.

"Tamar, know one thing: I will always find a way back to where you are," he said, gently brushing my hair out of my face. We were lying down on the sand, him next to me, propped up on his side.

I smiled and kissed him softly. When I pulled away, I suppose I had a look on my face, because he grinned and said, "What are you thinking about?"

I looked up at the vast sky that spread its loving arms over us. "Why do you stay with me? There is so much telling you to stay in the safety of your village."

He leaned his head back a bit, as if studying me intently, and I laughed. "Do I need a reason?"

"There is always a reason for everything," I said and shrugged.

"Well...you are beautiful; you have eyes that can make my heart stop and a smile that makes me want to stop time. You go out of your way to make someone happy, and you care for people selflessly. You have a pure soul and a good heart, and you continue to be so even after people take advantage of you. I am so lucky to have you by my side, Tamar. You are my greatest strength because I would do anything for you, and you are my greatest weakness because you are my everything."

My face flushed. "You must be a writer in your free time."

He leaned down and placed his lips on mine softly. It was like drowning—this feeling—and I never wanted to come up for air. His breath *was* my air.

When he left that night, he cupped my face in his hands and whispered, "I love you, Tamar. We shall soon be free."

I kissed him again. "What are we waiting for?"

"I am working during the day. I am gathering the money we need for the journey. I have asked a cousin to help me, and don't worry, he is to be trusted."

"Be safe, my love. Always come back to me," I murmured, leaning against his shoulder. I closed my eyes, sighing with the comfort I felt. I could go to sleep. I almost did. But then I felt his touch.

His fingers traced the contours of my face, as though he were planning a long and winding journey through the mystery that was me. He was slow and deliberate, stretching out the strands of time with his measured movements. I felt him linger sometimes, as if a certain spot needed more attention than the rest: the arch of my eyebrow, my lower lip, the line of my jaw. He tugged at the skin there, and I felt his breath catch. Through the darkness of my eyelids, I could almost see the look on his face. Just as he traced my face with his fingers, I traced his with my memory. My thoughts smoothed over his skin, over the hardness of his jaw, his set pursed lips that always seemed ready to say something but rarely did, his soft eyes that always gave his turbulent thoughts away. He traced the skin on my neck, and I lifted my chin, my lips parted in preparation for a kiss that I needed, a kiss that breathed life into me. But it did not come.

"Have you found it yet?" I breathed.

"Found what?" came his voice almost immediately.

"Whatever you are looking for."

There was silence, and he lifted his finger from my skin. Worried I had said something wrong, I blinked open my eyes. He was only a few inches away from my face. The starry sky was reflected in his dark eyes, and I gazed into them, mesmerized, certain he could see the same reflection in my eyes.

Without breaking his gaze, he put both hands on my cheeks and murmured, "I have already found the greatest treasure in all the world."

He kissed me then, his lips soft against mine.

It was anguish when it was time to part. He held onto my hand and kissed the veins at my wrist. With his other hand, he lifted my chin and caught my eyes. "I will see you soon."

"Must you leave already?"

He looked out at the sun that was beginning to peek over the horizon. "Yes, there is much to do. I must leave. But, Tamar," he said, his voice faltering.

"Yes?"

He looked down at me, a small smile on his face. "I can't let you go without making you mine first."

He pressed something into the palm of my hand and closed my fingers around it. With a firm kiss to my forehead, he said with resolve, "Soon." Then he jogged toward the water. I watched him wade into the waves, which sparkled like jewels in the reflection of the rising sun. I watched him until he was but a speck and I could not see him anymore, like a faded promise that echoed with the word, *Soon*.

I looked at the item in my hand—though my heart already knew what it was. Tears came to my eyes as I saw the ring. It was made with two thin pieces of metal, intertwined and twisted into each other. I knew that he had made it with his own hands, and the simple ring I looked at was more precious to me than anything I had ever known. It shone more brightly than the jewel-encrusted ring I wore with disdain on my finger.

I kissed Aleek's ring firmly and uttered the same prayer I had sighed at the lake for months. "Please bring him back to me, Lake Van."

⤙⤚

That night, when I arrived back at my castle, I noticed a figure in the shadows of my chambers. My hand flew to my side where I kept the dagger Aleek had made for me for my birthday. It was in my hands in a second, and I held it in front of me, but he threw up his hands in surrender.

"Tamar, it is I. It is Bedros."

"Tell me why I should not scream for the guards right now," I hissed.

I heard him move and strike a match to light the lantern. The room came to life with the light, and I saw him standing in the center of my room, watching me.

"I was worried about you. I came to ask if you were all right, but you were not here."

"You are not allowed in my chambers. Please get out."

"We are to be married."

"I do not care."

"We shall soon share a room."

"I do *not* care. We are not married yet. This is still *my* room."

"Please…Tamar, put the dagger away."

I realized I was holding it in front of me like a sword, and it looked ridiculous. I put it back in its spot. "I would have used it, Bedros."

"I know you would have. Where did you get it?"

"It was made for me."

"By whom?" I did not respond. "Tamar, by whom?"

"Get out of my room."

"Where were you tonight? Were you with *him*?"

"I was taking a walk."

"At this time of night?"

"It is a beautiful night."

"Why are you lying to me?"

"Why should I *not* lie to you? You betrayed me. You broke your promise. I do not have to tell you anything."

He pursed his lips. "You were using *my* boat, Tamar. I know you were going to the mainland, though I could not imagine why."

I stayed silent, fear and shock freezing my tongue. He knew where I was going? He seemed to take it as an invitation to continue speaking.

"I tried to ask you several times where you were going, but you did not trust me. You were only using my boat, so I did what I had to do—"

"So It *was* you!" He was taken aback by my sudden exclamation. "*You* stole the boat!"

"It was *my* boat. I only took back what was mine."

I slammed my hand onto my pillow, sending feathers flying into the air.

"It did not help. You still went. I do not know how." His face was flushed. He looked down at the ornate carpets. I saw the way his eyes traced the designs sewn into them, as if he was reading his words among the colored thread. I could see the child in him from this angle; the child that had ruined my grass strands and would pull at my hair or trip me. It infuriated me as the feelings came rushing back from the memories. "At the funeral, I saw how you danced next to him—the boy from Aleena's wedding, the *dancer*."

"What about him?"

"You were intimate with him. I saw it in the way you held hands. And as Aleena *died*, you let him touch you."

"He comforted me. And during the dances, we all have to hold hands. That is the way of the dance."

"It was *different*, Tamar. I am not stupid." He locked eyes with me, and we both pierced each other with steady glares. There was an electric current between us, angry and painful. My fists were clenched, and his jaw was locked.

"Are you meeting him?"

"No."

"You are."

"I said no."

"You should be *ashamed*."

"I have done nothing shameful."

"You are meeting a man with no escort, in the middle of the night. That is disgusting."

"Get out of my room!" I raised my voice slightly, and I could tell from the way he took a step back that he was afraid of the consequences of getting caught.

He made to leave, but as if on second thought, he took a step toward me and lowered his voice, muttering, "He is not meant to have you."

"No Bedros, *you* are not meant to have me," I said slowly, dangerously.

He turned and stalked out of the room into the hallway, and I watched as the dark shadows swallowed him whole without any mercy.

He is not meant to have you.

Shivers ran through my body.

He is not meant to have me.

It was a threat. I had to warn him.

⊷▰◉ ◉▰⊷

That thought spun through my mind over and over again, and I knew it was urgent. The next two days passed in a blur, and I could hardly wait to run to the beach and warn him.

Ideas flicked through my mind as to what we could do, and the arrow of my focus continually landed on *Run away*. It was either that or we end our meetings. But I could not imagine ending my love for him. It would not be possible.

But where would we go? How would we survive? My father would send his guards, and they would find me.

But they would not know where to find me. We would go where Aleek said: to Karin. We would escape to her and find shelter with her. We did not need to wait for money. I was a princess. I could steal money from my parents.

I longed for Aleena's guidance. The longing was overpowering, and I could not breathe with how it consumed me.

Dinner that night was torture. It was tedious and took ages, every word of conversation stabbing my heart. The empty space in front of me taunted me. It was as if Aleena was challenging me. *Go ahead*, she seemed to say. *Let us see if you could do it. Run away, as I did. Go show them who you really are.*

Could I?

A strong whistle brought me back sharply from my musings. All the heads at the table looked up toward the doors.

"What was that?" asked my mother.

"Storm," my father responded curtly. "Looks like it will be bad tonight."

My knife slipped from my tight grip, and I cut my finger, blood welling up out of the wound. I gave a small gasp of pain, but no one seemed to care. My mother, who normally would have scolded my intrusion, stayed silent.

The wind howled outside, laughing at my disgrace.

Storm.

Storm.

I felt Bedros's eyes on me, judging me, weighing my every move. I wanted to gouge them out with the knife in my hands.

I stood, unsteady on my feet. "If you would please excuse me. I am bleeding onto the table."

My mother nodded dismissively in my direction, looking so much older than she had a month ago.

I turned and strode out of the room, struggling against the tears that threatened to burst from my eyes. I began to run halfway to my chambers, and I arrived there in a flurry of agitation, slamming the door behind me.

I wasted no time in pulling on warm clothes, eager to escape these damned walls. I fumbled with the laces of my clothes, and my fingers slipped in anxiety.

I was ready, and I had an hour to go before I would normally light the candle. But I could not wait inside. I prayed and prayed that Aleek would not try swimming to me. He must know better than that. He knew about the legend, knew how much our story paralleled it. He must not try swimming to me.

I will always find a way back to where you are.

I thrust open my window and, with my usual routine, jumped out, my skirts flailing around me and hair catching the wind. But this time, I was not careful enough, and I hit the rooftops rather hard.

My stomach churned, and I felt I would be sick. But I needed to continue on.

I made my way on quick feet toward the beach. The candle and the matches were gripped tightly in my arms, as I bowed my head against the relentless wind.

I was surprised when I heard it over the din of the wind, but nevertheless, I veered wildly to the side when I heard a rustle in the bushes. A shadowy figure stepped into the path and lunged forward to grab me, clamping his hand down on my forearm.

"Bedros!" I shrieked in horror.

"Let go of those," he said, trying to grab the candle. "I know what you are trying to do."

"No!"

I tried to twist free, but his grip was strong. The matches and candle clattered to the ground. I scrambled after them, but he grabbed me around the waist, pulling me back. "You think this is a game? You think playing with the legend and the lives of those around you is a game?"

"Leave me be! This does not concern you," I shouted, my voice battling with the roar of the wind.

"This concerns everyone!" he shouted back. "Your entire future, Tamar. The entire future of Akhtamar."

"Stop it! Leave me alone! Leave us alone!" I cried.

"Come with me, Tamar. I will give you everything that you want. Just come with me."

"Get away from me!" I stumbled backward. I was blinded with panic.

"I do not want to have to hurt you, Tamar."

"Leave me be!"

"He is not worth this!"

"He is worth more than you will ever be worth," I spat.

I knew I had dealt a harsh blow to his pride, and I cursed myself for my foolishness. His face was frozen in a dull stare, as if he could not believe the change that had come over me. "Fine," he said. I was frightened at the tone in his voice.

"Fine?"

"You want your romantic legend; you can have it. But they do not call it a tragedy for nothing."

He took several steps forward, striding toward me fiercely, and grabbed me by the shoulders.

I really did not think he would do anything. It was *Bedros*. I had played with wooden toys with him as a baby. We had crawled all over the castle on all fours, unable to walk yet and still causing havoc among the bustling maids. Bedros would never have hurt me. Even as he grabbed a fistful of my hair in his fist, I believed he would just drop me to the ground and be off on his way.

Foolish girl.

I bent under the pressure of his pull on my hair. He began to pull me back toward the palace, though I struggled as hard as I could. "I am doing this for your own safety," he said, his voice straining.

"Please, Bedros. We will talk about this tomorrow!" I cried out in pain. "Please leave me be tonight!"

He took me to the stables, much to my dismay. The horses huffed and snorted in agitation as we burst into the stables loudly. I saw Asdgh, my horse, in his stable, stamping his hooves in frustration. Bedros dragged me to an empty stable and threw me inside.

When I leaped back to my feet, he jumped forward and suddenly twisted my hands behind me, tying the length of a rope around my wrists and around the rail where we usually tied the horses. I hadn't even seen the rope in his hands. "Bedros!" I cried. "What are you doing? Let me go!"

I twisted and tried to slam my head into him, but he had finished and had stepped back to watch me with a horrified expression on his face. "I'm sorry, Tamar," he said. He leaned down and took the candle and matches into his hands. "You do not understand. This has to end."

And with that, he turned and ran outside into the darkness with my screams of "You're mad!" following him.

→⊨⊜ ⊜⊨←

He had tied the rope very crudely. I wasted no time in wriggling back and forth. I needed to reach the dagger at my hips—which he had thankfully forgotten about. I writhed against the rough rope, and with a whimper, I felt the skin on my wrists break. But I did not stop; I kept going, grimacing and giving small grunts of pain as I felt the blood slip over my fingers. It felt as though my elbows would break with the effort I was putting in to reach the dagger. With a last cry of frustration, I finally managed to pull out Aleek's beautiful dagger. Sawing back and forth, I began to cut through the rope, and slowly the tendrils gave away until I was free. I fell to my knees and clutched at my blood-covered wrists in pain, but I only gave myself a few seconds. As soon as I was able, I jumped out of the stall and ran toward Asdgh, who neighed in joyful anticipation.

I opened the stable doors, leaped onto Asdgh's back, and driven by fear, love, anger, and panic, we dashed out into the storm.

I heard Princess Tamar's screams echo against the cliff walls and the roar of the lake as it devoured the man she was living for. I saw the dark clouds gathered over the horizon, the black sky overhead ominous and looming over the tiny island. The rain poured around me, washing over me and streaming into my eyes. I cried in fear, for I knew Aleek now swam in those treacherous waters, swimming toward a flame filled not with love, but with deceit.

At last, I saw the clearing appear in front of me, and I burst into it, stumbling blindly down the dark path toward the secluded beach. When my feet touched pebbles, I stopped running, disoriented when I saw the overhanging rock and a smooth glow shining from the inside. Right across from it, the beach was wild—wilder than I had ever seen it. The waters convulsed in agony and pain, arching and rearing up toward the skies. I was completely drenched in a matter of seconds, with the help of the spray and the rain.

I slid and stumbled over the smooth pebbles to reach the candle, and when I did, I saw it sitting there, alone and proud, calling my beloved to the shores of my island.

But where was Bedros? Had he come to his senses? Had he forsaken his violent revenge?

I neared the candle, my eyes filling with relief, but my head snapping back and forth to try and see where he was. A shadow suddenly passed behind me. I turned and cried out in horror as Bedros grabbed me, pulling me down to the sand. His hand clamped over my mouth, and he hissed, "Do not scream."

I quieted, but I tried to reach down with my hand to my waist. He beat me there, though. He pulled at the belt at my waist, sliding out my cherished knife. "This does not belong to you," he said, stepping away from me.

I was still on the floor, watching him with anger in my eyes. "You will kill him with the same dagger he made himself?"

"No."

"Then what?"

"You said you wanted your little tragic story, and I shall give it to you, Tamar. In a few minutes, I shall snuff out that candle, and we shall hear your lover cry out your name while the lake finishes him. *That* is his fate. *That* is what you both have been playing with."

"You are mad," I whispered.

"No, I am the only one thinking rationally. You are the mad one," he responded calmly, looking up at the lake.

I took that chance to release the most blood-curling shriek I was capable of. He stopped it halfway by jumping onto me and squeezing my cheeks with his fingers and thumb. I began to keen loudly as the skin broke under his fingers and my teeth felt close to breaking.

"I said, do not scream," he said, stepping back.

I cradled my face in my hands, the blood smearing onto my palms. Had Aleek heard my shriek? Why was he silent? I waited in tense suspense for any noise, but there was nothing. Was this it? Was he gone? Had the lake finished its work with him?

Then I heard it.

"Tamar!"

It was as if the lake had whispered it. Both our heads snapped up toward the thrashing waves. "Tamar!" I heard again, louder.

Bedros pointed the knife toward me. "Do not respond."

I ignored him. He wouldn't kill me. He was not so daft. "Aleek! Go back! Go back!" I shrieked as loud as I could, but I knew he could not go back. There was no light on his end. He was trapped.

Bedros lunged forward, and I flinched when I thought he would stab me with the knife. But he seemed to change his mind. He turned toward the overhanging rock, smiled at me in the most menacing way, leaned over, and blew out the candle.

The beach plunged into darkness, and I immediately began to bawl, the tears rolling down my face in great torrents. "No! No!" I screamed, lunging toward the candle. Bedros stepped forward and hoisted me up over his shoulder as if I were a rag doll. "Aleek!" I screamed over and over, my throat ripping from the force. Maybe he would hear me and swim toward the noise.

"Aleek!"

I was wild with panic and fear, crying and shrieking until I had no voice left. It was all to no avail. I heard nothing more.

The only echoes I heard were the ones that rang over and over in my mind.

Akhtamar...

Akhtamar...

Akh, Tamar.

Chapter 26

HE TOLD ME he would always find his way back to me. And he did.

They found him on the shores of my island, and some village children who had been playing on another beach had found him. No one knew what had happened to him, why he had been swimming in the lake in the middle of a violent storm. Confusion and sorrow rang through the villages, for he had been well known and loved by the people. They held a large funeral for him on the mainland. I was not allowed to go.

My window was closed, but through its thin glass, I could see the outline of the lake. I could smell it from where I sat. I could hear the roar of the waves as it smashed against the rocks. And farther out, so far, I heard it echo in the depths of my mind.

Tamar! Akh, Tamar…

The lake sighed and whispered the words. I heard it in every ebbing of a wave.

I was still, so still. My body had no will to move, my brain too preoccupied, for my entire being was stunned at the sudden state of my shattered heart.

My eyes were hazy; I could not focus on anything around me—for what was there to see within the walls of this miserable castle? All I saw were my thoughts, dark and tortured, vengeful and pained, heavy and numb.

I vaguely heard voices, dim and muffled in the background. I did not move my head; I could not. I heard Janna say, "You should not be here."

"I want to. Please let me in."

"Come see her another time," she said, but I heard her protests as he made his way inside. I sat still as the door closed and a single pair of footsteps neared me.

"Tamar," spoke a sullen voice.

"I'm sorry, Tamar; I could not keep him out," said Janna.

My heart ached at how much I wished another man to be in here right now. "Tamar, I am sorry."

They were all apologizing to me. For what? *Sorry* could not fix this. *Sorry* could not piece together all the pieces of my heart. *Sorry* could not save a life. He came closer and stooped to his knees at my side to try to look into my eyes. He was trying to be himself again, to make me forget the demon I saw in his eyes on that wretched night. But all I could remember was that side of him: the monster. "Tamar, I know I am the last person you want to see right now." His voice shook. "You probably hate me, and I understand that. But everything I did, I did for you. You must believe me. If your mother found out, it would have been your ruin—your downfall. You would not have had a good life ahead of you. If you marry me, Tamar, we could be happy together; we could start a better life. Just marry me, Tamar. I love you." There was silence when he stopped speaking, except for his labored breathing. "Tamar," he repeated, almost pleading. He leaned over and looked me in the eyes.

I looked away and pursed my lips, but a second after, I turned back to him and looked straight at him. He sat back a bit, unsure of what I would do. I ran my tongue over my cracked lips to moisten them, so I could speak. He waited. I stood slowly, my skirts rustling. He stayed on his knees, his eyes following my every move. I extended my hand to him. He took it in his, his eyes brightening with pleasant surprise. But when he looked down at my hand, he let go immediately, his eyes filling with horror. The blood had not been washed from my hands yet. The wounds from my wrists were crusted over and had become a dark brown, with beads of dark red blood seeping out of them.

"I am so grateful for all that you have done for me," I said in a flat voice.

"Tamar..."

I continued, "I will marry you, Bedros. But know that I would never give up anything for you."

He stood up as well. "I would never ask you to."

"And that is why you do not love me." I turned around to look outside.

After a moment, I heard him walk out of the room. I knew what I had to do. I knew what I would do. I wanted to hurt them. I had no other thought except revenge. I would marry him, and I would betray them all. I would not be a *good* girl, as the other Princess Tamar had possibly been. *Show them who you really are.* I knew who I was. I was Princess Tamar—the one they did not expect, the one who would change the legend's ending.

The marriage was rushed; none of the joyful traditions were used. I knew during Aleena's wedding that I would never experience those traditions. They gave me Aleena's dress to wear, and since she had been taller than me, they had to pin up the hem, so it would not drag on the floor. I felt as though I were Aleena, walking toward my doom instead of a wedding. But I knew what I had to do. I walked down the aisle once more to meet Bedros, but the fun lightheartedness had died. He watched me closely, as if I would crumble right there and become a dusty pile of bones on the church floor.

They all watched me with those worried, pitiful eyes. But they were fools.

My heart had broken, but my body and mind were stronger than ever. I would not crumble.

We were married, but the reception was not undertaken. I tried not to think about this night, for I would have to lie with Bedros and consummate the marriage. But what love could be found between water and fire? I knew it was necessary, however.

Father approached me with a gift. It was a large, flat parcel. I glanced at it, with surprise. When I opened the parcel, I swallowed over the sudden lump in my throat. It was Aleena's wedding portrait, but he had painted me beside her. It was crude, for it was obvious it was done in great haste. He had painted me with the same dress I had worn on the night of Aleena's death. The blue dress contrasted against Aleena's crimson dress, but the original colors of the painting shone through me. He did not have enough time to make me stronger in color. I was a pale shadow next to her—a ghost—with the background shining through. It seemed fitting that this would be the only portrait painted of me.

Night fell quickly, the sun bowing his head down at the events of the marriage. That night, the maids prepared me for what was to come.

They washed my skin with rosewater and dressed me in a cream nightgown made of the thinnest cloth. They were young women and, as such, blushed at the idea of the night, but my face stayed sullen and pale. Janna took care of my wrists, making sure the wounds were clean and wrapped in fresh bandages.

"Thank you, Janna."

She glanced up at me. "It is no trouble, Princess Tamar."

"No, for everything, thank you for everything."

I leaned forward and kissed her cheek, aware that she was worried at my actions. But I only smiled at her and walked away.

The bed was prepared in my chambers, for it was agreed by the parents that it would be best if done in my own bed. When I walked in, I was alone for the first time in a long time. I felt stupid in the flimsy nightgown. It was held together by a crisscross assortment of strings, but one pull from the end would open the entire dress. I sat on the chair at the foot of my bed and turned my eyes to my window to watch the dark night outside where the lake glittered like diamonds. The pomegranate was not at my windowsill anymore, and I assumed that Janna had thrown it away. I could see the sky so clearly.

The stars blinked down at me, the only witnesses to my meetings with Aleek. They watched me without a sound, without any expression. Did they think I had been shameful? Had they slandered my name? No, they wouldn't. Aleek was right; they had watched over us with affection. But as I gazed back at them from my seat, I realized that they were looking at me *now* with shame in their eyes.

Love is a powerful thing, no matter who it is found with. The stars understood this. And they scorned my marriage with Bedros, not my union with Aleek. They scorned this night above all.

I did not move when the door opened and closed behind me, and I heard him walk in. I did not move when he placed his hands lightly on my shoulders.

He placed a kiss on the top of my head, and when I still did not move, he stepped in front of me and kneeled to look at me in the face. I saw his eyes wander over the bruises on my face and the cut on my forehead. He was the only one who had seen them—as he should, for he had put them there.

He traced a finger lightly over the cuts, and I winced, more from his touch than from the pain. He took my wounded hands in his and kissed my knuckle. I hated that he did that. It was not his move to do.

"I am sorry."

I remained silent.

"You are my wife now."

I was still silent.

"You must…pretend to like me…at least for the night, for our parents."

I merely looked at him quietly.

His face was flushed as his finger strayed near the string that would undo the nightgown. He played with it, unsure if he should pull it or not.

"I suppose it must happen in the bed, and not in this chair," I said coolly.

He pulled his hand away, as if I had struck him. "Ah yes! Of course, of course."

He helped me stand and led me to the bed. I lay down on my back stiffly and looked up at the ceiling, preparing myself mentally.

He undressed himself, fumbling with his strings until he stood with only a loose shirt on. He climbed onto the bed and slowly lay across my body. His weight pushed out my breath slightly. I turned my head, so I would not have to look at him. I watched the lake through the open window. It glistened in the moonlight and looked at me quietly with a million stars as my audience.

Not having my lips available to kiss, he instead placed his lips on my jawline, kissing the skin that was stretched tight there. When he was ready, he reached down and pulled the string, slowly but steadily. My nightgown fell loose, and I shut my eyes, pursing my lips at this disgrace. *The stars slandered at impudent, shameless Tamar. How dare she give herself to this man? How dare she betray the one she loves, when he is not yet cold in his grave?*

I tried to imagine it was someone else, but my heart could not be deceived. It knew too well.

They did not slander Tamar. This time, they slandered *me*.

The stars outside in the vast sky were unblinking, and I wished to be one with them, shining high in the darkness with not a care for what happens on the earth—much less on a tiny beautiful island.

I noticed in the sudden stiffness of his body that he realized I had already been taken by Aleek. I was surprised at his surprise; had he not assumed it already?

But at that point, he no longer cared. He had nothing else to say to me.

Chapter 27

And so, I find myself here. Back where I began this story.

Back on the rowboat I stole from Bedros. I found out where he kept it from his servant, and I took it from him. It was the least I could steal, after everything he had taken from me. They did not suspect anything, for I had become a ghost of a girl for a week. But I had been planning, scheming. They were fools to think I was weak enough to endure all that for the rest of my life.

I would never *endure*. I would *live*. I told Aleek I would leave this island with or without his company, and I would prove that.

The day after my wedding, I sent off a letter to Lilit to tell her everything and ask for help. Her reply came within several days, and she had sent money as well as some supplies, and a note: "Always write to me!" My last night in the palace, I went to my mother and father and made sure to hug them before we all separated. They were surprised but pleased at my affection. I would write to them one day.

I set off in the boat, looking back once at my beautiful little island. I would return one day. Before heading off into the unknown, I went first to Aleek's family to express my condolences, for I would not have rested easy had I left his family without closure. It had been hard doing it, but it was necessary. They did not know, of course, of our nightly encounters, any more than the rest of the village did. They were just as much in the dark. I bowed my head and hid my guilt as they thanked me for my visit and gave me food and fresh juice in a tight bag, for I told them I would be leaving on a journey.

At first, I knew not where I would be going. But when I looked up and saw the bright star in the sky that he had pointed out to me once, I knew I had to follow it. I knew it would lead me to where I needed to go.

So now, I row and I row relentlessly, crying and smiling at the memories I am leaving behind me. I pretend that Aleena and Aleek are with me in the boat, helping me row, making me laugh with their silly jokes and mischievous glances.

I know I will somehow never be alone, as long as I keep flying on my own path. The Tamar in this new legend would not go back home and live a dutiful life. She will fly away, past the places she knows, and she will be free.

Be free, Tamar.

Be free.

>⟫ ⟪⟪

A year has passed and I walk down the cobblestone streets of Yerevan, our capital city that I had never been to until now. I look around myself, aware that no one can notice me here. No one knows who I am. Princess Tamar is a legend, a mystery from a tiny island far away. But I know of one who still knows me.

I see her on a lonely bench, her head bowed to read a book. A blue and silver scarf is wrapped around her neck, and her hair is wrapped tight in a bun. I stand still for a moment and take a deep breath; then I continue toward her. When I approach her, I stand across from her and grin. "Hello," I say to the young woman.

She looks up, and for a moment, I can see what she is seeing: a young woman, older than herself by a few years, her clothing torn and old and her hair hanging about her pale face.

"Hello," she says uncertainly.

"It is a rather warm day for that scarf; do you not think so?"

She fingers the scarf at her neck. "I wear this every day."

I sit beside her on the bench, facing her, and she leans back slightly, unnerved by this odd woman. "I also have something I carry about with me every day."

"Oh, yes…," she says, getting ready to put her book away, but her eyes catch the object I am holding in my hand.

She leans forward and sees the small portrait. Her eyes widen. The girl in the portrait is wearing a pale pink beautiful dress, and the shawl is thrown over the bottom half of her face. Her brown eyes peer out merrily. A crown rests on her head.

"Karin, do you not recognize me?" I say quietly.

Her eyes widen, and I see the disbelief in them. She looks at me, and I see her eyes travel over my face. It is the first time she has seen me without my scarf.

"Lo…Lori?" she asks hesitantly.

"I am not Lori," I respond, but she already knows. I see the recognition dawning in her widening eyes.

"You are Tamar. Princess Tamar! This entire time!" she cries, the book dropping from her lap. She tries to stand, but I grab her hands, pulling her down.

"Karin, it is still me," I exclaim. "Oh, Karin, I have missed you."

She throws her arms around me, and I feel her shoulders shaking as she cries into my neck.

"My brother...," she sobs.

"I know, Karin, I know," I say, holding her even tighter.

That is when I truly know.

I know that we will continue together, as a force that has been beaten over and over again by the cruel waves of our lives. But we are still strong, and we have found each other after all these years.

That is when I know I am not alone.

Tamar never went back to her duties after her happiness was taken from her. No, she continued on. She would never let her life be dictated by others again.

The heart is too strong to be kept caged.

Be free, Tamar. Go show them all who you really are.

→═◉ ◉═←

Author Biography

Meli Sarkissian holds a bachelor's degree in European studies and psychology and is currently earning a master's degree in forensic psychology. Born in Cyprus, Sarkissian was raised in an Armenian household. The family's proud traditions, particularly the folk-dance group that Sarkissian was part of, sparked the inspiration for this novel.